Mrs Collins, Against Her Wishes

MELANIE SCHERTZ

ISBN:1497478227
ISBN-13:9781497478220

DEDICATION

This book is dedicated to my parents, and my daughter. My parents, Deryl and Diana Schertz, lived for nearly 45 years as husband and wife, setting an example of love for my brothers and myself. My daughter, Caitlin Brianne (Cate), has said for many years that she wishes to find the same sort of marriage for herself, long lasting and durable, surviving the bad times and enjoying the good.

ACKNOWLEDGMENTS

I am grateful for my many friends at A Happy Assembly and DarcyandLizzy.com, for their support, suggestions and giving me the courage to write.
Of course, I am grateful for Jane Austen's stories, which have touched and inspired so many people for over 200 years.

I am so grateful for my friends, Pat Weston and Elaine Tibbs, who both Beta'd my writing and helped me correct my errors. Pat has been my friend for many years, and I am grateful for her dedication. Elaine has become my friend through my writing, and I am grateful for her wisdom and kindness to me.

Chapter 1

As she looked at herself in the peer glass, Elizabeth Bennet knew it was most likely the worst day of her life.

Being the second born of five daughters of a country gentleman who had his estate entailed away from the female line, Elizabeth knew that her lot in life was slim, but she would never have believed it would sink so low.

Her elder sister, Jane, was the most beautiful of the five sisters; at least that is what their mother had told them her entire life. Mrs Bennet had never been fond of her second born. Not only was Elizabeth not the heir her mother insisted she was carrying, but Elizabeth was unlike all of her other daughters by using wit and wisdom to make her way through life. The girl was also quite independent and a great lover of nature. It was not uncommon for Elizabeth to wander off into the park surrounding their home of Longbourn, only to return with dirt covering her dress or a tear in the fabric from her less than ladylike behavior.

The past few months had been intriguing, as the next estate from Longbourn, Netherfield Park, had finally been leased. The young man who leased it was single and extremely amiable, and he instantly fell in love with Jane. It was his sisters who were lacking in manners, their caustic tongues spilt bitterness against all in the neighborhood. The Bingleys were new money, with their wealth stemming from trade. Miss Bingley and her elder sister, Mrs Hurst, seemed to have forgotten their lowly beginnings as they looked down on the country folk with disdain, not realizing that the Bennets' were far above the Bingleys by society's standards. The Bennet family had been landed gentry for more than six generations.

The other member of the Netherfield party was Bingley's closest friend, Mr Fitzwilliam Darcy. Mr Darcy was one of the wealthiest men in all of England, with his family well established in society. He was also one of the most sought after bachelors in England, which was frustrating to him. He disliked society, preferring to keep a simple life at his estate of Pemberley, in Derbyshire. Darcy was also the opposite of his friend, shy and withdrawn from large groups of people. This attitude had given the people in the neighborhood of Longbourn and the nearby village of Meryton the feeling that Mr Darcy looked down his nose at them.

From the start, Bingley and Jane took a great liking to each other. Miss Bingley was adamant in her desire to separate her brother from Miss Bennet, and had finally succeeded in removing Bingley from Netherfield, claiming the desire to stay in London for

the upcoming holiday season. Unbeknownst to
Bingley, his sister also planted seeds of doubt in the
mind of Jane Bennet, claiming a desire for Bingley to
marry Darcy's younger sister, Miss Georgiana Darcy.
There had never been a desire by Bingley for such a
match, nor would Darcy have allowed such, as his
sister was far too young to be married. But neither of
the men were aware of the letter Miss Bingley had
sent to Jane, expressing her brother's devotion to the
young Miss Darcy.

The day after the Netherfield party had left for
Town, Elizabeth's world began spinning out of
control. With no proposal to Jane, and their family in
danger of being homeless, if their father was to die
soon, Mrs Bennet's prayers were answered in the
form of the heir to the estate, as he arrived at
Longbourn, wishing to choose from his fair cousins a
bride.

At first, Mr William Collins had preferred Jane.
This would not do, as Mrs Bennet had not given up
completely on Mr Bingley returning to Netherfield
and wishing Jane to be his wife. So Mr Collins
transferred his preference to the next eldest daughter,
Miss Elizabeth Bennet.

The morning Mr Collins asked to speak to
Elizabeth, the young lady wished she was anywhere
else. Even spending an afternoon locked in a room
with Miss Caroline Bingley would be preferable to
such torment as to be in Mr Collins' presence. The

man was a clergyman, and a complete idiot. Short and round, balding on top and quite disgusting to be near, he was also the sort of man who idolized the wealthy, especially his patroness, Lady Catherine de Bourgh, of Rosings Park, in Kent.

"Miss Elizabeth, I wish to speak with you of my affection for you. You must already be aware that, after arriving here at your beloved father's home, I soon singled you out as the lady with whom I wish to spend the rest of my life. I know you have no dowry to speak of, and after today, I will never speak of it again. As your dear mother has already given her blessing on our marriage, I feel all that is required is for me to express the depths of my devotion to you."

"Mr Collins, you forget yourself. You have not proposed to me, nor have I accepted any offer of marriage. I must say that I cannot marry you, for I do not believe I could make you happy, and I am certain you will never be able to make me happy."

"Ah, my dear cousin, I see you are practicing the honorable method of young ladies to deny an offer from the man she intends to accept, expecting me to increase my feelings for you. I know you mean to accept me, as you might never receive another proposal. And, as I have mentioned, your own mother has sanctioned our union, and I am sure you would never go against your parents in such a situation. My esteemed patroness, Lady Catherine de Bourgh will be pleased with my choice of wife, as she has told me

'Mr Collins, you must marry, and make sure she is gentle born. Then you must bring her to Hunsford, and I will pay a call on her.' What a true gift from such an important lady of society. And the added relief of knowing your mother and sisters will be provided for after your father is in his grave, all of these must prove to you my devotion to you, as well as the honor I give you in making such an offer."

Elizabeth was frustrated. "Mr Collins, I do not tease you when I say I will not marry you. It is not my custom to mislead anyone. I cannot marry you."

Mr Collins was not to be stopped. "I am sure that, once you have spoken with your parents, you will change your mind." He smiled, believing her to already be his fiancé.

Just then, Mrs Bennet entered the room. "Oh, Lizzy, is it not wonderful? You will one day be mistress of this estate, and will be able to provide homes for myself and your sisters, once your father has left this world."

"Mamma, I have refused Mr Collins, as I cannot see myself married to him."

"You will come with me immediately, Lizzy. Mr Collins, you should remain here, as I have asked Mrs Hill to bring refreshments. I am certain Mr Bennet will be able to sort this all out, and we can begin to prepare for the wedding."

~~ ** ~~

Thinking about that morning, Elizabeth could not help but remember the meeting with her father. After Mrs Bennet pulled Elizabeth with her as she stormed into Mr Bennet's study, the elder lady ranted to her husband of how ungrateful their daughter was, and how she demanded he force their daughter to marry Mr Collins.

"Mrs Bennet, would you please allow me to speak alone with Elizabeth?"

His wife nodded her head, giving Elizabeth a stern glare before she left the father and daughter alone.

"My dear Lizzy, so Mr Collins has proposed to you, and you have refused him." Mr Bennet watched his beloved daughter nod her head. "Lizzy, I must insist you accept Mr Collins' offer."

"Papa, I cannot. Mr Collins is a foolish man, ignorant and appalling. How could I ever be married to a man such as him? It would kill me to be married to him, as it would destroy any chance at happiness."

"Lizzy, I am afraid you must. You see, I am not in good health. Had Mr Bingley offered for Jane, I would not ask such a sacrifice from you, but Mr Bingley is gone and I must take steps to protect our family. Mr Collins is my heir, therefore, he will have this estate when I am gone. Your mother will not have to find a home, and your sisters will be given protection as well. I know you dislike Mr Collins, but it is the only way to afford the rest of our family the comfort of a home when I am gone."

"Papa, please, why can it not be Mary instead of me? She likes Mr Collins, and I am certain she would approve of marrying him." Elizabeth pleaded.

"Mr Collins has determined you would bring him the greatest joy in life. Mary is plain, where you are quite handsome, so your cousin is naturally drawn to you. He is vain, so he would prefer to have a beautiful lady as his wife." Mr Bennet stood and walked to the window. "If there were any other way to protect the family, I would refuse to allow you to marry Mr Collins. But there is not. I am pleading with you, Lizzy. Please think of the family."

"What is wrong with you, Papa?" Elizabeth asked, tears streaming down her cheeks.

"Mr Jones has spoken with his fellow apothecaries as well as a physician. They believe I have a tumor near my heart. It is causing the heart to not function properly. From all reports, if I am fortunate, I will have near six more months with you all. If I am not fortunate, well...let us not think of that at the moment. Can you see now, why I am adamant you must marry Mr Collins? What would happen if you do not? Your mother and sisters would be destitute, as would you. I know you would be able to find your way in life, but your sisters and mother could not endure such."

"My spirit would be crushed, married to such a man as Mr Collins."

Mr Bennet shook his head. "My dear girl, you have always been the strongest of my daughters. You will be able to find a way to endure his foolishness. I believe you will be able to find a way to be happy, you only need to convince yourself."

"So, I must marry Mr Collins? You insist on me sacrificing my happiness for the family?"

"As I said, my beloved Lizzy, it is the only way. If you do not marry him, your mother will insist you be turned out from our home. And I will be forced to do as she wishes. Please, Lizzy, allow me the remaining months of my life to be able to keep in contact with you, and not to have to disown you. Please allow me the peace of mind, knowing you are all safe and secure, once I am gone from the world. I regret that you are forced to make up for my neglect of protecting your futures. There is simply nothing else I can think to do."

Elizabeth knew she had no choice. She knew she had to do her duty to her family. "Very well, Papa. Though, I pray you understand, I am not pleased with the situation. I feel as if I am being punished for the rest of my life for your not taking better care of our family." Elizabeth stood and left the room, walking directly to her room.

The banns were read and all was being prepared for Elizabeth's wedding to Mr William Collins. The wedding would be on the second of January, and the couple would leave after the wedding breakfast for Hunsford parsonage immediately. Mr Collins was certain his patroness would wish to meet his wife as soon as possible, as Lady Catherine would not travel to the wedding. She felt it was more important for her clergyman to bring his bride home and begin their married life as soon as possible, so there would be no need for her to go out of her way to come to the wedding. Little did Mr Collins know, but Lady Catherine absolutely refused to consider lowering herself by visiting the home of someone who was beneath her in consequence.

Elizabeth's wedding clothes were made, though she did not care how they looked. Her heart was not prepared for such sacrifice, so nothing could matter to her. Feeling as if she were an empty shell rather than the young lady she had been, Elizabeth allowed her mother to make decisions. Mr Bennet watched his favorite daughter become melancholy and withdrawn from her family. He knew she was unhappy, but what else could he do to protect the entire family?

To give his daughter a break from the preparations for her wedding, he sent her to Town to visit her aunt and uncle, the Gardiners. The Gardiners were kind and caring, and loved Jane and Elizabeth as if they were their own children. Mrs Gardiner was close to the eldest two Bennet sisters, and they adored their aunt in return.

Upon arriving at the Gardiner home, Elizabeth went to her aunt's parlor so the two could have a talk. "Lizzy, I know from your letters of your displeasure in having to marry Mr Collins. But seeing you here, oh, my dear girl, you look miserable."

"I have to do my duty, Aunt Helen. Father is dying, and it is the only way to protect my family." Elizabeth said in a manner of fact tone. "My happiness is not important, as my family will be protected."

"Your father should have taken better care of the situation, and your mother should have been thrifty in her spending. If either of them had taken responsibility for their actions, you would not be in this mess."

"Aunt Helen, wishing for the past to have been different will make no changes on the future. What is done is done, and nothing can change the facts. When Papa is gone, I will make certain Mamma knows her place. She will move to the dower house as soon as possible and I will be in charge of the main house."

"Fanny will not approve of your decision, but I do. Fanny has never taken the time to be a proper mother to you girls. Now, tell me what has happened with Jane and Mr Bingley. I could not believe your letter stating that he and his party had left Netherfield, giving no farewells to the neighbors or giving a date of return. How is our dear Jane fairing?"

"Aunt, I have never seen Jane so sad. She struggles to keep a smile on her face, but I can see the pain in her eyes. Every time I think of the situation, I become furious. How could someone as amiable and kind as Mr Bingley behave so appallingly towards my dearest sister? I am certain his sisters and his friend have convinced him that Jane does not care for him. If they only knew how much pain they have caused my sister, but it would not matter to them. Despicable people."

"Well, my dear Lizzy, to help take your mind from all the worries you have and to lift your spirit, your uncle has purchased tickets for us to attend the theatre. We will be seeing *Much Ado About Nothing*. I am sure you will be entertained."

"Thank you, Aunt Helen. I appreciate your kindness more than I can say. I shall enjoy the performance, for it is most likely to be my last. I cannot imagine Mr Collins attending the theatre, unless his patroness commanded him to attend." Elizabeth said with a touch of sadness in her voice.

The night of the performance, Elizabeth had finally put a pleasant outlook on life for the evening, and was looking forward to the performance. She was wearing a pale lavender gown, one of her finest. As she prepared for the evening, she thought to herself that it was most likely the last evening she would have to wear such a fine gown. Being the wife of a clergyman, especially one as pompous as Mr Collins, would not include such frills as balls and dances, theatre and opera. Her future husband had already informed her of Lady Catherine's dislike for such activities, and he instructed Elizabeth that she would start to appreciate what her ladyship did. So, for this final evening, Elizabeth would behave as if all was as it had been six months before, when there was no word of William Collins or Lady Catherine de Bourgh, and when Elizabeth still felt alive.

The carriage arrived at the theatre shortly before the performance. They made their way to their seats, prepared to enjoy the evening. As the performance began, Elizabeth noticed one of the occupied boxes contained people whom she knew. Mr Darcy and Mr Bingley were seated with a young lady between them. *Could this be the reason Mr Bingley has not returned to Netherfield? Is this the young lady Miss Bingley hinted would become her sister? The young lady is handsome, though nothing in comparison to Jane. Is she Mr Darcy's sister?*

From the moment Elizabeth caught sight of Bingley, she felt anger building up inside her. She had never felt herself capable of such feelings as hatred, but at that moment, she knew she was feeling hatred. Hatred for Bingley, his amiable and smiling person, a man who had altered her life by deserting her dear sister, breaking Jane's heart, and forcing the need for

Elizabeth to marry such a man as William Collins. Here Bingley sat, enjoying the performance, with his friend and the young lady, without a care in the world, while Elizabeth's life was spiraling to an end.

It was difficult for Elizabeth to concentrate, and when the intermission came, she rushed to the necessary room, as she felt she would be ill. It was as she came out of the room that she nearly collided with the young lady she had seen in the box with Bingley and Darcy. Up close, it was easy to tell that, though tall and having a womanly figure, the lady's features showed she was much younger. She could not remember how old Darcy's sister was, it seemed to her that Miss Darcy was near the age of Elizabeth's youngest sister, Lydia's, age. The young lady was attractive, with her golden blonde hair and bright blue eyes. Just as Jane had. Was Mr Bingley transferring his attraction for Jane to Miss Darcy, due to Jane's lack of fortune and Miss Darcy's large dowry?

The young lady looked strangely at Elizabeth, as if she were curious as to whom she was. "Excuse me, I did not mean to be in your way."

Elizabeth was not in the mood to be polite to this lady, as she wished to spread her hatred to all who were in the Darcy box. "It is I who should beg forgiveness, Miss. I was not watching where I was walking. Please forgive me."

As Elizabeth moved to step passed her, the young

lady spoke again. "Forgive me, my name is Georgiana Darcy. I cannot help but feel that you are upset. Is something wrong? Is there something I can do to be of assistance?"

Why does she have to be so nice? Why must she speak to me, when all I wish is to hate her and her brother and Mr Bingley? "Thank you, Miss Darcy, but I am fine. I will make my way back to my aunt and uncle, they are waiting for me."

"Might I ask your name?" Georgiana asked.

"Miss Elizabeth Bennet." Was the reply.

"Miss Elizabeth, from Longbourn?" Seeing Elizabeth nod her head, Georgiana became excited. "My brother has told me so much of you. Every letter he sent from Netherfield told me more of you. Please, will you not come to our box and greet my brother and his friend?"

"I am here with my aunt and uncle, and I know your brother will not be pleased to meet them, as my uncle is in trade and they live near Cheapside. It is best that your brother does not know we are here." Elizabeth began to walk away.

"Please, Miss Elizabeth, I am certain my brother and Mr Bingley would be grateful to see you." Georgiana was surprised at her own daring. From reading her brother's letters, the young lady had come to the conclusion that her brother was half in love with the very lady standing in front of her. After seeing Elizabeth Bennet for herself, Georgiana was even more convinced.

"It was a pleasure meeting you, Miss Darcy. I must return to my seat before my relatives come searching for me."

Elizabeth made her way to her seat, though her aunt could tell something was wrong. "Lizzy, are you well?"

"I am fine, Aunt Helen. I just encountered someone in the lobby I was not prepared to see, and it has me a bit out of sorts."

Mrs Gardiner could not imagine who could have caused her niece to be so jittery. "Who did you meet?"

"Never mind, Aunt, let us enjoy the rest of the performance."

~~ ** ~~

Georgiana hurried as fast as she could to her brother. "William, you will never guess who I met?"

"Very well, dearest, who have you met?" Darcy smiled slightly at his sister's excitement.

"Miss Elizabeth Bennet. She is here, with her aunt and uncle. I asked her to come greet you, but she stated you would not approve of her relations, as they were from Cheapside."

"Where did you see her?" Darcy asked as his eyes

began to search the crowd.

"She was leaving the necessary room as I was going in. We nearly collided. I was surprised to learn her name. She is beautiful, William. But something was wrong, she appeared to be upset." Georgiana's eyebrows nearly knitted as she attempted to determine what could be wrong with her brother's friend.

"Miss Elizabeth is a strong lady, Georgie, have no fear for her. Even when she was worried for her sister, when Miss Bennet took so ill at Netherfield, Miss Elizabeth did not allow it to bring her down." Darcy was still attempting to spy the familiar face of the woman who was in his thoughts constantly. "Perhaps it is best that we return to our box, as the play with begin again shortly."

Throughout the remaining portion of the play, Darcy ignored the performance on the stage, as he searched the theatre for Elizabeth Bennet. He continued looking throughout the building, wishing for a glimpse of her. If only he could see the sparkle in her eyes, the impish turn of her lips when she smiled. Perhaps the sight of her would calm his restless heart for a little while.

~~~~~~~ ** ~~~~~~~

Chapter 2

Darcy spent the following day with his solicitor on matters of business. He was distracted, his mind wandering back to the evening before, and his lost chance of seeing Miss Elizabeth Bennet.

Bingley had been sad to have not been able to greet the sister of the angel to whom he had given over his heart. Ever since he left Netherfield, his mind continued to return there, to the incredible Miss Jane Bennet, with beautiful pale blue eyes, golden hair, and the sweetest nature. After all of their talks, Bingley thought he knew Jane Bennet better than anyone else in the world. His heart was broken when his sisters and Darcy insisted there was no sign of any attachment on Jane's part, and he was devastated when Darcy suggested Jane was acting according to her mother's demands for her to marry a rich man, whether she loved him or not.

Seeing Bingley's anxious face at the possibility of seeing Jane's sister, Darcy realized the depths of his friend's devotion for Miss Bennet of Longbourn. Could he tell his friend the truth? Could he tell Bingley that his own sisters had come to Darcy House, begging for Darcy's assistance in keeping their brother from Miss Bennet?

If he told Bingley the truth of the matter, it could destroy their friendship forever. And there was a part of the truth to which he could not admit, not to anyone. For Darcy's greatest fear was his friend would marry Miss Bennet. If Bingley did, Darcy would be in the company of Miss Elizabeth Bennet often. Darcy did not feel strong enough to be able to control his feelings for the country miss who had haunted his thoughts, day and night, since he met her.

Seeing the beautiful, teasing Miss Elizabeth while he was visiting Bingley at the estate he leased was difficult, especially the week Miss Elizabeth stayed at Netherfield, Bingley's estate, to nurse her ill sister. Knowing that his vision of perfection was sleeping three doors away, under the same roof, Darcy could not sleep at night. Every time he saw her, his tongue became tied and he could not find the words to speak to her. So he would stand across the room from her and stare.

The chestnut curls always seemed to be trying to escape the pins holding them on top of her head. Darcy longed to see her hair flowing freely, and to be able to run his fingers through those curls. Her eyes sparkled with delight, especially when she was particularly mischievous. She always spoke her mind, not giving in to those who, like Miss Caroline Bingley, thought themselves better than a young lady from the country. Her intelligence was far above most ladies her age, as Elizabeth had been taught as if she were a son.

Darcy was quite melancholy at not having had the opportunity to see Elizabeth Bennet, and yet, he knew it was for the best. If he had seen her again, he knew there was no way he would be strong enough to let her go a second time. Though she was extremely inappropriate to make a proper wife, especially with her crude relations and lack of dowry, Darcy's heart could not be swayed.

~~ ** ~~

As she prepared for the day, the morning of the second of January, Elizabeth's thoughts returned to the night at the theatre and how she had hidden in her seat, using her uncle's large frame to block Darcy from seeing her. She did not wish to spend the evening, knowing he was watching her, and knowing he was looking to find fault in her. What fault could there be in her attending a play? He did not own the building, and she was nowhere near his box, so he could not find fault in her being there.

The confusing part was the fact that his sister knew who she was. Miss Darcy even stated her brother's letters from Netherfield told of her. Why would he write to his sister, mentioning her name and her exploits? Elizabeth chuckled at the thought that Darcy was most likely setting examples of things his sister should not do.

The numbness she had been feeling since her father informed her she would marry Mr Collins, had returned in greater proportions, overwhelming her every thought. After this morning, she would no longer be herself, she would be Elizabeth Collins, wife of Mr Collins and expected to do her duty as his wife. Such duties included the marriage bed to produce an heir for him. Remembering the chat with her mother, the night before, Elizabeth shuddered. How was she to submit to such a man in that way? No matter what she thought to try to distract herself, Elizabeth's mind continued to return to this fact. She was to submit to him, allow him to do things to her body which she could not imagine being true, and hope for a son. Her mother stated that once men had their heir, they were less demanding on their wives and even took mistresses to give their wives a break.

Sarah, the maid who took care of all of the Bennet daughters, came in to assist Elizabeth in her preparations for the day. Not long after, Jane came to assist with her sister's hair. Since the decision had been made by their father, Jane had noticed the melancholy that had engulfed her sister. How Jane wished she could protect Elizabeth, as she knew her sister would be miserable married to the imbecilic clergyman.

Soon, Elizabeth was dressed in the gown her mother had had made for the wedding. The necklace her father had gifted her, which had been her grandmother's, was placed around her neck. Everyone claimed how beautiful she was, how perfect a bride she was. Elizabeth could only feel the numbness wrapped around her body. She tried to smile and greet everyone with a pleasant word or two. But she felt it was forced and unnatural, and Elizabeth was certain others would see through the falseness.

It seemed like no time at all had passed when Mr Bennet knocked on his daughter's door and announced it was time to go to the church. At this announcement, Elizabeth's legs felt like they were made of jam, and she required assistance in walking. Jane was on one side, and Mr Bennet was on the other, as they led Elizabeth downstairs and out to the carriage. Once at the church, Elizabeth felt as if her limbs had turned to stone. It was difficult to force herself to take each step forward, all the while her heart was slowly beating until, just before the altar, and Elizabeth felt as if her heart stopped completely.

She did not hear the words, only her name being spoken. She heard herself repeating her vows, doing as she was told to do. When the clergyman asked if there was anyone who could think of any reason the two should not marry, Elizabeth found it difficult not to scream out. *Please, anyone, save me from this sham of a marriage. Find some kind of reason, anything, to say the marriage could not happen.* But no one said a word. No one came to her rescue. No one knew that, at that moment, Elizabeth Bennet died a cruel death, leaving only the shell of a person standing beside Mr Collins, being pronounced as his wife.

The wedding breakfast was soon underway, with

everyone coming to wish the couple all the joy in the world. Elizabeth could not remember anyone, her mind was coated in ice as she went through the motions of being a happy bride.

The food was enjoyed by many and before long, Mr Collins declared it was time for them to take their leave for Hunsford. Her stone limbs were difficult to control, forcing herself to take each step forward until she reached the carriage which would convey them. She could hear the voices of people wishing them well and congratulations, though not one of the voices could be recognized. As she sat back against the carriage seat, Elizabeth's eyes closed. She prayed her new husband would take the hint and allow her some peace, at least until they reached her new home. Finally, peace overtook her, and Elizabeth fell asleep.

~~ ** ~~

Suddenly, Elizabeth felt her body being tossed about. She could hear Mr Collins' screams, and the carriage lurched to the side, before rolling down a hillside. The horses could be heard, their voices protesting whatever was happening. Feeling the carriage come to a halt, upside down, she noticed there was something heavy laying on top of her body, trapping it against the ceiling of the carriage. It was difficult to breathe, and all she could see was darkness. The pain inside her head was tremendous, until, she felt nothing more.

~~ ** ~~

Darcy was seated at his desk in his study of Darcy House, the Darcy family townhouse he had inherited five years before, when his father died. Though Darcy had inherited the family estate of Pemberley, a smaller estate in Scotland, and property in Ireland, there was something about the study at his London townhouse which was comfortable. Perhaps it was due to his father having preference to the study at Pemberley, and that particular room had not been updated since Gerald Darcy's death. The townhouse study had been refurbished before his father's death, making it more to Darcy's liking.

It had been nearly a month since the theatre, though every moment he was not occupied, Darcy's mind was thinking of Miss Elizabeth Bennet. He was in love with her, there was no doubt about it. He loved everything about the country lass who wrapped him around her little finger. Her chestnut colored hair which curled so much that it defied any attempts to be pinned, her sparkling chocolate brown eyes which held so much life inside them, her cheeks which blushed so prettily, her lips which tempted him to possess. Her slim body had the most perfect curvature to it, in all of the right places, making him desperate to caress each and every inch of her.

How he had wished he could have seen her the night of the theatre. Darcy felt as if he were in the desert, and Elizabeth Bennet was the tall, cool glass of water which he desperately needed to survive. Perhaps he was wrong in discouraging Bingley from returning to Netherfield, but Darcy feared being in Her presence for too long.

All the arguments he had made for not becoming involved with Elizabeth were for naught. Yes, her family was obnoxious, with her overbearing mother and her two youngest sisters who behaved abhorrently. There was no dowry to speak of, and the estate was entailed to a cousin. Mr Bennet was known to only be worth two thousand per annum, and he preferred to hide away in his study rather than correct the misbehaviors of his family. Mrs Bennet's family came from trade, with her father having been a solicitor, her brother-in-law took over the business after her father's death. Mrs Bennet's brother was in trade and lived near Cheapside. So a relationship with Elizabeth would bring no connections to it.

Darcy knew that his feelings towards the young lady from Longbourn were inappropriate and would never come to pass. He had his family to consider. He had inherited guardianship of Georgiana, who was only ten years old when their father died. Their mother died shortly after Georgiana's first birthday. If Darcy were to marry the wrong sort of lady, it could damage Georgiana's future and her potential for marrying well.

Darcy also knew his mother's brother, Lord Matlock, would not approve of such a lady as

Elizabeth Bennet. Nor would his mother's sister, Lady Catherine de Bourgh. Lady Catherine insisted that he was to marry her daughter, Anne, and unite their two estates. Anne was a sickly and nearly useless lady, as she had been sheltered all of her life. When Anne was a child, she was stricken with a terrible fever, which left her heart weakened. After Anne recovered, Lady Catherine refused to allow her to go out of doors or any activity which would include her exerting herself. Darcy had no desire to marry Anne, and he attempted to tell his aunt constantly.

So, when a letter arrived from Rosings Park, Lady Catherine's home, Darcy prepared himself for another tedious letter filled with asking him when he would be coming to Rosings to ask for Anne's hand in marriage. Dreading the letter's contents, he began to read.

My dear nephew,

I require your assistance immediately at Rosings. We are in a despair over what to do. Mr Collins, my clergyman at Hunsford, recently married. On his way to bring his wife home, their carriage had some sort of breakdown which caused an accident. Mr Collins was killed, and his wife was injured.

The carriage he was in was one of my old ones, but I still need to have it repaired. And, now, I am forced to search again for a clergyman. It took me many months to find Mr Collins, and now he has left me in the most terrible position of searching again. This is not to be borne. And we need to remove his wife, who was taken to Hunsford Parsonage, so the apothecary could tend to her injuries. She should be returned to her family rather than remain here, for we need to prepare the cottage for the next clergyman I select. Mr Wilkens, the apothecary claims she is far too weak to be moved, but I do not believe him. If she is to die, it is best she do so elsewhere, not in my parsonage.

Please come as soon as possible. I cannot get through this trying time without you.

Lady Catherine de Bourgh

Mr Collins, was that not the name of the man he met in Hertfordshire? The one who was cousin to Miss Elizabeth? If the new Mrs Collins was so badly injured, why had Darcy's aunt not sent for a physician, rather than the apothecary? Darcy never had much faith in Mr Wilkens.

Though Darcy was not pleased with having to travel to Rosings, he decided it would be best if he did assist his aunt and see to the widowed bride of Mr Collins. It would be best if he went the following day, so he could return to Town by the following week. And if Darcy could manage to correct the ledgers for Rosings Park quickly, there would be no need for him to return at Easter.

Darcy quickly penned a letter to a friend of his, Mr Raymond Lowe, who was a physician. If Mr Lowe were available, Darcy would take him along on the trip to see to Mrs Collins. Though Lady Catherine was more put out with having Mrs Collins on the estate than she was worried for the young lady, Darcy would make certain of the care taken of the lady.

~~ ** ~~

The following morning, Darcy's carriage left London for Rosings Park. With Darcy was Mr Lowe and Darcy's cousin, the second son of Lord Matlock, Colonel Richard Fitzwilliam.

"So, had you met this Collins before?" Colonel Fitzwilliam asked his cousin.

"I did. I met him while I was visiting Bingley at the estate he had leased. As you can well remember the last clergyman Aunt Catherine had, I am certain you can conjure up an image of this one." Darcy stated as he looked out the window of the carriage. "Actually, he is worse than the previous one, if you can imagine it."

"Did you meet his, then, fiancé?"

"No, and to be honest, I am shocked any woman would ever accept a man such as he to marry. It makes me wonder what sort of lady would lower herself to marry him. She must have been quite desperate to make such a choice."

Lowe chuckled. "Well, after meeting you, it would be difficult for any lady. I am sure you left behind many a broken heart, just as you did when we were at Cambridge together."

"I have no desire to cause anyone heartache." Darcy began to feel uncomfortable. "I have always attempted to conduct myself in a manner so as not to lead ladies to believe I favor them."

"Darcy, you have always behaved properly. That does not mean you do not break hearts, especially of those who fall head over heels for you, only to never gain your acknowledgement." Lowe stated. "You must understand that one can fall in love with someone from across a crowded room."

This comment struck deep within Darcy's heart. *Yes, of all people, I should know about falling in love from across a room.* His attention to the conversation returned when Colonel Fitzwilliam asked if he knew Mr Collins' bride.

"I was not informed he had become engaged before I left Netherfield, so I cannot say who the young lady is. There were a couple of ladies who were close to being 'on the shelf', and Collins may have made one of them an offer. I cannot imagine any other lady being foolish enough to marry such a man. Well, perhaps Miss Mary Bennet would. She was forever reading Fordyce."

"Who is Miss Mary Bennet?" Colonel Fitzwilliam

asked.

"The middle daughter of Mr Thomas Bennet, of Longbourn. It is the estate which borders Netherfield. I believe I wrote to you about the family, when the eldest was sent to Netherfield on horseback when it was about to rain. She became quite ill and had to remain at Bingley's house for some time. Bingley was quite taken with Miss Bennet. They just so happen to be Mr Collins' cousins, and he would have inherited the estate."

"Ah, yes, I do remember you writing about the family. You were pleased to have been able assist Bingley in leaving the neighborhood before he proposed to her. Did you not say the two youngest daughters were quite wild?"

Darcy nodded his head. "And their mother was vulgar, and quite the matchmaking mamma. That is the reason Miss Bennet arrived on horseback, her mother wished for a reason to keep her daughter at Netherfield to win Bingley's heart. Miss Bennet is a sweet natured young lady, and quite pretty as well, but I could not detect any partiality on her side towards my friend. So Bingley's sisters and I convinced him it was wiser to remain in Town, once we arrived there for a short visit. Bingley has not been the same since leaving Netherfield. He thought Miss Bennet returned his regard, and now he is unsure if he can trust his own judgment. I have been trying to decide a way to bring him out of this mood, but can only think of inviting him to Pemberley in the summer."

Colonel Fitzwilliam nodded his head. "A change of scenery, especially to a place as grand as Pemberley, would do wonders for anyone's melancholy. It is a magical place to recover, as I stand proof. I do not believe I would have recovered so fully from my battle wounds if it had not been for my time at Pemberley. It soothed my body and my soul."

"I will have to remember your words, Cousin." Darcy smiled as he turned his view out the window. "Ah, we have almost arrived. I will be glad when this is over, I wish to be returned to Town as soon as possible. I promised Georgiana we would take in the exhibit at the museum before it moves on."

~~ ** ~~

Arriving at Rosings, Darcy, Colonel Fitzwilliam, and Mr Lowe made their way into the drawing room, where Lady Catherine was seated in her throne like chair.

"Darcy, it is about time. I have been at a loss as to what to do. It has been a fortnight since Mr Collins died, and I have yet to remove his wife from the parsonage or find a replacement for him. I am at my wit's end."

"A fortnight? Why did you only send the express to me yesterday?" Darcy frowned as he attempted to discover what was happening.

"Well, at first, we did not know he was dead. The newlywed couple were to leave Hertfordshire shortly after their wedding breakfast. When they did not arrive at the parsonage, as had been planned, I thought Mr Collins had decided to change his plans and not contacted me. Then, one of my tenants discovered an injured horse on his property. It turned out to be one of my horses, one which had gone with the carriage to retrieve Mr Collins and his wife. My steward insisted on a search of the area, and that was when it was discovered that the carriage had overturned. I am rather vexed at the condition of the carriage, as I am certain it will cost a great deal to repair it. And the driver, I will need to hire another driver, for he was killed as well. This is all too much for me to bear."

"How many days between when they should have arrived and they were found?" Mr Lowe asked.

"The carriage was found six days after the day of the wedding. Oh, and Darcy, I will need more horses. Only one of the horses survived the wreck, and it is extremely lame. Perhaps we should have it put down, as it will never be able to pull a carriage again."

"Aunt Catherine, have you no compassion for what this accident has done to others?" Colonel Fitzwilliam asked, his ire building with his desire to throttle his aunt. "All you care about is how you are affected, and not about the two men who died, the horses, and especially not having any care for the young lady who is not only injured, but is now a widow. Instead of giving a thought to her care, you wish her removed from the parsonage so she no longer inconvenience you."

Lady Catherine was not in a mood to accept such comments from her nephew. "It is none of your concern, Fitzwilliam. Mind your own business or I will inform your father of your meddling."

"Richard, perhaps you should take a walk down to the stables. You are a good judge of horses, I wish for your opinion of the lame horse, whether we should put it down or find someone who can tend it. Also, I would like you to look at the carriage remains. Give me your opinion as to how the accident occurred and if the carriage is salvageable." Darcy took charge of the situation.

"Yes, Cousin. I welcome the chance to be of assistance. Will you go to the parsonage with Mr Lowe to check on Mrs Collins?" Colonel Fitzwilliam was pleased to remove himself from his aunt's presence.

Darcy nodded his head. "Lowe, are you ready?"

"Darcy, you cannot leave me at this time of my greatest need." Cried Lady Catherine. "Your physician can most assuredly tend to the young lady without you."

"Aunt Catherine, I wish to see for myself the condition the lady is in, and to ensure everything that needs to be done for her is done. We cannot move her from the parsonage until she is well enough, so it is wisest to do what we can to make her well." Darcy was close to losing his composure.

"Very well. Go to the parsonage. But return before long, as it will soon be tea time." Lady Catherine huffed.

~~~~~~~ ** ~~~~~~~

Chapter 3

Darcy and Mr Lowe made their way to the parsonage, and were welcomed into the cottage. Mrs Johnston, the housekeeper for the parsonage, was pleased to see Darcy. "Sir, I am so grateful you have come. Your aunt has been so very angry that the young lady was brought here, but there was nowhere else to take her. And Mrs Collins is very ill indeed. The apothecary, Mr Wilkens, has begged for your aunt to send for a physician for Mrs Collins, but Lady Catherine has flat refused."

"Where is the lady?" Lowe asked.

"I will take you to her. Due to Lady Catherine's anger, we felt it wiser to have the young lady placed in my rooms, as it would be easier to hide her. Lady Catherine has been here three times, ranting about being inconvenienced by Mr Collins' death and having to find another clergyman. She has even stated it was Mrs Collins' fault, for if they had been married from Hunsford rather than the young lady's home, they would not have been traveling as they were."

Darcy knew his aunt's behavior had always been rude and unkind, but this was far worse than he could ever have imagined. He followed Mrs Johnston and Lowe towards the back of the house, to the servants' area. As they reached Mrs Johnston's door, Darcy remembered he had a question to ask. "Mrs Johnston, do you, by chance, know the lady's family name? I was led to believe she was from Hertfordshire, near where I recently stayed with a friend of mine. I met Mr Collins there, he was visiting his cousins."

"It is one of his cousins he married." Mrs Johnston replied.

"I will send word to Mr Bennet, as I am familiar with the gentleman." Darcy replied. "Would the young lady have been Miss Mary Bennet?"

Mrs Johnston frowned as she opened the door and stepped inside the bedchamber. "No, Sir, Mrs Collins' name was Miss Elizabeth Bennet."

Darcy stumbled as he heard the name. Looking at the bed, seeing the unrecognizable person lying on it, Darcy's heart began to shatter into bits. "Elizabeth...no, it cannot possibly be Elizabeth." Tears welled in his eyes as he attempted to find something familiar about her.

The wounds Elizabeth sustained were severe. Her head was bandaged, including her eyes. Her left arm was bandaged as well. She was so still and lifeless, he had to watch the blankets which covered her to assure himself that she was breathing.

"Darcy, do you know the young lady?" Lowe asked, seeing his friend pale.

"Whatever you need to do for Elizabeth, please, see that it is done. Damn the cost, do all you can for her." Darcy said, still unable to look anywhere but at the woman he loved.

"Mr Wilkens is sleeping, as he was up all night with Mrs Collins. Shall I awaken him?" Mrs Johnston asked.

"Yes, if you would. The sooner Mr Lowe knows about her condition, the sooner he will be able to tend her." Darcy insisted.

Moments later, Mr Wilkens arrived, looking quite exhausted. "Mr Darcy, I cannot thank you enough on behalf of my patient. She is in need of more care than I can provide."

"What is her condition?" Lowe inquired.

"When she was found, the carriage was upside down, after rolling several times. It had rolled down the hill, two miles from here. The carriage was upside down and Mrs Collins was lying on what was the ceiling. Mr Collins' body was pinning her, draped across her torso and legs. Once we removed his body, we found she was in a terrible way. She has several ribs cracked, the collarbone is broken on the left side, and a terrible cut on her left forearm. She had lost a good portion of blood, which caused me to fear for her survival. To be honest, I am amazed she has lived this long."

Darcy was shaking as he took a seat in the chair next to the bed. Listening to the apothecary describe Elizabeth's injuries was taking a toll on him.

"What of her head?" Lowe asked. "What is the bandaging covering?"

"Mrs Collins has not been awake since we found her. We found a rather sizeable lump on the back of her head, and several areas of bruising and cuts on her face. There was scrapes across her forehead and the bridge of her nose, which is why her eyes are covered. We applied an herbal blend to the wounds, after they had been cleaned. There is a cut along her right lower leg, and it appears that she has some toes broken."

"The housekeeper stated that Mrs Collins was restless last night." Darcy said in a whisper.

Mr Wilkens nodded his head. "She thrashes about at times, though she is still unconscious. If we could locate any of her family, perhaps this might calm her during these fits."

"I know her family and will send an express to them as soon as possible. Has she been conscious at all?" Darcy was finding it difficult to control the fear which was racing through him.

"Not conscious, though she moves about and moans at times. I fear giving her any more laudanum, though I feel she must be in pain." Mr Wilkens replied.

Mr Lowe agreed. "Too much laudanum can suppress the mind if she is attempting to return to the world. We will be able to judge better the damage if she is not sedated the same as she would for the other injuries alone. Darcy, you said you know her. What sort of lady is she?"

"Forgive me, I do not understand."

"Is she of a sickly nature or normally strong and healthy?"

"Miss Elizabeth was known to walk out of doors most every day the weather was nice. When her sister was ill, last year, and Miss Bennet was a guest at my friend's estate, Miss Elizabeth walked the three miles from her home to Netherfield to tend to her sister. She has always seemed to be a strong and vibrant young lady, full of life."

"Do you know much of her marriage? Would knowing her husband is dead weigh heavily upon her and cause melancholy?" Lowe continued his questions.

"As far as I can remember, Miss Elizabeth disliked Mr Collins and found him to be ridiculous. That was the reason I was shocked to learn it was she who had married Mr Collins and not her next sister, Miss Mary. In my opinion, after meeting Mr Collins and being near him for only a short time, it is my belief that Miss Elizabeth would not be saddened by his loss. I would think her more likely to be saddened by the driver of the carriage dying."

"Very well. Darcy, would you mind stepping out of

the room so I might examine her? I will let you know when you can return." Lowe knew there was more to his friend's behavior that Darcy had let on.

Nodding his head, Darcy stepped into the hallway. He began pacing, back and forth, over and over. After what seemed an eternity, the door to the bedchamber opened again. Mr Lowe stepped out into the hall to speak with his friend.

"Send the express as soon as possible. Her family needs to be here. I do not understand how she is still alive, Darcy. She is weak, extremely weak. Make haste, get her loved ones here as quickly as possible, for I do not know how much longer she will live."

Those words were as if someone had grabbed hold of his own heart and yanked it from his chest. Elizabeth was dying. This was not possible. How could she be here, at the parsonage, married to Mr Collins, and now was dying? *This has to be a nightmare, it cannot possibly be real.*

Darcy made his way to the desk in the parlor, and extracted the items needed to write the letter. *How do I write this letter to her family? How do I tell them she will die soon?*

He wrote several drafts before finally having a letter he felt proper to send. After sending for one of his men who had traveled on the carriage with them, Darcy sanded the letter and sealed it.

As the footman who had been sent for arrived at the cottage, so did Colonel Fitzwilliam. The look upon his cousin's face told Darcy that Richard was quite displeased.

The letter was handed over to the footman and the young man took leave, with the understanding the letter was to be received by the Bennet family as soon as possible. The young man had acted as personal courier for Darcy before, so the task was not unusual for him. Once he was off, Darcy and his cousin took a seat in the parlor.

"Richard, tell me, what did you find out?"

"Aunt Catherine should be whipped for her negligence. I found out that the carriage involved had not been maintained due to our aunt being miserly and refusing to spend a single coin on it. It was also the oldest carriage Aunt Catherine owns. From what I was told, it should never have been used. The axle broke clean through. And the road was full of holes, causing the carriage to bounce about. Remember where we were when my horse stumbled last year? That is where the accident occurred. The carriage rolled at least three times completely before coming to rest on its top. I looked inside the carriage, it is behind the stables. Even having been in the battlefields, I was not prepared for the amount of blood I witnessed in the carriage. How is Mrs Collins? Was it the young lady you thought might have accepted the man?"

Darcy stood and walked towards the window. Having grown up with Darcy, Richard Fitzwilliam knew his cousin was in turmoil. After a few moments, Richard walked over to Darcy and stood beside him. "Tell me, Will. Who is she?"

"Miss Elizabeth Bennet. I know I should be referring to her as Mrs Collins, but I cannot think of her as the wife of that imbecile, even if he is dead. She is the one I wrote about, the sister of Bingley's angel."

"And she has your heart in the palm of her hand?" Richard asked.

Darcy could not speak, so he simply nodded his head. "She is an amazing lady, so filled with life, intelligent, witty, and very beautiful. Why would she be the one to have married Mr Collins? I know she disliked him, it was quite clear she thought him to be ridiculous."

"Perhaps it was a marriage of convenience. You said her father's estate was entailed to Collins. Would that not be a reason for her to accept such an offer?"

Looking into his cousin's eyes, Darcy shook his head. "No, not Elizabeth. She is not the sort to marry without affection for her partner."

"How is she?" Richard asked, seeing the pain in Darcy's eyes.

"Lowe said we should bring her family here as soon as possible. He is amazed she has survived this long, and does not feel she will last much longer." A lump had formed in Darcy's throat as he spoke, causing him difficulty in speaking the words. "She is dying, Richard. The most perfect woman in the world is dying."

"Then, perhaps you should be with her, so she can find some comfort from a familiar voice until her family arrives. I will have some coffee brought up to you, as well as some food. You could read to her, allow her to hear your voice."

Darcy nodded his head. If he could do no more, he would bring her some comfort. He walked back to the bedchamber, knocking softly on the door. Lowe opened the door and allowed his friend to enter. "She is restless, Darcy. We are attempting to calm her without having to sedate her."

"Would you allow me to sit beside her and read to her?"

"Of course, she would be more at ease with a voice she has heard previously. That would be a splendid idea." Lowe motioned to the chair beside the bed.

Darcy sat down, taking hold of her right hand. "Miss Elizabeth, do not fret. I am seeing to everything being done for you. I have sent a letter by express to your family, informing them of your accident and injuries. I pray they will be on their way soon and be here by tomorrow at the latest. Perhaps you will wake to find Miss Jane beside you. You and your elder sister are so dear to each other. I can remember you're walking to Netherfield to tend to Miss Bennet when she took ill and was required to stay there. I am sure she will wish to do the same for you."

Soon, Elizabeth seemed to calm her thrashing about and began to breathe easier. Mr Lowe was pleased to see the change in his patient's condition. "Keep talking to her."

Darcy opened the book his cousin had brought him and began to read. The longer Darcy read, the calmer Elizabeth became. Mr Lowe was shocked to see such a change in his patient's condition. "Darcy, I am going to step out and refresh myself. Would you mind staying with Mrs Collins while I am in the other room?"

"Of course not. The maid will be here as well, so there should be no cause for reproach. Have something to eat as well. We need to keep you healthy and strong, so you can tend to Miss Elizabeth."

~~ ** ~~

Elizabeth felt trapped inside her mind and body. The last memory she had was of being inside the carriage, leaving her home and family, as she journeyed to her new home. Vaguely she could remember the carriage shaking and rocking, and then she remembered feeling as if she was trapped under a boulder, the air being forced from her lungs and making it difficult to take in any air. She could remember feeling wet, as if it had rained on her. Nothing was making sense to her muddled mind, as she was unable to comprehend where she was or what had happened.

Trying desperately to open her eyes or move her arms and legs, Elizabeth struggled in vain. No matter how hard she tried, she could not command her body to act as she wished.

The pain she felt was constant, and grew in intensity whenever she attempted to move her body. Being unable to determine where she was or who was with her, Elizabeth began to feel panic setting in.

What happened to me? I feel as if I have been trampled by a hundred horses. If only I could open my eyes, determine where I am, I would feel better. Is Mr Collins here with me? Am I ill or injured? If something is wrong with me, would not Mr Collins send word to Papa and Jane? They would come, I am sure of it. Oh, Jane, how I wish you were here to tell me what was going on.

But that voice that is speaking now, there is something familiar about it. The depth of the baritone voice, the warmth it has created, so very soothing. I could listen to that voice forever. It is making me sleepy. So comforting...

Elizabeth drifted off to sleep, unbeknownst to the man behind the voice. The calm which came over her was painless and easy, and she prayed the voice would stay close to her until she could figure a way to make her body function properly.

~~ ** ~~

Mr Bennet had just read through the letter he had just received from Darcy's courier. He sent the young man to the kitchen to have something to eat so he could compose himself enough to write a letter in return for the man to take to Darcy.

Stepping to the hallway outside his study, Mr Bennet called for his housekeeper to locate Jane.

Several minutes passed by before Jane knocked on her father's study door. "Enter." She heard her father call out to her.

"Papa, Mrs Hill said you asked for me. Is something wrong?"

"Sit down, my dear. I just received an express from none other than Mr Darcy."

Jane was shocked. "Mr Darcy, whatever could cause him to be sending an express to us?"

"You remember he is the nephew of Lady Catherine de Bourgh of Rosings Park? Well, his aunt sent for him to resolve a problem. Upon his arrival at Rosings, he learned the truth of her 'problem'. There was an accident with the carriage in which Lizzy and Mr Collins traveled to Hunsford. I do not know all the details, but it appears as if the carriage ended up overturning down a hillside. The driver of the carriage and Mr Collins are both dead, and Lizzy is badly injured. Mr Darcy had taken a friend with him who is a physician, for Lady Catherine had stated that Mr Collins' wife had been injured and was being seen by the apothecary. Of course, Mr Darcy had no way of knowing Mrs Collins was Lizzy. The physician has urged us to come to Hunsford as soon as possible, as he is unsure Lizzy will be able to survive all her injuries."

Tears were steadily rolling down Jane's cheeks as she began to sob. "Oh, Lizzy, my dear sister. Papa, tell me we are leaving immediately."

"Go up and pack some belongings. We will leave within the hour. I will send the courier back to Mr Darcy, letting him know we are on our way." Mr Bennet pulled out his handkerchief and dried his own cheeks. "Let us pray Lizzy will hold on. She has always been strong."

"She has, but the wedding has taken its toll on her spirit. And now she is a widow, on the same day she became a wife." Jane shook her head. "It is too much to endure. Poor Lizzy."

"All we can do at the moment is pray. Be off now and hurry. I will have our carriage made ready."

It was not long before Mr Bennet and his eldest

daughter set out for Hunsford parsonage. Neither of them wished to speak, their thoughts were wrapped around the young lady who was fighting for her life at the parsonage. There was nothing either could say to calm each other's nerves, so the father and daughter stared out the windows of the carriage, watching the scenery as they rolled passed.

Finally, the carriage came to a halt in front of the parsonage. It was late at night, yet the cottage was well lit. Darcy had come down to welcome the Bennets.

"Mr Bennet, Miss Bennet, I wish I could say it was a pleasure to see you right now. But under these circumstances, I wish things were quite different."

"Mr Darcy, I wish to express my gratitude for informing us as to my daughter's condition. Why were we not notified before this? The wedding was a little over a fortnight ago and your letter stated the accident was the day of the wedding, as they were coming here?"

"The accident was not known for almost a week. Then there had to be a search conducted to locate the carriage and your daughter. From what my cousin and I have been able to discover, our aunt did not become alarmed at Mr Collins' continued absence, and only realized there was a problem when one of her horses, which had been used to pull the carriage, was found at one of the tenant's farm. The carriage appears to have had the axle break, and it lost control, overturning several times, before coming to rest upside down. Miss Elizabeth was trapped underneath the body of Mr Collins. The driver had been thrown from the carriage and crushed as it rolled. Once your daughter was found, they brought her here, unfortunately against my aunt's wishes. My cousin and I are handling Lady Catherine for the moment, as she is behaving quite selfishly in demanding Miss Elizabeth be removed from here so a new parson can be found and moved in here."

"From listening to my cousin, I was confident that Lady Catherine was an eccentric person who demanded her own way in everything. Now I see I am correct." Mr Bennet stated. "And how is my daughter?"

"She is badly injured. But I will have the physician speak to you on those matters. I wish you to know, I have instructed Mr Lowe to spare no expense on caring for Miss Elizabeth. I will be handling the bills, and will not allow you to argue the point with me. Had my aunt behaved properly, none of this would have happened. Now, allow me to show you to your daughter. The housekeeper here at Hunsford put Miss Elizabeth in her rooms, in an attempt to protect your daughter. My aunt made several trips here in her anger over having to hire a new clergyman, and Mrs Johnston did not wish for Lady Catherine to take her ire out on Miss Elizabeth. I would have her moved to one of the better rooms, but we cannot do so until Mr Lowe and the apothecary agree she can be moved."

Jane could see the pain in the eyes of the man before her. "Mr Darcy, I add my gratitude to that of my father. We are completely in your debt."

Darcy led the Bennets to the room and to Elizabeth's bedside. Mr Bennet stood back, looking distraught at the sight before him. Jane instantly sat on the side of the bed and took hold of her sister's right hand. "Oh, Lizzy, my dear sister, please return to us. Do not leave me, Lizzy."

"Mr Bennet, if you wish, perhaps you should sit in the chair." Darcy attempted to guide the elder man to the chair he had been occupying.

Seeing a book on the chair, Mr Bennet was curious for some sort of diversion. "Who has been reading?"

"Mr Lowe felt it would be calming for her to hear a voice which she could recognize reading to her. Though our acquaintance is of a short duration, I was the only one here she has known. So I have been reading to her." Darcy explained.

Lowe stepped forward. "It has had an amazing effect on her, Mr Bennet. There have been times of her thrashing about, but as soon as Darcy began reading to her, she calmed and became quite peaceful. In just the time I have been here, I can see a remarkable change in her breathing and heartbeats. If we can keep her calm, allow her body to use the calmness to work towards healing itself, she may have a chance at recovery."

These words were like a balm on the souls of the three people who cared for Elizabeth. Darcy felt peace in knowing his simple action had been helpful to the woman he loved. Mr Bennet was surprised at the kindness of Darcy, after hearing of his aunt's selfish distain for his beloved daughter. And Jane, sweet natured as she was, expressed her gratitude to Mr Darcy for his kind attention which was saving her dearest sister.

After half an hour, Mr Bennet was showing signs of weariness. "Mr Bennet, we have a room prepared for you upstairs. I can have Mrs Johnston show you to it, if you would like." Darcy expressed, concerned for the man who was appearing to be weaker than the last time he had seen him.

"Mr Darcy, might I ask you to show me to the room? I would like a moment with you." Mr Bennet said, making it clear he had some questions for the younger man.

Darcy nodded his head. "Of course, Sir. Come with me."

Slowly, the two men made their way up the stairs and to the room. Once inside, Mr Bennet asked Darcy to take a seat so they could talk.

"Mr Darcy, I must say that I am shocked at all I have learned today. First, to learn of the accident, and of the death of my cousin, then to learn of my dear Lizzy's condition. Then we arrive here, to find Lizzy in such a fragile state. But the greatest shock is to learn of your ignoring propriety by being in my daughter's bedchamber, and reading to her. I am shocked at such behavior from someone of the highest circle of society."

"Mr Bennet, I must admit, the behavior has shocked more than just you. My cousin, Colonel Fitzwilliam, accompanied Mr Lowe and myself here. He has not said in words as you have, but the looks he has given me are ones of surprise and shock. Mr Lowe and I have been friends for many years, and he has stated his surprise at my willingness. Now I am going to admit to you, what I have admitted to no one else. I love your daughter, Miss Elizabeth. She captured my attention shortly after I arrived in your neighborhood."

Mr Bennet was even more amazed by this man's confession. "Forgive me, Sir, but are you not the one who stated at the Assembly that Elizabeth was tolerable, but not handsome enough to tempt you?"

"You know of those words I spoke in frustration? I was tired of Bingley attempting to engage me in dancing with one of the young ladies, and did not even look at which young lady he pointed. Later, when I realized he was speaking of Miss Elizabeth, I was appalled at my own behavior."

"Unfortunately, my daughter overheard you. I must tell you, my wife has always insisted Elizabeth was not pretty, always making remarks to dampen Elizabeth's opinion of her own beauty. Your remarks only reinforced my wife's opinion in Elizabeth's mind."

"Mr Bennet, it has been some time now since I came to the conclusion that Miss Elizabeth is the handsomest young lady of my acquaintance."

~~~~~~~ ** ~~~~~~~

Chapter 4

"The handsomest of your acquaintance? I must admit that I am shocked."

Darcy grinned. "I believe I hid my feelings well, though perhaps too well. Yes, Mr Bennet, I have loved your daughter since shortly after meeting her. To be completely honest, the main reason I did not ask to court her is the difference in our situations. I had also found the behavior of your wife and younger daughters to be a detriment to such a union as well. But today, as I sat in that room, reading to your daughter, knowing that my aunt is ultimately responsible for what happened and the negligence which was perpetrated, I know who the truly revolting family member is. I cannot imagine your wife, as vulgar as she can be, to be capable of denying medical care to someone who is terribly injured in an accident which claimed the lives of the other two people. I cannot imagine your wife wishing to have someone removed from the cottage so that she can find a new parson to move into the cottage, the risk to the young lady's health be damned. No, Mr Bennet, it is my family member who is truly revolting and it has humbled me to see this."

"I appreciate your willingness to admit your aunt's failings. It would not have been unusual for someone of your standing to cover up the fault of your relations." Mr Bennet acknowledged.

"I admit I have been a fool. I have allowed society to lead me in the wrong direction, and, in doing so, have nearly lost the only lady I could ever love as I do your daughter." Darcy wiped his hands over his face, attempting to rein in his feelings. "Mr Bennet, I must ask. How is it Miss Elizabeth ended up becoming married to the likes of Mr Collins?"

"That is due to my foolishness." Mr Bennet replied. "I never took the time to put aside the money to have proper dowries for my daughters or protect them when I am gone. By the time we admitted there would be no son to break the entail, it was too late. Mr Darcy, what I am about to tell you is only known by four other people besides me. One is my physician, then my solicitor, my wife's brother, and Lizzy. I thought we were rescued from my foolishness when Mr Bingley began to pay Jane notice. You see, I am dying. I do not have much time left in this world. If Mr Bingley had offered for Jane, I felt sure he would protect the rest of my family when I am gone. When Mr Bingley went to Town, and then, never returned, I became desperate. My only option was that of Mr Collins. He was to inherit upon my death. If he was married to one of my daughters, he would be more willing to protect my family. He was dead set on the daughter being Lizzy or Jane, and my wife refused to allow it to be Jane. So my beautiful, delightful girl made the sacrifice. It nearly killed me to watch her go through the motions, as she was displeased with the entire situation. Lizzy disliked Mr Collins, and held no respect for him. The only way she could stomach the thought of marrying him was to shut down her emotions. It was as if she built a strong stone wall around her to protect herself. My wife's brother and his wife hosted Lizzy in Town for a week before the wedding. They were concerned for her, she did not even enjoy the trip to the theatre, as she had always done in the past."

"I am afraid her enjoyment at the theatre may have been ruined by me. You see, my sister met Miss Elizabeth as she was coming from the necessary room. It is my belief she saw myself, my sister and Mr Bingley in my box. If she felt Bingley's departure from Netherfield led to her being forced to marry Collins, it would be natural for her to be angry at my friend. And to blame me for my part in Bingley remaining in Town. I did not believe Miss Bennet returned his regard."

"Jane is a private person, Mr Darcy. Her feelings, not unlike your own, are very private and held from those around her. Only those who are closest to her know how deeply she was wounded by the loss of Mr Bingley." Mr Bennet watched closely as Darcy heard his words.

"This proves I am an even bigger fool. You are correct, I do not allow people to know me well. Why would I not realize and recognize the same in Miss

Bennet? What an idiot I am. I will write to Bingley, if you approve. I wish to apologize to him for giving him bad advice and inform him that my impression of Miss Bennet has changed."

"I believe Jane would not be averse to meeting Mr Bingley again." Mr Bennet smiled.

Darcy immediately walked to the nearby desk and pulled out supplies from the drawers. In a matter of moments, he had penned his letter to Bingley. It was simple and to the point. *I was wrong with regards to Miss Bennet's feelings towards you. Come to Hunsford parsonage, you will find her and her father tending to Miss Elizabeth here, as am I. You are welcome, no matter the time.*

"I will have my courier take this to Bingley as soon as possible. It would not surprise me to find him knocking on the door before sunrise." Smiling, Darcy stepped towards the door.

When the door opened and Darcy prepared to remove from the room, Jane's voice could be heard calling for him. "Mr Darcy, we need your assistance. It is urgent."

Darcy nearly ran down the stairs to find Jane near the kitchen area. "What has happened?"

"Mr Lowe asked for you to come. My sister is restless and is thrashing about. He is afraid she will injure herself further. Mr Lowe stated your reading to her calmed Lizzy earlier. Will you not try reading to her again? If she continues in this manner, she may die." Tears were freely flowing from Jane's blue eyes.

"Of course, Miss Bennet." Darcy hurried to reclaim his chair next to Elizabeth's bedside. He could see the way Elizabeth's body tossed itself about, tangling in the bedding. "Elizabeth, shh, calm yourself. You are safe and need to rest. Please, Elizabeth, calm yourself. All is well. Your father and sister are here to see you now, so you must recover for them. I will read to you some more, as you seemed to enjoy it earlier." With that, he opened the book and began reading again.

It was clear to all in the room that the moment Darcy had begun to speak, Elizabeth began to calm. Within a matter of moments, she was completely relaxed and resting peacefully. Jane was amazed at the change, especially the caring nature of the man who had calmed her sister.

~~ ** ~~

Where was the voice which was so soothing? I can hear others around me, though they are not him. The pain is too much, I wish it would end. Why can I not open my eyes to see who the voice belongs to? Why can I not move without such severe pain? Please, Father in Heaven, take me from this pain or bring the voice back to me. The voice was so kind, so caring. It made me feel loved and wanted. It has been so long since I felt such, I do not wish it to end.

That soft lady's voice is familiar. Who is it? Could it be my dear Jane? If I could open my eyes, I could see if it is Jane. Jane, not even you could save me from such a life as I now have. You would have offered to take my place, but Mamma would never have allowed it. How can I ever tell you how empty I am since Papa told me of his health? How can I explain how dead I feel inside?

OOOH, there is the voice. It has returned. He must be an angel, come to take me to heaven. Thank you, God, for sending the voice back to me. My personal angel. My salvation...my peace...

~~ ** ~~

For the next two days, a routine was achieved. Whenever Elizabeth became agitated or thrashed out, Darcy would speak with her or read to her. He described his home estate, Pemberley, in great detail. He read from Shakespeare and from a book of poetry. He spoke to her of his love and how dearly he wished for her to return so he could spend the rest of his life with her. And he told her he had sent for Bingley.

As predicted, Charles Bingley arrived in the wee hours of the morning after receiving the express from Darcy. He was confused as to what had happened, and why the Bennets were at Hunsford, but he could not wait to see Jane and renew his attentions to her. By the afternoon, Jane Bennet and Charles Bingley were officially engaged.

Mr Bennet spoke with the newly engaged couple,

explaining to them of his declining health. "Mr Bingley, I believe it would be best if you could obtain a special license, and we can have the wedding as soon as possible. I would prefer to know my daughter is happily settled before I die."

"I will do just that, Mr Bennet. And I will do whatever is needed to protect Mrs Bennet and the younger daughters." Bingley replied. "My dearest, Jane, are you comfortable with such arrangements? I know it will not allow you the fancy wedding your mother would demand."

"All that is important is the man I am to marry, and that Papa will be with us. No frills are important compared to the two of you." Jane patted the hand of Bingley's that held hers. "Papa, what will happen now, with Mr Collins death? Who inherits Longbourn?"

"I do not know. There are no other male family members. I will write to Mr Phillips. Your uncle is well acquainted with the situation and is a good solicitor. Hopefully he will be able to figure it all out."

Darcy entered the room, hearing Mr Bennet's words. "Sir, perhaps it would be possible to break the entail, with enough money to back the process. I pledge to you my assistance in seeing this done, and I will pay the costs."

"Mr Darcy, I appreciate your kindness, but I could not accept such generosity."

"Considering my feelings towards your daughter, I pray we are one day to be family. It is in my best interest to protect the family in such a manner."

"Darcy, as I am officially engaged to Jane, it should be me who pays for such a venture. If, in the future, you become my brother, I will allow you to reimburse me." Bingley stated, attempting to appear strong and decisive.

Mr Bennet laughed. "Gentlemen, I am grateful for the two of you falling in love with my daughters. I will be able to die peacefully, knowing Fanny and the girls are looked after."

A knock was heard on the cottage's front door. Hearing a loud, female voice, only Darcy knew what was about to happen. Without waiting for the housekeeper to open the door, Lady Catherine de Bourgh opened the door and entered the house.

"Where is my nephew? I demand my nephew attend me immediately."

Darcy walked to the door of the parlor. "Aunt Catherine, keep your voice lowered. There is no need to shout."

"Darcy, it is time you came to Rosings. Anne is quite distraught over all of the happenings, and is especially upset after hearing a rumor that you have been seen in the bedchamber of Mrs Collins. This is not to be tolerated. You will come to Rosings and refrain from coming here again. And I want everyone who is staying here to leave the property immediately. They should take Mrs Collins with them. She has no right to remain here. I need to have the cottage available for the next clergyman when he is found."

"No, Aunt Catherine, I am not following you to Rosings. I am remaining here, as are these people who are members of Miss Elizabeth's family."

"Who is Miss Elizabeth?" Lady Catherine was confused, but determined. "It does not matter, for she has no right to be in this house. I want them gone from here before the sun sets today."

Colonel Fitzwilliam had been walking to the parsonage when he heard his aunt's tirade. He opened the door and entered behind her. "Aunt Catherine, I would suggest you return to Rosings and stay there. I have sent an express to my father, your brother, who is the head of our family. He sent a message in return. Father is on his way here, and he is quite angry with you. I would go so far as to say he is furious beyond words. I informed him of your negligence for the care and upkeep of the carriage, the callous manner in which you treated the deaths of men who were a part of your estate, how the deaths were on your head from your refusal to properly maintain your equipage. And especially, how you demanded William to move Mrs Collins from this house, while she is barely hanging on to life. How dare you be such a selfish old harpy? I have just been to the main house, where I spoke to Anne. You have never considered Anne's feelings, not once in her life. You have been so self-righteous that you have never noticed Anne's feelings for another man. She has no desire to marry Darcy. She and William have spoken of this, and came to the decision long ago. Anne loves me. And I love her. If Anne is to marry, it will be to me."

"No, my daughter is to marry Darcy. My sister and I made the decision when Anne was just a babe in her cradle. She will never marry a second son, you have no prospects for the future."

"Aunt Catherine, I believe it is high time you removed yourself from this cottage and await your brother's arrival. The Bennets will remain here until Mr Lowe pronounces Miss Elizabeth healthy enough to be moved." Darcy moved to stand beside his cousin, and the two men utilized their towering frames to intimidate their aunt. Finally, Lady Catherine turned and marched towards the front entrance.

"I know how to handle this situation. You have not heard the last of me." She said as she left the cottage.

With their aunt gone, Darcy gently punched his cousin on the shoulder. "Perfect timing, Richard. Thank you for your assistance."

"It has been a long time coming, but I know my mother will be pleased with me when she learns it was I who told the old hag what was what."

Darcy chuckled at his cousin's words. "I will be proud to verify your story, if your mother requires it. And congratulations on finally telling her of you and Anne's love for each other. It is about time everyone knows it and you can move forward."

~~ ** ~~

Elizabeth continued to struggle, having episodes of thrashing about, followed by a peaceful calm when Darcy would speak to her. She still had not awakened, and Mr Lowe became concerned. The longer she went locked inside herself, the more difficult it would be for her to return to her loved ones.

A fever began several days after the arrival of her family. Beginning slowly, the fever increased until Lowe feared Elizabeth had only hours until she would most assuredly die. Darcy refused to leave her side, as Lowe, Jane and one of the maids assisted in trying to cool Elizabeth's fevered brow with cool wet cloths. Time and again, Lowe gave her tonics and elixirs to aid in her recovery. For a full week, the fever threatened to take Elizabeth's life. For a full week, Darcy was at her side, sleeping for moments at a time, until he heard any movements from the young lady whom he loved. Then he was at her side again, begging her to hear his words of love, begging her to live.

~~ ** ~~

Why am I still here, trapped in this life? Please God,

end my suffering. I did my duty, I married the idiotic fool, is that not enough?

Do I have to spend years at his side, allowing him to touch me as a husband has right to? Do I have to spend each day, for the rest of my life, listening to his groveling at his patroness' every word? Please, release me from such torture.

I am sure Mr Collins will honor his pledge to take care of Mamma and my sisters. He does not need me at his side. Do I not deserve some sort of compensation for my devotion to my family? I gave up all of my dreams and my future happiness, does that not count for something? The pain is too great, I only wish to be released from it. The only comfort I find in this place is that heavenly voice. I know not who it is, but he makes me feel loved.

~~ ** ~~

"Mr Bennet, your daughter is not recovering as I would hope. I must ask you, could there be something which has caused her to give up on life?" Mr Lowe asked.

Jane was sitting beside her father, holding his hand. Tears were coming easily to both father and daughter. Finally, Jane spoke. "When Lizzy was proposed to by Mr Collins, she refused him. Papa insisted Lizzy do her duty to the family and accept Mr Collins' proposal. When Lizzy did as Papa instructed, it was as if she were lifeless. Nothing seemed to bring her joy, she no longer found happiness in life. The day of the wedding was the worst. It was as if she were only a shell of herself, with no emotions at all."

"I was a terrible father, asking my dearest daughter to make such a sacrifice. I should have seen to protecting my family for when I was gone, but I did not, and Lizzy paid the price for my lack of preparation." Mr Bennet said as he leaned heavily against his eldest daughter. "Is this now to rob us of Lizzy completely? Have I killed my beloved girl by my behavior?"

"No, Papa. Lizzy will live. I am certain of it. She has suffered so much since the accident, God would not allow her to suffer, only to take her from us."

From the back of the cottage, Darcy's voice was shouting for assistance. Lowe hurried towards the bedchamber where he found a nearly lifeless form of Elizabeth Bennet Collins and a desperate Darcy begging for her to live.

~~~~~~~ ** ~~~~~~~

Chapter 5

"Do not leave me, Elizabeth. My dearest love, please, do not leave me. Elizabeth, I need you. If you leave me, I will not be able to live. Please, dearest one, stay with me." Darcy was desperate.

"What has happened?" Lowe asked as he entered the room.

"She is hardly breathing, and her heartbeat is weak. She is dying." Darcy sobbed.

"William, she needs to know that Collins is dead. She needs to have a reason to live, to know she will not be trapped in a marriage to that man. Tell her."

Darcy leaned close to Elizabeth's ear. "Lizzy, you do not need to leave. Mr Collins is dead. You will never have to be with him. You have so much to live for, my love. Mr Collins is dead. He will no longer be a part of your life."

That voice, the sweet sound of his voice. Can I not know who the voice belongs to before I join you, God?

"Lizzy, wake, my dearest. Come back to me. Please, Lizzy, I beg you to stay here with me."

He sounds so sad, as if he were in pain. His voice is so sweet, so caring. He has brought me so much peace.

"My love, I wish to marry you, take you to Pemberley, give you the life you deserve. Lizzy, there is no need to fret, Mr Collins is dead. He will no longer cause you any strife. Mr Collins is dead. You need to stay here with me."

What did he say? Mr Collins is dead? Who is the voice, how does he know of Mr Collins? The voice is familiar, but I cannot tell who it is. Mr Collins is dead? I am a widow? I do not have to be married to him, share his bed, make a life with him? God, is this true? Am I free to make a new life, one free of the shackles which marrying Mr Collins placed upon my soul? Can this be true?

"Lizzy, please, try to come back to me. If you can hear me, squeeze my hand, dearest."

Faintly, Darcy could feel some movement of Elizabeth's fingers.

So hard to move. It feels as if I am frozen. Do I wish to stay here, not go to heaven? Do I wish to know who is behind the voice? He seems to care deeply. But who could he be? Who could be so loving and kind? It is not Mr Collins, he never truly loved me. The only other man...no it cannot be him. He did not find me handsome enough with whom to even dance. Who is this man with such warmth to his voice? I want to know who he is...

Surprised, Darcy could feel Elizabeth's fingers lightly squeeze Darcy's hand. Lowe watched, smiling at the sight of Elizabeth's breathing deeper. He leaned over and could feel her heartbeat becoming stronger. "Darcy, I believe you are reaching her. Keep it up."

"My dearest Elizabeth, I vow to make you happy, to love you every day for the rest of our lives. Just return to me. Keep fighting. I know you are tired, but you have to keep fighting. You have a reason to live. Mr Collins is gone, he is dead. You are free from that burden. Please, Lizzy, my Lizzy, come back to me."

I want to stay. I want to know this man. I want to live, now that there is a reason to stay. Who is this man?

"Who?" Came a whispered voice from Elizabeth.

Darcy was thrilled to hear her voice. He knew then, she would live. "If you are asking who I am, dearest love, I am Fitzwilliam Darcy."

"Mr Darcy?" Came another whisper. "Cannot be."

"Why is that, my love?"

"Mr Darcy…not handsome…to dance."

Wiping the tears from his eyes, Darcy laughed. "Even if I live to be one hundred years old, I will regret those words each and every day of my life. My dearest Elizabeth, you are the most handsome lady I have ever known. I could not keep from staring at you whenever you were in the same room with me. You own my heart. I only wish I had had the strength to tell you before. I could have saved you from all of this torment you have endured. But now, now I have a second chance to make things right. I love you, Elizabeth. I love you so very much."

"Mr Collins?"

"He died, my dearest. The carriage overturned. The day of your wedding. Mr Collins is dead and buried. You will never have to live with him. You are free from the commitment you made to save your family. I know about your father's illness. He and your sister are here. Your sister, Miss Bennet, has wonderful news for you. And I will do all in my power to protect your mother and younger sisters."

"Jane...here? Papa...too?"

"Yes, dearest. Would you like them to come to you?" Darcy asked as he motioned for Mr Bennet and Jane to enter the room.

Jane nearly threw herself on the side of the bed. "Lizzy, my dear sister, you have come back to us. Oh, Lizzy, you must stay with us. I can never marry without you by my side."

"Marry?"

"Yes, Lizzy. Mr Darcy sent for Charles...Mr Bingley. Charles asked for my hand, and I accepted him. We are to marry, thanks to Mr Darcy. So, you see, you must recover. We need you so desperately. Especially Mr Darcy. Lizzy, he loves you dearly."

"Papa?"

"Yes, my baby girl, I am here. I am here with you, Lizzy Bee. You have been so brave, so giving to everyone else. Now, my beloved daughter, you shall reap the rewards. You sacrificed your happiness for your family, now it is time for you to be happy...and loved as you should be."

"Mr Collins...dead?"

"Yes, my cousin died in the wreck. You are free of your obligation to him. You are free to make a new life, one with love." Mr Bennet said, leaning over to place a kiss on his favorite daughter's head. "You rest now, but only rest. We need you with us, Lizzy. And we love you."

"Eyes?"

Lowe stepped forward. "Miss Elizabeth, you suffered a head injury in the accident. You also have several cuts and scrapes. We have been placing salve on the wounds and should be able to remove the bandages in a day or two."

"Since you cannot see him, Elizabeth, Mr Lowe is a friend of mine from Cambridge, who has become a very well respected physician." Darcy decided to assist her confused mind. "I brought him to tend to your injuries."

"Thank..."

"Rest, dearest. No need to thank me for anything." Darcy lifted her hand to his lips and placed a gentle kiss on it. "I will stay here at your side while you rest. If you need anything, you only need to ask."

Elizabeth reached out a hand and found Darcy's face. She felt his chin, the days of growth which had developed into a beard. "You...rest...take care."

"I will, Elizabeth. As soon as you rest and become stronger." Darcy smiled as he spoke. Without seeing him, she was able to discern he had been neglecting his own care. When she recovered, he knew he would never be able to hide anything from her.

Not long after, it was easy to see Elizabeth had drifted off to sleep. Mr Lowe checked her pulse and breathing, and for a fever. Looking at the haggard appearance of his friend, Lowe could not stop the corners of his mouth from lifting. "Her fever appears to have broken, and her heart is beating normally, and strong. Even her breathing appears to be normal. I believe, if she continues in this manner, she will recover."

Darcy clasped his hands together and raised them to his lips. "Thank God."

Mr Bennet embraced his eldest daughter. Looking at the young man who was deeply in love with his dearest daughter, Mr Bennet knew that it was Darcy who had somehow found a way through to his daughter and gave her a reason to live.

~~ ** ~~

Lady Catherine was furious at the treatment she was receiving, especially due to the fact that it was her own family treating her in such a manner. Lord Matlock, Henry Fitzwilliam, had arrived at Rosings after receiving an express from his son, Richard. During his long journey from Matlock, in Derbyshire, to his sister's estate, in Kent, Lord Matlock continued to review all he had learned. He had to stop at his townhouse in London, retrieving copies of his late brother in law's will and other papers. Lord Matlock also left word with his solicitor that he might have need of the man at Rosings. The solicitor, Mr Meagle, agreed he would make the journey upon receiving an express from Lord Matlock.

Learning of his sister's negligence was bad enough, but to learn of her demands for Elizabeth to be removed immediately from the parsonage, and her refusal to send for a physician, the normally calm Lord Matlock was ready to join his son in the desire to throttle his elder sister.

"Catherine, with all of your resources, why would you have a carriage which was in great need of repair? Why would you not just repair it? Or better yet, get rid of it? You have no need of it, you have three others and rarely go anywhere."

"How am I to know the carriage was in such bad shape?" Lady Catherine fumed. "I have people paid to take care of them, they are the ones responsible."

"No, Aunt Catherine, you will take responsibility for this accident. Your men told you, several times, the carriage was in need of repairs. You refused to allow them to spend the funds necessary. In fact, Mr Bogs stated he told you, the day you insisted that carriage be sent to Hertfordshire, that the carriage was not in any condition to travel such a distance without repairs."

"Then I must have been confused by his words, thinking he meant a different carriage." Lady Catherine refused to accept her role in the accident. "He should have sent a different carriage."

"Mr Bogs made such a suggestion, a suggestion which resulted in his being berated by you and to have his job threatened." Richard was in no mood to allow his aunt any kindness. "I have been speaking with many people who work here at Rosings. You demand my cousin to come here each year to see to problems, yet, as soon as he has left, you insist the changes he has made be stopped and ignored. Your only reason to bring Darcy here is in attempt to bring about a marriage between him and Anne. My Anne. The woman I love, and who loves me in return."

"Catherine, I have told you before, and I will tell you one final time. Anne and William are not ever going to marry each other. Get that thought out of your mind. Anne loves Richard, and, if I am not mistaken, William is very taken with the young lady who is recovering at the parsonage."

"How dare you, Henry, how dare you make such a

statement. Are the shades of Pemberley to be thus polluted with the likes of some unknown country hussy, someone who first uses her wiles to trap my clergyman, to become Mistress of my nephew's estate? Not as long as I draw breath. I will see that no marriage to Mrs Collins ever comes about." Lady Catherine was shouting her disapproval.

"No, Mother, you will not cause any further harm to that poor young lady." Anne stated as she walked towards her mother, her fists clenched at her side. "I was proposed to by Richard, and have accepted him. And if Mrs Collins loves my cousin Darcy, even half as much as Richard has stated William loves her, she will be welcomed by me."

"Not in this house." Lady Catherine declared.

"Well, there again, you are wrong." Anne declared. "The house is mine. I have allowed you freedom to rule over everything, but no more. Your foolishness has left us in a delicate position. I have spoken with Richard, and we will be setting up funds for the widow of Mr Franks, the carriage driver, as well as for Mrs Collins. Mrs Collins not only became a widow, but she was severely injured in the accident. She deserves to be compensated for her pain and loss, that is, if she survives. If she had died, from your negligence and refusal of sending for a physician, I would have had you locked away for the remainder of your life. I have decided the funds for the two widows is to come from your settlement from when you married Father. You have lived off of the estate long enough. From this day forward, things are going to change."

"How dare you speak to me in such a manner?" Lady Catherine fumed. "You have no authority to do anything with regards to the estate or the accounts."

"Catherine, you are a bigger fool than I thought you were." Lord Matlock stated. "Anne is the rightful heir to Rosings, not you. She is now stepping forward and claiming her rights."

"Ah, but I had Anne declared unfit the year before she would have inherited. The solicitor made sure I would retain control of Rosings, and Anne would never inherit." Lady Catherine looked quite smug at her announcement.

Colonel Fitzwilliam lost his control. "You arrogant hag. You dared to treat your daughter as if she were your plaything, forcing her to do as you bid, and then have her declared unfit? If she had gone against you at any time, you would have also said she was unfit. You are the one who is unfit. You are a selfish, good for nothing harpy who sees fit to bring harm to others for your own pleasure."

"Have no fear, Richard, I will contact our family's solicitor firm and have this resolved. In the meantime, we can have Lady Catherine pronounced deranged and in need of being placed in a sanitarium for her own safety. I know that de Bourgh wrote in his will that if Catherine is unable to be handle her duties, I am the next in line." Lord Matlock smiled as he dashed his sister's hopes.

"I am well and of sound mind, Henry. You cannot have me placed in a sanitarium." Shouted Lady Catherine.

"Oh, but I can. There just so happens to be a physician nearby who can examine you and render a diagnosis. After what the physician has seen of the victim of your neglect, I have no doubt you will be finding your next home at a sanitarium." Colonel Fitzwilliam added.

"That man is not a physician. Darcy brought some friend of his, not a physician. And if you try to force me from my home, I will send for the constable to come and have you all removed from Rosings, including your precious Mrs Collins."

Lord Matlock could not believe his ears. His sister had always been difficult and head strong, but she had become impossible and delusional. "Catherine, you are ill. You are behaving more like our mother did before she died."

"There was nothing wrong with our mother!" Lady Catherine screamed.

"She was ill, Catherine, delusional, just as you have become. You see nothing wrong with your actions, and when you are made aware of the results of your behavior, you blame someone else. It is ridiculous.

You are the one who has ruled this estate with an iron fist. No one can do anything against you, for fear you will bring harm to them or their family. And you went so far as to have your daughter declared unfit, so you could continue to control Rosings and the finances."

"Anne is too delicate to run an estate, and she has never had a head for figures. That is why she was to marry Darcy, until your son interfered. I blame your son, Henry, for he has made both Darcy and Anne forget what they owe to me."

"Richard, if you would, send to the parsonage to have Mr Lowe come here. I insist he give an opinion on my sister's well-being as soon as possible." Lord Matlock decided that the argument would be endless with Lady Catherine. "Anne, have no fear, you are not unfit to run the estate. I will see that Rosings and the money are placed in your control as soon as possible."

Lady Catherine shouted out to her butler. "Joseph, send for the constable. My brother and his son, as well as the interlopers at the parsonage, need to be escorted from my property."

"Joseph, ignore my sister's request. I am sure you are aware of her illness, and you must also have your concerns for your position and income. Have no fear, I will see you retain your position."

Standing in front of her brother, Lady Catherine placed her hands on his chest, shoving him backwards. "Out of my house, Henry. Out of here, immediately. I am going to my rooms. Be gone before I return."

With that, Lady Catherine marched from the room and up the stairs, locking her bedchamber door behind her.

~~ ** ~~

A message was sent to the parsonage to request Mr Lowe to come to Rosings. The message in return was that Mr Lowe was attending to Mrs Collins' wounds and would come to the grand house within the hour.

Lord Matlock decided to allow his sister the chance to calm herself before confronting her again. He would leave her to be alone until after Mr Lowe arrived and they could speak with him. In the meantime, Lord Matlock sent an express to his solicitor. He would expect the man the following day, and they would begin the daunting task of correcting all the mistakes his sister had made.

"Have no fear, Anne, you will have your estate and your freedom from your mother. I will see that you will not be under Catherine's thumb any longer." Lord Matlock stated as he stepped to the sideboard of the drawing room, pouring himself a glass of port. Turning to his son and niece, he offered to pour them a glass as well, which both accepted. It was not often Anne imbibed, but after all she had heard from her mother, she felt the need to calm her nerves.

"How could Mother treat me in such a manner? To have me declared unfit to inherit my estate, just so she could keep control of my inheritance and my life? The woman is unbelievable."

"I will begin going over the books and speak with William. He knows more of the goings on here, with the exception of the steward. But that man has only been here for a few months. I wish I could contact Mr Hanson, have him come and go over everything with us."

"Uncle, I doubt Mr Hanson will ever wish to return here, not after how Mother treated him. After ten years of his loyalty, he stood up to her when it came to the necessary repairs which were needed on the tenant cottages. Without some of the repairs, the homes would be dangerous to occupy and might have led to some deaths. Mr Hanson would not allow Mother's tight fist on the finances cause any of the tenants to lose their lives. So he made the necessary repairs, against Mother's instructions, and, when she discovered his actions, she sent him away, without reference. I believe he is living in Dover, he has relations there."

Lord Matlock downed the contents of his glass and walked over to refill it. "Catherine is ill, that is the only explanation. I never would have expected her to behave this disgustingly. To place peoples' lives in danger, the very people who are responsible for making her a rich woman, how ridiculous."

"I will speak to the men about the estate, learn what I can. Mr Bogs has told me some things in the stables and carriage up keep. I am sure there are others who can assist me with regards to the other aspects of the estate." Richard offered his aid to his father and his betrothed. "Have no fear, Anne, Father and I will protect you, as, I am certain, will William."

"I trust you, my love. We will make everything right." Anne said as she patted Richard's hand. "Thank you for standing by me. Many men would have fled from Mother's tirade long ago."

"But you have to remember, I have known your mother all of my life. And winning your hand is a true gift, nothing your mother can say or do will change that." Richard leaned over to place a kiss on his betrothed's cheek.

~~~~~~~ ** ~~~~~~~

Chapter 6

Lady Catherine had gone the back way from her bedchambers, through a secret hallway which led downstairs and outside the house. No one knew she had left the room, and she was determined to deal with the main problem which had led to the others. She was going to remove Mrs Collins from the parsonage, no matter what she had to do to be rid of the woman.

Sneaking through the rear door of the parsonage, and counted herself fortunate that no one was in the area. She knew the layout of the building, and knew the rooms which Mrs Johnston used. Opening the door carefully, Lady Catherine peeked inside, noting only the young lady lying on the bed. *It appears Darcy has abandoned his harlot.*

He must have realized the truth of his feelings for Anne. This tramp has only made him forget for a little while. Now he will marry Anne, and he needs to be rid of this trollop permanently. We cannot have him lured away from Anne again. No, only when Mrs Collins is gone forever, will we be safe and sound.

What can I do to end this? *She does not look to be strong enough to live long anyway, I would be doing her a service by releasing her from her pain. I could give her a large dose of medicine.* Lady Catherine picked up the bottle of laudanum. *There is hardly any in here. Certainly not enough to finish this trollop. I refuse to contend with blood. Oh, I can do like I did to my husband. I can smother her with her pillow. It should not be as difficult as it was with Louis de Bourgh. He put up a struggle.*

Lady Catherine stepped to the side of the bed, pulling the pillow from beneath Elizabeth's head. Placing the pillow over the young lady's face, Lady Catherine began to press down.

Elizabeth began to struggle, knocking over a glass which fell to the floor, shattering. Mrs Johnston had been coming to check on Elizabeth, and heard the breaking glass. She opened the door, peering around the wood to see if Elizabeth was sleeping. Seeing what was happening, Mrs Johnston cried out. "Lady Catherine, what are you doing? Step away from Mrs Collins, please. Please, Lady Catherine, stop what you are doing."

Lady Catherine was determined, and refused to be deterred from her goal. "Unhand me." She shouted, attempting to remove the housekeeper's hands from her arms. Mrs Johnston had managed to pull Lady Catherine slightly away from the bed, though the Mistress of Rosings was not willing to stop. Finally moving her arm to her advantage, Lady Catherine pulled it forward and then shoved backwards, striking the housekeeper hard in the belly. The force of the strike knocked Mrs Johnston backwards, falling to the floor.

Just as Mrs Johnston fell, Bingley and Jane came rushing into the room. Bingley quickly realized what was happening, and he grabbed hold of Lady Catherine's arms, pulling the woman from the side of the bed, where she was again preparing to smother Elizabeth. Shouting as loud as possible, Bingley called for assistance. Mr Bennet came quickly, and between the two men, they were able to subdue Lady Catherine, tying her hands and feet with some bandages from the tabletop. Jane was bent over the housekeeper, but to no use. Mrs Johnston had struck her head, killing her quickly.

Once Jane determined Mrs Johnston's condition, she made her way to the bed to check on Elizabeth. Fortunately, her dearest sister was breathing. "Lizzy, please, squeeze my hand or speak to me. I need to know you are unharmed."

Tears were free flowing when a slight squeeze came from her sister's hand. "J...J...Jane? W...W...What happened?"

"Do not fret, dearest. Just rest and be well. Can I bring you something to drink?" Jane said as she wiped her eyes.

"Y...Y...Yes please."

While Jane was ensuring her sister's welfare, Mr Bennet sent one of the maids to Rosings to fetch Darcy and Mr Lowe back to the parsonage, as well as some men to deal with Lady Catherine.

Bingley looked at his future father in law, as Mr Bennet stemmed the flow of obscenities flowing from Lady Catherine's lips, by placing a wad of fabric in the offending woman's mouth. "She has murdered Mrs Johnston and attempted to kill your daughter." Bingley stated the obvious to Mr Bennet.

"Darcy's family will have their hands full dealing with this woman. It is plain to see she is deranged and a danger to all. Fortunately, Lady Catherine's brother is here to contend with her."

"And I thought my sister was bad." Bingley shook his head. "Caroline is many things, but a murderer, I cannot believe."

"Count your blessings, Bingley. Be grateful if your sister remains as she is and does not slip over the edge, as this self-proclaimed woman of importance has."

~~ ** ~~

After reading the message sent from Rosings for Mr Lowe to meet Lord Matlock at the main house, Darcy decided it was time to confront his aunt for her treatment of his beloved. Elizabeth was stable, and resting peacefully, so Darcy felt it safe for him to leave her for a short time.

Arriving at the house, Darcy greeted his uncle with pleasure. "Where is Aunt Rebecca?"

"She is with Marcus and his wife, as she is in

confinement. The babe is due any day now and Rebecca could not stand the thought of leaving when her first grandchild was soon to arrive." Lord Matlock replied. "I wish I was there with her, as this entire situation is beyond belief."

"Where is Lady Catherine?" Darcy asked.

"She has locked herself in her bedchambers, and we decided to leave her there until Mr Lowe could be here to evaluate her condition. William, we have learned from Catherine's own lips that she has taken legal steps to have Anne declared unfit to inherit the estate and her fortune, attempting to keep Anne her prisoner."

"Good God, what was she thinking?"

"That is the problem, she was not thinking. She thinks she can do whatever she wishes and damn the consequences. Her hatred for Mrs Collins is growing by the moment. It is my belief that my sister blames that poor lady for all that is going against the grand and powerful, Lady Catherine de Bourgh."

"She has never even met Elizabeth, how can she blame the innocent party of being at fault?"

Lord Matlock chuckled. "My dear boy, my sister has never taken responsibility for her actions. Rather than blame any of us, she would rather place the blame on someone else, namely your Mrs Collins."

Anne and Richard joined the discussion with Lord

Matlock, informing Mr Lowe of Lady Catherine's behavior. Mr Lowe was shocked at what he had heard, but he decided that it would be for the best to have Lady Catherine placed in an asylum. "I fear for the safety of all around her if she continues this behavior." He stated. "I can send word to a friend of mine who is the head of Lockhead Asylum, hopefully he will have room to take her in."

Just then, the butler knocked on the door of the drawing room. "Lord Matlock, I just received word from the parsonage that Lady Catherine is there, and she has committed murder."

Without another word, Darcy was running from the room, all the while tears were flowing as he was certain his aunt had murdered Elizabeth. *Please God, do not let it be. Not my love, not Elizabeth. Please, she has only begun to heal.*

When Darcy arrived at the parsonage, he did not waste time in knocking, he entered the cottage quickly and went straight to the room where Elizabeth was.

"Darcy, I am glad you are here so quickly." Bingley said. "Your aunt was attempting to smother Elizabeth, and Mrs Johnston appears to have tried to stop her. Your aunt somehow killed the housekeeper, as you can see Mrs Johnston's body." He pointed towards the side of the room, where a sheet covered Mrs Johnston's body.

"Elizabeth?" Darcy was able to force the name from his lips. He felt as if all the air had been removed from his body, and there was a huge lump blocking his throat.

Jane stepped to Darcy, placing her hand on his arm. "She is well. She spoke to me, and even took some drink after all this happened. I believe she is sleeping again."

"Thank God."

Darcy moved to Elizabeth's bedside, kneeling on the floor and grasping hold of her hand. "My love, forgive me. I left you alone and a member of my own family nearly kills you. I would never have been able to live with myself if she had succeeded."

Hearing more people entering the room, Bingley turned his attention towards them. Mr Lowe went straight to his patient, and once he was convinced she was alive and resting, he went to the draped body of Mrs Johnston. Mr Lowe checked for any signs of life, and, finding none, re-covered the housekeeper's form.

Lord Matlock stood in disbelief as he looked about the room. On the floor was a draped body, on the bed, a heavily bandaged young lady who had been through so much. Next to the bed, his nephew was kneeling and ignoring propriety as he was grateful for his beloved still living. And then Lord Matlock turned to see his sister, seated on the floor, her hands and feet bound and cloth protruding from her mouth. Even with the cloth, his sister was shouting. And her main focus was at Darcy. Lord Matlock could hear vague words, and the ones he could determine clearest were aimed at removing Darcy from Mrs Collins' side.

Richard and Anne had arrived, as they were slower than the rest, due to Anne's health. With them were a dozen men from Rosings. Anne suggested the men stay in the parlor while she and Richard learned what had happened.

Seeing her mother thrust up, Anne turned into Richard's embrace, her face hiding in his shoulder, as she wept.

"Mr Bennet, would you mind stepping into another room?" Lord Matlock asked. "And you, as well, Mr Bingley?"

The men agreed, and stepped into the hallway. Mr Bennet motioned to a room he had been using as a study, and the men and Anne entered, leaving Darcy, Jane and Mr Lowe to attend to Elizabeth and ignore Lady Catherine.

Bingley and Mr Bennet informed Lord Matlock, Richard and Anne of what had occurred. Bingley described the difficulty he had in restraining Lady Catherine, having to pull her from the bedside as she was attempting to strangle Elizabeth. Anne sobbed at the realization that her mother had completely lost her mind.

"And Mrs Collins, she did not suffer further injury from my sister's attack?"

"It does not appear she has, as Lizzy spoke to my eldest daughter, Jane." Mr Bennet stated. "We were overwhelmed with fear until Lizzy held her sister's hand and then spoke. Jane was even able to get her sister to drink some water, before Lizzy went back to sleep. It was terrifying to witness such violence, but to know its intended victim was my own child, my dearest daughter, I found that I could have easily killed Lady Catherine if I had been stronger. The only reason your sister is still alive is due to my failing health."

Lord Matlock understood. "It may sound heartless, but a part of me wishes you had killed her. We have much to repair here, as Catherine has done a great deal of damage."

"Uncle, what will we do?" Anne asked, as she still held firmly to her betrothed.

"Mr Lowe is to contact his friend to determine if there is room for Catherine at his asylum. We had best send that message express, as soon as possible. Once we know where we will take her, we can make the rest of the decisions. My solicitor will be here tomorrow, so the legal issues can be resolved. We will protect you as much as possible, Anne, but with Mrs Johnston's murder, we may be forced to endure scrutiny. There will be much talk about this situation, as there are too many people aware of it to keep it private."

"Mrs Johnston's daughter lives in Hunsford. We should send word to her. We must see to the expense of her funeral and compensation to her family." Anne stated. Richard patted her gently on the back.

"Do not fret, Anne, all will be taken care of. One of the things I plan to ask the solicitor is for him to procure a special license for us to marry." Richard said. "The sooner the name de Bourgh is eliminated from Rosings, the better. You will be a Fitzwilliam, and we will begin our life together as soon as possible."

"The name Fitzwilliam may also take some damage, Richard." Lord Matlock stated. "After all, Catherine was born a Fitzwilliam."

"But if we cut all ties to her, it will be to our advantage." Richard countered.

"We will know more tomorrow. Until then, what should we do with Catherine? We will need to have at least two people with her at all times."

"And they will need to be strong." Bingley declared. "I was amazed to find such a small built woman could be so strong. She looks so frail."

Richard nodded his head. "It should be men, and at least one of us from the family with her. I do not think it wise to have William with her, he might wrap his fingers around her scrawny throat and squeeze the life from her."

"You and I will need to take turns, Richard. Then, tomorrow, we will know how to go forward." Lord Matlock said with a sigh. "Perhaps it would be best for Mr Lowe to sedate Catherine. If we keep her sedated, it may make our lives easier for the time being."

"Mr Lowe was nearly out of laudanum, so he asked Mr Wilkens to bring some." Mr Bennet announced. "I expected Mr Wilkens to arrive in a few hours."

"Good. We may need him to supply more, if we need it to sedate Catherine and be of comfort for the pain Mrs Collins is most likely experiencing."

"Mr Lowe has kept from giving Lizzy much, as she has been so delicate. Mr Lowe did not wish to suppress her in her weakened state." Mr Bennet was worn from the emotional upheaval.

"Now that she is awake, her pain will be more strongly felt." Richard responded. "We will make certain that Wilkens stocks more in, just in case there is a need for it."

Bingley stood and walked to the window. It was clear to see that the usually amiable young man was deeply affected by what had come about. "If I had been even a moment slower at getting to Lady Catherine, Elizabeth might not be with us. If Mrs Johnston had not paid the ultimate price in delaying

Lady Catherine, again, Elizabeth might be dead. To come so close to witnessing the murder of my betrothed's most cherished sister, forgive me, it is overwhelming."

Lord Matlock walked to Bingley, placing a hand gently on the young man's shoulder. "I am grateful for the fact that you saved Mrs Collins from my sister, Mr Bingley. And I am sure I speak for my nephew as well. You have done us a great service this day, and I will never forget it."

~~ ** ~~

Lady Catherine was struggling against her restraints, attempting to shout at her nephew. Kicking her feet about, she finally had scooted herself near him. Finally, Darcy turned his attention towards her.

"How dare you attempt to speak to me? Do not come near me. As far as I am concerned, you are no longer a member of my family. I hate you, you miserable hag. You are a bitter harpy, willing to harm anyone who does not agree with your decisions. You murdered a kind and caring woman. Mrs Johnston did not deserve being killed. And Elizabeth certainly did not deserve to have you try to kill her. The only reasons you had to dislike her is that she was here, when you did not wish her to be, and that I love her. Yes, I love her, more than anything else in this world. I LOVE ELIZABETH BENNET! I will always love her. I will never marry Anne. It is time for all of us to move forward with our lives, against your dictates and demands. Anne and Richard will marry, and they will live at Rosings. I pray that Elizabeth will accept my hand in marriage. And you, you will rot in an asylum. You will be placed where you can never harm anyone again."

It was obvious that Lady Catherine did not agree with her nephew. Though she still had the cloth in her mouth, her displeasure was clear.

"Go on, *Lady Catherine de Bourgh.* Your wealth and audacity will not save you from the grave you have dug yourself. You attempted to rule all of our lives, and now, we will rule your life. We will decide where you will live, what you will wear, when you are allowed to eat and exactly what you are given to eat. Your every movement and everything in your life will be guided by the choices of those you attempted to control."

Darcy heard a movement from the bed. He turned his attention towards the lady he loved. "M…Mr Darcy. I…Is that y…y…you?"

"Yes, Elizabeth, I am here. Are you well? Do you need anything?"

"W…W…What happened? Y…you sound so angry?"

"Not with you, dearest. With my aunt, for her cruelty towards others."

"Y…you are well?" Elizabeth asked in a soft voice.

"Hearing your voice, knowing you are growing stronger, I am very well indeed. Your father is down the hall, speaking with my uncle, Lord Matlock. Your sister is refreshing herself, she will be back in a moment."

"Mrs Collins, if you can remember, I am Mr Lowe. I am the physician Mr Darcy brought to tend you. How are you faring?"

After a moment of hesitation, Elizabeth answered. "T...tired, pain. Frustrated. Wish to see...everyone."

"Tomorrow, we will take off the bandages. Would you be able to take some broth? We also have some bread and cheese for you. The nourishment will assist in your recovery." Mr Lowe spoke with a fatherly voice.

Jane Bennet returned to the room, and was thrilled to hear her sister speaking with the men. "Lizzy, we have some chicken broth ready, I know you prefer chicken. I will fetch some for you."

"T...thank you, Jane." Elizabeth replied.

"Mrs Collins, I wish to know where the pain you are feeling is located. Can you tell me?"

"All over. F...feels like...had a horse...t...trample me."

"Close, as it was actually the carriage throwing you about and you were crushed beneath items inside the carriage." Darcy stated. He did not wish to bring up the fact that it was her deceased husband's body which crushed her.

While Darcy was attending to his beloved, Lady Catherine moved closer to him. Finally, she struck out her leg, kicking her nephew in his leg. Darcy cried out as he fell to the ground. Lady Catherine had finally managed to expel the cloth from her mouth.

"How dare you speak to this harlot as if she matters? She should be dead. She has no right to be alive. You are to marry Anne, not have your head turned by the likes of some nobody who has worked her wiles on you, making you forget what you owe me, owe the family."

Darcy lost his temper. Grabbing hold of his aunt's shoulders, he began to shake her. "You are the wickedest person I have ever known. How dare you treat us in such a manner?"

Mr Lowe was attempting to separate Darcy from Lady Catherine, while Elizabeth cried out to know what was happening. Jane came running into the room, crying out for help. The men and Anne hurried to the bedchambers, finding Mr Lowe had wedged his way between his friend and Lady Catherine, attempting to hold Darcy's hands from the old woman's throat. Jane was beside the bed, trying desperately to calm her sister who was begging for information as to what was happening. Elizabeth began pulling at her bandaging around her head, until she had uncovered her eyes.

"NO!" Elizabeth exclaimed.

Darcy instantly stopped what he was doing, as he became aware of the pain he heard in his beloved's voice. Finally, her need of him penetrated his mental fog and caused him to abandon his attempts to inflict pain on his aunt.

"I am here, Elizabeth. What is wrong? Are you in pain?"

Elizabeth's hands were at her face, her agony was clear to everyone. Richard took hold of Lady Catherine, tossing her over his shoulder and carrying her from the room. Mr Lowe went to the other side of the bed, preparing to assist his patient.

"Jane, where are you?" Elizabeth begged for her sister.

"Lizzy, dearest, I am here, beside you."

"I cannot see you, Jane. I cannot see anything."

~~~~~~~ ** ~~~~~~~

Chapter 7

Lord Matlock stood beside his nephew as they watched Mr Lowe attend Elizabeth. Having Bingley hold a candle close, Mr Lowe looked into Elizabeth's eyes, finding no response from her. The eyes which had always sparkled appeared lifeless, as if they belonged to someone else. Darcy held one of Elizabeth's hands, while Jane held the other, each speaking to her in gentle voices, attempting to sooth the despondent young lady.

After his examination, Mr Lowe suggested they wrap Elizabeth's eyes again. She had another opinion.

"I do not wish to have anything covering my eyes. I feel as if I am lost in a pitch black cave as it is, the cloth will only make me feel worse."

"Mrs Collins, I wish to place some medicine on your cuts, which are near your eyes. It would be necessary to cover the cuts, which would mean covering your eyes."

"Mr Lowe, please, I do not wish to have my eyes covered." Elizabeth's voice sounded like a small child, frightened of the world.

"Very well, but I may change my mind at a later time. How are you feeling otherwise? Are you in much pain?"

"Some, though I wish to have a few moments alone, with my sister. Jane, will you speak with me?"

"Of course, Lizzy. Allow me to see the others out of the room, then we can speak. Would you like some refreshments while we speak?" Jane remembered she had left a tray of tea, broth, and some sweet biscuits which she was sure Elizabeth would enjoy. "The tray is in the kitchen, I can have a maid bring it to us?"

"Perhaps after we speak." Elizabeth said tentatively.

"Very well. Gentlemen, might I ask for you to step down the hall?" Jane encouraged. Seeing Darcy reluctant to move, Jane smiled at him. "Mr Darcy, no harm will come to my sister, I will see that she is safe. Remember, she has only returned to us this morning, and there are many things which must be confusing to her."

Darcy nodded his head, though his eyes never left Elizabeth's sweet face. "Elizabeth, I will be down the hall, with your father and Bingley. Please know you are safe, I will not allow anything or anyone to cause you further harm. If you require anything, anything at all, have your sister send for me."

"You have my gratitude, Mr Darcy." Elizabeth returned, desperately attempting to control her voice.

The men left the room, allowing the sisters some privacy. "What did you wish to speak of, Lizzy?"

"What has happened? One moment, I had just married Mr Collins, and the next, I cannot see and Mr Darcy is sitting in my bedchamber, speaking of loving me and calling me by my Christian name. I am so confused."

"Your wedding was nearly a month ago. On your journey here, to Hunsford parsonage, the carriage broke an axel and overturned on the side of a hill. It is believed that it overturned several times, before landing upside down. It was over a week before anyone knew you were missing, as one of Lady Catherine's tenants found one of the horses. Once they found you, you were brought here. Mr Collins was killed in the accident."

"Did he suffer?" Elizabeth asked.

"From what we were told, it appeared he died quickly, as the apothecary told Papa that Mr Collins' neck was broken in the accident. Lady Catherine, Mr Collins' patroness, is Mr Darcy's aunt. She wrote to him, begging him to come here and deal with the situation which frustrated her. She wished you removed so she could find someone to take Mr Collins' position. Mr Darcy was angry when he learned of his aunt's behavior towards a young lady who was injured, as well as becoming a widow. It was only when he arrived at the parsonage that he learned that you were the young lady. He had no notion that you had married Mr Collins. He told Papa that he truly believed it would have been Mary who would have made a proper wife for our cousin."

"Poor Mary. I would not wish such a life on any of my sisters." Elizabeth stated bitterly.

"Lizzy, Mr Collins is dead. There is no reason to think cruelly of him now."

"I am not as good as you are Jane. It has been difficult."

"I know, Lizzy. Once Mr Darcy learned it was you, he became overwrought. He told Papa that he had fallen in love with you while staying at Netherfield, though he was afraid to declare his feelings to you. And yes, you are most likely thinking that Mamma and our younger sisters had some influence on his being frightened away. It was only when Mr Darcy realized that it was his aunt who was far worse than our mother that he felt he could declare his love for you. Papa and Mr Darcy have spoken openly. When there has been time for mourning your husband, Papa has given Mr Darcy permission to court you, if you approve of him."

"Mr Darcy, wishes to court...*me*? I cannot believe all of this has happened."

"Lizzy, if only you had been awake to hear Mr Darcy, the love in his voice as he spoke. He described his home in great detail, as well as reading to you for hours on end."

"THE VOICE!" Elizabeth became agitated. "He was

the one speaking to me? Reading to me?"

"You could hear him? He rarely left your side. And when you were agitated and thrashing about, his voice seemed to calm you tremendously."

"It was such a peaceful pleasure. I kept thinking he was an angel, sent to take me to heaven."

"I am so grateful that he was able to keep you here, with us. I cannot begin to think how it would be without you by my side. Anyway, Mr Darcy realized he had made a mistake in how he spoke to Mr Bingley, with regards to how I felt about him. He sent a letter to Town, to Mr Bingley, who came here directly. Within just a few moments our speaking with one another, we decided to marry. I am betrothed to Mr Bingley. So I will need you to recover soon, for I will require you by my side when I wed."

"There is so much going through my mind, Jane. If I am no longer married, where do I live? Do I return to Longbourn? What if I am blind for the rest of my life? Papa is ill, he will not be able to take care of me. And when Papa is gone, Mamma will be in a terrible state."

"When Charles and I are married, you will come to live with us. And I am certain you will fully recover. You have always been strong and healthy. And you have the love and support of all of us. Mr Darcy's cousin, Miss de Bourgh, has stated that she is planning to set up funds for you, as she feels her mother was responsible for the accident. The carriage was in need of repairs and Lady Catherine refused to allow them. So Miss de Bourgh plans to make sure you are taken care of for the future. With your own money, you can live as you wish."

"Jane, I will need someone to assist me all the time. I cannot see. I will not be able to do for myself."

"That is selfish, Lizzy. You are intelligent, and will be able to overcome any obstacles in your path. We can have someone come to teach you how to do things for yourself. I have heard many things they can teach blind people to do. If you are blind permanently, we will deal with it in the future. You are strong, I have faith you will recover fully."

"Why do I feel as if I am close to Mr Darcy, and yet, I cannot think of a time we ever got along? Mr Darcy has only ever looked at me to find fault."

"No, Lizzy, he only looked at you with love. But he was so shy, and it was difficult for him to speak with you. Well, it was difficult until he found you here. The way he speaks to you now, oh, Lizzy, my heart nearly broke to hear the pain in his voice as he begged you not to die and leave him. He truly loves you."

"I am becoming sleepy, Jane. All of this is wearing on me, and I am fatigued."

"I insist you have something to eat first, then you may rest. Would you be opposed to Mr Darcy returning to the room while you eat? I am certain he is outside the door, fretting over you and needing to be comforted by being here with you."

"Very well, I will agree to eat and to allow Mr Darcy to join us. Thank you, Jane. You are the dearest sister I could have ever hoped for."

~~ ** ~~

When Darcy entered the room, Elizabeth was nearly asleep. He whispered to Jane, asking her if Elizabeth was well.

"I am still awake, Mr Darcy." She said, a sweet smile gracing her lips.

"I do not wish to disturb you, but I wished to see for myself that you were well and inquire if you have need of anything which would bring you comfort."

"I am as well as can be, after being in a carriage wreck weeks ago. Jane has discussed what happened with me. I must also tell you how grateful I am for your kindness, while I was in such a bad way. While I was unconscious, I prayed to be released from my pain and misery, and I heard a most soothing voice speaking to me. I believed it was an angel, sent by God to help lead me to heaven. When I was at my worst, only that sweet voice was able to comfort me. I now learn that it was your voice which saved me. You have no way of knowing how dear your voice is to me."

"I did nothing more than talk to you, read to you from several books."

"Mr Darcy, I believe you have said more to me today than you have in all the time we have known each other combined." Elizabeth teased. "You rarely conversed with me when you were at Netherfield, and never so friendly as you have been here."

"Has your sister spoken to you of my feelings for you?" Darcy asked.

"She has, though it would be best if you and I spoke honestly. You are a gentle and kind man, as has become apparent since I woke here. Your devotion is also clear, though, I must tell you, it is unnerving to me. I barely know you, and yet I wake to hear you call me by my Christian name and speak to me in such caring terms."

"Forgive me, Miss Elizabeth. I did not mean to cause you pain or anguish, it has been difficult to watch you, so terribly injured and nearly dead. It brought all my feelings for you to the surface, everything I attempted to hide from the beginning of our acquaintance."

Elizabeth was nearly asleep. "Mr Darcy, I have so many questions for you, as well as wish to know more about you. I have heard such differing versions of who you are. But I am fatigued."

"I will be here, when you wake. And you are

welcome to ask me all the questions you wish. I will answer you honestly. Now, sleep. You have been through far too much." Darcy lifted Elizabeth's hand to his lips. The gesture made a shiver course through Elizabeth's body.

Darcy picked up a book and began to read aloud. Within moments, Elizabeth was fast asleep.

Mr Darcy...his voice...oh, how wonderful his voice is. Is that enough to make me forget what I have heard from others, and from his own lips? His proud manners, his behavior? Who is this man? So much I want to know, so much I wish to learn about him. Will he truly be here when I wake?

As Elizabeth slept, a dream began to emerge.

She was sitting in a grand drawing room, with her fingers lightly gracing the keys of a most remarkable pianoforte. The music was flowing beautifully, and there was a man standing beside the pianoforte, instructing her on her fingering.

"Madame, you are playing much better this week. You have come a long way since we began your training."

"My thanks to you, Mr Pollack, as you have been a most patient teacher. I am so very grateful for your guidance."

"You have a keen ear, and that has allowed you to be able to play without needing sheet music. That is a

blessing, for it would have been difficult for you to learn some of these songs without being able to see the sheets."

"My wife has a very wonderful talent, Mr Pollack. She amazes me as she moves about, accepting her impairment in stride and making the best of life." Darcy stated as he entered the room, walking straight to Elizabeth's side. "I am truly blessed to have her as my wife, for she brings joy to my life every day."

"William, I thought you were to be gone this morning. Did you not have a meeting to attend?"

"I did, dearest, but I could not stay away from you any longer. I have brought a gift for you." Darcy placed a bundle of flowers in Elizabeth's hands, asking her to take a sniff.

"Oh, William, roses. How wonderful. They smell so heavenly."

"I stopped at a shop on my way home. I wished to purchase every flower in the shop, after the news you gave me last night." He leaned towards her, kissing her on the cheek.

"Not here, William. What will Mr Pollack think?"

"Our time is finished for the day, Mrs Darcy, and I am on my way out. I wish you both a pleasant day and I will see you next week." Mr Pollack walked quickly from the room.

"My love, I cannot contain my happiness. You have given me the greatest gift in the world. I am to be a father. Oh, Lizzy, you are such a wondrous woman, and I treasure the day you accepted my hand."

Elizabeth laughed. "William, you are truly a silly man. I never would have expected you to behave in such a manner. You are almost giddy."

"Do you wish for a son or daughter first? I wish for a daughter, with your beautiful dark curls and sparkling brown eyes."

"My eyes must not sparkle as they once did, William. Things have changed since you first met me."

"The only things that have changed in the sparkle in your eyes is that you can no longer see them. The sparkle is still there, I can see it when you are excited. My only wish is for you to be able to see our babe when it is born."

"You will have to be my eyes. I wish to have a son, a handsome boy with his father's blue eyes and a wavy mop of black hair. And a dimple in one cheek, as I have felt on yours. I wish I had seen you smile more when we first knew each other. I would have liked to have the memory of your smile and the sweet dimple."

"I wish I had done a great many things back then. Perhaps we would have married sooner, and you would never have been in the accident which took your sight."

"You cannot take the blame for what happened,

William. We are together now, and that is all that matters."

"I will always be here with you. You are my heart and life."

"As you are to me."

"As you are to me." Elizabeth mumbled in her sleep. Darcy smiled, hoping that she was finding peace in her dreams. Not long after, when Jane came to check on her sister, she found Darcy had fallen asleep, with his head resting against the side of the bed. It was easy to discern a smile on Darcy's lips, and his left cheek showed a dimple which she had not noticed before. She hoped that this great man would be able to win her sister's heart and hand.

~~ ** ~~

Mrs Johnston's family came to the parsonage, and were informed by Lord Matlock of the unfortunate situation. Her daughter, Olivia, was married with three children of her own. Olivia broke into tears, devastated by the loss of her beloved mother.

Lord Matlock, Richard and Anne spoke with the family, informing them of the plans to pay for the funeral and burial, as well as set up a fund of one thousand pounds to assist with Mrs Johnston's grandchildren. Olivia's husband was a soft spoken man, a clerk at the general store in Hunsford village.

"I appreciate your generosity, Lord Matlock. My

wife's mother was devoted to her grandchildren, and I am certain she would be pleased to know there is a means to pay for the education of our son, as well as assist the girls when they are older."

Mr Bennet entered the parlor, and Lord Matlock introduced him. "Mrs Johnston saved my daughter's life. I cannot say enough to tell you how grateful I am for her devotion and I am deeply sorrowed by your loss. She was a kind and caring lady, and I am in her debt."

"Ma was deeply sorrowed by your daughter's accident. She stated she was amazed at the strength the young lady had. Last Ma told me, your daughter was near dead, but suddenly was growing stronger."

"She is, she has even been awake twice now, and has spoken to us." Mr Bennet said with a slight smile.

Olivia nodded her head. "I will pray for her, as Ma would have."

"You have my gratitude."

Olivia turned towards her husband. "It is best we return to our house. When can we return to collect Ma's belongings?"

"We hope to move Mrs Collins to another bedchamber tomorrow or the next day, depending on her strength. Once we have her out of the rooms which were Mrs Johnston's we will send word." Lord Matlock decided.

"Thank you, Lord Matlock. Miss de Bourgh, thank you." Olivia said as she walked, leaning heavily on her husband's arm, out of the parsonage.

Lord Matlock was worn from the events of the day. "Richard, has Mr Wilkens returned with the laudanum? I wish to sedate my sister and find some peace for an hour or two. This entire mess has been a bloody disaster and I will never forgive Catherine for it."

"Father, your language." Richard exclaimed.

"Forgive me, Anne, Mr Bennet, Mr Bingley. I am certain you men will understand my frustration."

"Of course, Lord Matlock." Mr Bennet replied. "I am not offended, therefore, there is no need to forgive you."

Richard contained a smile. "I will check to see if Wilkens has returned. Mr Lowe went to rest, as he was awake most of last night. Poor man, he has had quite an ordeal to contend with by coming here with William."

"He is a good man, and a good physician. Mr Bennet, have you had a chance to have him examine you?"

"I thought it wiser to allow him to concentrate on Lizzy. But, now that she is doing better, perhaps I should consult with him. I am amazed I have not required more of the powders the apothecary at home gave me."

"Perhaps you are growing stronger." Lord Matlock said hopefully.

"I can only pray that there was a misdiagnosis and that I might recover. But I doubt that very much. Well, shall we have the men haul Lady Catherine to Rosings and put her into a secure room, where she can do no further harm?"

Lord Matlock nodded his head. "Anne, dearest girl, would you prefer to go ahead of us and have a room prepared for your mother, or would you rather remain here? I can send one of the men ahead to have the housekeeper prepare a simple room. I believe there is one in the basement which was a servant's room, no window and only one door. A bed and a few chairs are all that will be required until we know more from Mr Lowe's friend."

"Uncle, if it is agreeable with you, I would prefer to remain here. I do not wish to contend with Mother any more today, though I know I should." Anne was exhausted, physically and emotionally.

"You have endured your Mother, day in and day out, all of your life, with no one to protect you from her since your father died. It is time you are given a chance to recover your strength, so you might think of the future."

Anne nodded. Jane entered the parlor and offered

the use of her bedchamber for Anne to rest. The young heiress agreed and followed Jane up the stairs.

"Miss Bennet, I am grateful for your kindness. It would be understandable to be greeted with you anger at all that has happened to your sister, due to my mother."

"Miss de Bourgh, due to your mother's writing to Mr Darcy, he came here. Due to Mr Darcy's arrival, all is being made right. With the exception of Mrs Johnston's death, all will be better. Your mother will receive the care she requires, and my sister will recover. Had Mr Darcy not come when he did, I am afraid...I am afraid Lizzy would be dead now. And we would not have been notified. And I would not be engaged to Mr Bingley. I prefer to look at the wonderful things which have come forth from all of this."

Anne smiled. "And I would not be engaged to Richard. Yes, I can see your wisdom, Miss Bennet."

"Please, my name is Jane. I wish for you to call me by my name."

"And mine is Anne. I thank you, Jane, for giving me a reason to be pleased, rather dwelling on the negativity of my mother."

"Rest now. I will check on you later."

~~~~~~~ ** ~~~~~~~

Chapter 8

The following morning, Mr Meagle and his assistant arrived at Rosings, as did an express from Mr Lowe's friend, Mr Simmons.

The express announced that there was room for Lady Catherine to be housed at the sanitarium, and Mr Simmons would send a special carriage with two of his men to transport the lady to the facility. The transport would arrive by the afternoon. Lord Matlock asked Richard to accompany the transport and see that all was handled at the sanitarium.

Mr Meagle had begun to research the information Lord Matlock had sent to him, and uncovered some interesting information.

The solicitor who had been utilized by Lady Catherine was no longer in good standing with the courts in London, as his practice was quite shady and illegal. The paperwork Lady Catherine had been given by the man, claiming Anne de Bourgh was unfit, was false. He had not filed anything with any courts as he should have, thereby, the papers were null and void. The man had bilked Lady Catherine for a substantial amount, and she never knew the difference.

Anne was the rightful Mistress of Rosings, and all the inheritance, which her father had set in motion in his will, were rightfully hers. Lord Matlock sighed with relief. They would need to make certain there were no copies of any papers with the sham solicitor, but that bridge could be crossed another day.

Mr Meagle was certain that special licenses could be obtained for not only Richard and Anne to marry, but also for Bingley and Jane. It was discussed that they could have a double wedding, at the chapel at Rosings. Mr Bennet had encouraged his future son to move swiftly, as he wished to have everything completed to protect his family as soon as possible.

Mr Bennet had also written to his brother in law, Mr Phillips. Mr Phillips had replied regarding the entailment of Longbourn, as Elizabeth's deceased husband was the sole heir. It was believed, by Mr Phillips, that the entail could be broken. Mr Bennet consulted with Mr Meagle, who agreed with Mr Phillips. Mr Meagle promised to write to Mr Phillips and work with the country solicitor on the proper means to go about it.

"Mr Bennet, I would be more than happy to back your petition at the House of Lords." Lord Matlock declared. "It is the least I can do for your family. Who would you wish the estate to be given to?"

"Lord Matlock, I appreciate your offer, but there is no possible way I could afford the fees that would be required." Mr Bennet was shocked at the offer.

Bingley stepped to his future father's side. "There

is no need to worry over the cost. If I am unable to afford the cost, Darcy will be more than willing to assist me. I can reimburse him at a later date. It would be of no consequence, as it would bring peace of mind to all of us, as well as take care of Mrs Bennet and the younger daughters. Jane has already stated that she wishes to have Miss Elizabeth live with us, after we are wed. I have readily agreed to her request, and Miss Elizabeth will have a companion as well as anything else she should require."

"See, Bennet, all will be well. So, who do you wish to have inherit? If by chance it is too late to accomplish it all before your time, I will ensure it is done for you." Lord Matlock was quite serious. He was also certain that his nephew would become one of the Bennet son in laws within a short time.

Mr Bennet thought for a few moments before replying. "I believe it should be my first born, Jane." Mr Bennet stated. "With Mr Bingley and Jane marrying and will be living at Netherfield, they would be able to allow my wife and younger daughters to remain at Longbourn, yet watch over them easily."

"Mr Bennet, know I will watch over your family, as they will soon be mine as well. Care will be taken of the estate, and you will be proud of how Longbourn thrives." Bingley stood tall and was pleased with the prospects of his future.

"I am grateful to you all." Mr Bennet stated, a soft

sob escaping him. "So very grateful, indeed."

~~ ** ~~

Elizabeth began to wake, a sense of calm wrapped about her. Her eyes opened, though still it was black in the room. "Is anyone there?"

A soft male voice, the one who had brought so much peace to her in the hours she was unconscious spoke. "I am here, Elizabeth. I will always be at your side."

"Mr Darcy, you sound as if you have had little sleep. You should go to your rooms and rest."

"I took a short rest while you slept. I will be fine." Darcy smiled at the thought of her mothering him.

"Sir, how long has it been since you slept in a bed rather than in a chair?"

Jane entered the room, unbeknownst to the occupants. "I believe it has been at least a week since Mr Darcy has utilized his bedchamber for more than a few moments. If you could feel his chin, you would find he has quite an impressive beard growing there, as he has not taken the time to shave in some time."

"Mr Darcy, you must take better care of yourself." Elizabeth chastised him. "How am I to get to know you better if you do not and become ill because of it? I demand you go to your bedchamber immediately, and do not return here until you have had a proper amount of sleep."

"I am well, there is no need to worry on my account." Darcy attempted to justify his behavior. "I feared leaving your side, that you would be gone when I returned. You were quite ill, and even Mr Lowe was certain you would not survive. I could not stand the thought of your leaving me."

"I am going nowhere, Mr Darcy. Please, for me, go to your bedchambers and sleep properly." Elizabeth smiled. "If you do, when you return, I promise to give you my answer on whether you may court me. If you do not do as I have asked, I will give you an answer this very moment, and you will not be pleased."

"Blackmail, Miss Elizabeth? I never would have thought you capable of such behavior." Darcy laughed. "Very well, I surrender. I will be upstairs. And I suggest you rest as much as possible as well, madam, for I will expect my reward when I wake."

Jane was laughing at the two. It was clear that her sister was realizing the true man Darcy was. "Before she sleeps, I am having a tray brought in for her to take some refreshments. There will be broth, some bread, some fruit from the orangery of Rosings, and some tea. After that, if you have eaten well, perhaps I will allow you some of the delicious pastries which Miss de Bourgh sent from Rosings as well. Her cook is sending food to us."

"I have had the pastries from Rosings, if I were

you, I would do as your sister commands, for you will be well rewarded for it." Darcy placed a kiss on Elizabeth's hand as he stood to leave. "Promise you will behave while I am sleeping?"

"I promise, Mr Darcy. Now, off with you."

~~ ** ~~

Elizabeth ate more than she thought possible, but the smell of everything heightened her appetite, and when she was sated, she felt as if she would burst.

Filled with the nourishment, Elizabeth soon found herself sleepy. Before falling asleep, her father came to speak with her. "How are you, my dear girl?"

"I believe I am feeling slightly better, Papa. I am pleased you are here with me."

Mr Bennet kissed her forehead. "I could not imagine not being here, Lizzy. You have scared us terribly, I will not tolerate such scares from you again." He smiled.

"Forgive me, Papa, it was not intentional. At least, I do not believe I broke the axel on the carriage, though, as big as I am, I likely might have." Elizabeth chuckled. She was of slight build, Mr Bennet often teased her that a strong wind would turn her into a kite.

"Yes, that must be the reason for the axel to have broken, as you are as large as a house...a house for a mouse, perhaps. I am so very grateful to Mr Darcy for all he has done for our family. Not only what he has done for you, but for sending word to us and more. It was painful, not receiving word from you for a fortnight, had he not sent word, who knows how long it would have been before we learned the news. And by then, would you have left this world? And he sent for Mr Bingley, who is now to be your brother."

"I am amazed at his behavior. He is not at all what he was like at Netherfield." Elizabeth was pondering the change in him.

"He told me that he was concerned with your mother's behavior, as well as those of your younger sisters. I admit, Fanny and the youngest two girls are foolish and can be quite vulgar. But, after learning of his aunt's behavior towards you, how she wished to have her recently deceased parson's widow removed from the parsonage, when the young lady was near death, just because it was inconvenient to her, Darcy realized that the truly vulgar person was his aunt. He commented to me that your mother would never have evacuated such a young lady under such conditions, yet his aunt demanded it. That was when he decided it was time to live his life the way he wished, expressing his love for you."

"So, he told you he has loved me before all this? For how long?"

"Not long after he first met you. And the Assembly, he had not even looked at the person Bingley was pointing to, and he is rightly ashamed of his words, and that you heard him. All the time he stared across the room at you, he was not looking for faults. He was deeply in love with you, but unable to speak clearly in your presence."

"Papa, what will happen to me if my eyesight does not return? I doubt very much that such a man as Mr Darcy would wish to have a Mistress of his estate who is blind."

Mr Bennet shook his head. "That is a discussion between you and Mr Darcy, Lizzy. I cannot speak for him. But, if it were me, I would take you no matter if you could see or not. Mr Darcy is a wise man, I am certain he will feel the same way."

Elizabeth yawned. "I am so sleepy, though I feel as if I have slept for a year."

"Your body needs to recover, which means it needs extra sleep. Would you like me to read you a bedtime story, as I did when you were a small child?"

A smile graced Elizabeth's face. "Thank you, Papa, but that will not be necessary."

"Then sleep, my dearest daughter. We will speak more, later."

~~ ** ~~

Caroline Bingley had received a letter from her brother, Charles. She was visiting Scarborough with her elder sister and her brother in law, Louisa and Gilbert Hurst. Charles had written to them to say he would not be joining them, as he had urgent business with Darcy in Kent. Knowing Darcy's aunt lived in Kent, and that his aunt wished a union between her daughter and Darcy, Caroline feared Darcy had finally given in and married his cousin. She could not imagine any other reason for Darcy to require Charles immediately, no reason other than to stand up with him at the wedding. This thought made Caroline ill.

It had been several years since Caroline had set her sights on capturing Fitzwilliam Darcy as her own husband, and becoming Mistress of Pemberley was a goal she intended to attain. For the past four years, Caroline had tried everything to impress Darcy, and in the past year, she had become desperate enough to attempt to compromise him. Nothing seemed to work, no matter what she tried.

But she was not pleased with her brother rushing to Kent to aid Darcy, especially if it was to stand up with him as he married Miss de Bourgh. Caroline had always heard that Darcy was adamant that he would not marry his cousin, he had desired a marriage built on love rather than a society marriage.

When they were staying at Netherfield Park, Caroline was fearful of Darcy becoming attached to Elizabeth Bennet. She had never seen the man act as he did when he was in Elizabeth's presence, staring at her in such a manner and asking for dances with her.

The danger was clear, with her own brother favoring Miss Jane Bennet, Darcy would be thrown into Elizabeth's path often if Charles were to marry the elder Miss Bennet.

Fortunately, that was put to a halt, and Caroline, with the assistance of Darcy, informed Charles that Jane Bennet felt nothing for him. Once that was finished, Caroline felt confident in her plans to capture the allusive Darcy for herself.

Now her mind was frantically attempting to find a reason for her to join her brother. Caroline felt she had to find a way to travel to Kent, to stop Darcy from marrying Miss de Bourgh. If he could see the two ladies, side by side, Caroline was certain Darcy would realize he was making a mistake and make her Caroline Darcy as soon as possible.

"Louisa, I believe you and Hurst were talking of journeying to Ramsgate soon. Why do we not leave now? We could meet Charles in Kent, and then make our way to the seaside. It would be such a pleasant time, I am sure."

"Mr Hurst and I have decided to go to Brighton instead, and not until next month. We are waiting for his brother and mother to visit us. Which reminds me, while they are visiting, you will be required to stay with our aunt. Gilbert's mother does not care for your manners, and I will not offend my mother in law by having you here, irritating her."

"I dislike that woman. She is so filled with her own self-worth, looking down on me. Her son is of little consequence, and far below what I aspire to for my social circle."

"Caroline, I will not have you speak of my husband in such a manner. And you think far too high of yourself, sister. I cannot imagine how you think you, the daughter of a tradesman, is higher socially than the heir to an estate, who comes from a long line of landed gentry."

"I plan to be of the first circle of society, Louisa, not your low level. My husband will make me one of the cream of society."

Louisa laughed. "And just who might your husband be? Let me guess, a duke? No, a prince. Come, Caroline, you must face reality."

The sneer Caroline gave her sister was cold and unfeeling. "You will never be allowed to visit Pemberley when I am Mistress. You do not deserve to be noticed by Fitzwilliam and myself."

"Fitzwilliam, is it? When did you two settle your arrangement?"

"We have yet to settle everything, but it is only a matter of time." Caroline stated, her nose sticking in the air.

"Caroline, it is time you give up on your dreams. Mr Darcy will never marry the likes of you, and would good reason. You are a hateful lady, with no feelings of love for the man. You only wish for what he represents, wealth, power, society. He wishes to be loved for himself, not what he has." Louisa stood and walked from the room.

"I will find a way to make him see that he should marry me, instead of his sickly cousin. Now, how do I find a reason to journey to Kent as soon as possible?"

~~ ** ~~

Lord Matlock decided to write a letter to his wife before taking the next watch of his sister.

My dearest Rebecca,

How I miss you and your calming ways at this very moment. You will be quite shocked when you learn of everything happening here at Rosings.

First, the young lady who was in the carriage accident happens to be the very lady whom Georgiana spoke of, the one William wrote to her about when he stayed in Hertfordshire. The marriage to Mr Collins, my sister's clergyman, was one to protect her family, there was definitely no love between her and her late husband. As it turns out, I believe our nephew is quite taken with Mrs Collins.

When I first arrived, I learned that Mrs Collins

was near death, and had been severely injured in the accident. It has been nearly a month since the accident, and only today, has she awakened for the first time.

Of course, Catherine refused to hear any of this, and insisted Mrs Collins be removed immediately, for it was inconvenient to her search for a new clergyman. Can you believe my sister being so heartless? Yes, I am certain you can.

In confronting Catherine, we learned that she had spoken with a solicitor about having Anne declared impaired and unable to inherit the estate, leaving Catherine in control. Fortunately, we have learned from Mr Meagle that the man Catherine hired was a sham and the papers were not legal. Now we are going through all the paperwork to transfer the estate and assets to Anne.

The worst of the situation is that Catherine, in her fits of self-righteousness, made her way to the parsonage to deal with Mrs Collins. She attempted to murder the defenseless young lady, by smothering her while she slept. The housekeeper for the parsonage, Mrs Johnston, entered the room and attempted to prevent the attack, only to end up being victim to Catherine's violence. Catherine murdered Mrs Johnston, and went back to trying to finish off Mrs Collins. Fortunately, William's friend, Mr Bingley, was here and arrived in the room in the nick of time. He is to marry Mrs Collins' eldest sister, so you can understand why he was at the parsonage. While Catherine was attacking Mrs Collins, William and his physician, Mr Lowe, were at Rosings to speak with Anne, Richard and me of what we should do with Catherine. By the time we learned of the situation, and arrived at the parsonage, Mr Bingley and Mr Bennet, Mrs Collins' father, had bound and gagged Catherine.

To say that Catherine came close to losing her own life is an understatement. William was ready to kill my sister, as was Richard. Part of me wishes they had, it would have been easier to deal with the aftermath than what we now face. But it is not proper, and I will not allow the boys to take such upon their shoulders.

Mrs Collins is beginning to do better, though it will be quite a long road to recovery. But William appears quite smitten with the young lady, and I can foresee the couple marrying sometime in the future. They will make a wonderful couple.

Now, for some well-deserved good news. Richard has asked Anne for her hand in marriage, and Anne has accepted. This has been a difficult time for our poor niece, but, with Richard at her side, she seems to be handling things much better than I expected.

The transport carriage arrived a few moments ago. It will leave in the morning to take Catherine to London, to the sanitarium where the lead physician is a friend of Mr

Lowe's. I asked Richard to make the journey with them, to ensure Catherine arrives there safely and is settled in. I plan to remain here, watching over Anne, and awaiting further news from my solicitor. Hopefully, within a fortnight, I will be able to return to Matlock and meet my grandchild. How dearly I wish to hold an innocent babe in my arms at this moment, see the world fresh and new, through their eyes.

I had best finish for now. Know how much I love you and miss you. You are always in my thoughts.

Your loving husband,

Henry F.

Lord Matlock sanded and sealed the letter, placing it to be posted the following day. All of which the man could think was how peaceful Rosings would be, once Lady Catherine de Bourgh was removed from it.

~~~~~~~ ** ~~~~~~~

Chapter 9

Darcy woke to a sunny day. Though it was nearly February, the day appeared to be shaping up as a warm one. He stretched out his body, feeling more alive than he had in weeks. Since his arrival at Hunsford parsonage, he had not had a full night's sleep, and especially not in a bed.

He stepped to the peer glass and was astounded to see his reflection. Jane Bennet had been correct, he had not been taking proper care of himself. Darcy sent for his valet, Jenkins, and requested a bath be drawn and preparations made to shave his beard.

Once he was bathed, shaved and dressed, Darcy made his way downstairs, to the bedchamber where his heart was to be found. She appeared to be awake and he carefully entered the room.

"Mr Darcy, is that you?" Elizabeth inquired.

"It is I, though I am not certain as to how you determined it was I."

"The way you walk, you have such a long stride. As you are taller than my father and Mr Bingley, and Mr Lowe has just retired for some rest, I could only imagine it was you." A smile graced her lips as she spoke. "I am attempting to learn how to rely on my other senses, since my sight is not functioning."

"I am certain you will be able to see again, Elizabeth. Give it time. Your body has been through so much in such a short time, it needs for you to build up your strength."

"Mr Darcy, I must face the very real possibility that I might never be able to see again. It is difficult for me to accept, but I must learn how to do things without my eyes. And I feel it is only fair to tell you that I cannot accept being a burden to anyone."

"You would never be a burden to me, Elizabeth. Even if you never recover your sight, I wish to be with you always."

Elizabeth took a moment. "Mr Darcy, I must insist on time. I need to learn who I am now. I am a widow on the very day I am a wife, and I do not even know what has happened for nearly a month, due to my own impairments. Then I learn what a kind and caring man you are, and that, instead of watching me to find fault, you were deeply in love with me. And now, there is a chance I will never see again. My father is dying, my sister is to marry Mr Bingley. So much is happening around me and I am deeply confused."

Tears were streaming from Elizabeth's eyes. Darcy picked up her hand, lifting it to his cheek. "Dearest Elizabeth, I can understand your emotions. I, too, have been through many changes these past weeks. Since I learned of your accident, of my aunt's callous and negligent manners, even learned it was you who had married Mr Collins, my heart was torn apart. Seeing you, day after day, hour after hour, so lifeless and near death; I felt as if I were dying along with you. All I ask is that you give me a chance to win your heart. If you are blind permanently, we can hire whomever is needed to instruct you on how to do things, so you can have a bit more independence. And you can have a companion to assist you when need be."

"I have not yet decided where I will live when we leave here. Jane said she and Mr Bingley will be married here, at Rosings. They have offered to let me live with them at Netherfield, yet I know Longbourn by heart. I would also wish to be near my father for what time he has left with us."

"When we leave here, I plan to journey to Netherfield myself. I wish to be near you. Bingley has also invited my sister, Georgiana, to come, so she can meet you and come to know you." Darcy enlightened her. "And I have no plans to go anywhere until I know what you wish to do for the future. Only when you tell me, from the bottom of your heart that you cannot possibly find it in you to marry me, will I give up hope. But know this, if you do not accept me, I will never marry. My heart will always belong to you and only you."

"Mr Darcy, you must not make such a pledge. You may come to despise me, or decide I would be unfit to be Mistress of your estate. It is not fair to make a decision for the rest of your life at this moment. Who knows, you might even decide that there is someone else who is perfect to be your wife."

"Never, dearest. I have met many young ladies in my lifetime. In all the time I have been a part of society, not one lady ever came close to owning my heart as you have. Now and forever, my heart is yours." Darcy kissed the palm of her hand. "But I will allow you to heal and be strong again. In that time, will you give me the opportunity to court you?"

Elizabeth thought for a few moments. All the emotions coursing through her told her it was too much, she could not possibly be a proper wife for him. But her heart wished to be loved. Love that she had desperately wished for all of her life. "Yes, Mr Darcy, I will allow you to court me. I cannot promise I will agree to marriage, but I wish to know you better."

"Then you have made me the happiest man in the world." Darcy leaned towards Elizabeth, placing a gentle kiss on her forehead. "I am truly grateful for this second chance."

~~ ** ~~

Mrs Bennet had been beside herself with worry. With Mr Collins dead, her daughter near death, what would happen to her and her other daughters when her husband died? She thought all of the problems were resolved with Elizabeth's marriage, but now, there was no heir at all. Would the estate be taken away from the Bennet family, given to some stranger they never knew? As Longbourn was entailed to the male line, what would happen to the ladies?

Mrs Bennet knew a little of entails, as her father was a solicitor, and she knew that it would be expensive to petition for it to be broken. There was no possible means for the Bennets to be able to afford such, which would leave the ladies destitute.

So the Mistress of Longbourn kept to her rooms, wailing about her future, blaming the world for her misfortunes.

Mary Bennet, the middle daughter of the Bennet family, had just taken possession of the express which had arrived from Hunsford, and hurried to her mother's side.

"Mamma, Papa has written to us. He sent it express, so it must be important."

"Most likely telling us Lizzy has died without fulfilling her duty to her family, leaving us to be thrown to the hedgerow when your father dies." Mrs Bennet cried.

Mary broke the seal and began to read. "Mamma, Lizzy is alive. She has finally awoken, and is improving. Is that not wonderful news?"

"Only if it says she is with child by Mr Collins and there is hope that it is a son."

"Please, Mamma, we should be grateful that my sister is to live. Oh, and Papa has written that Lady Catherine's brother, Lord Matlock, has arrived at Rosings to take care of matters there. Lord Matlock has offered to assist with the petition to the House of Lords to break the entailment, and his personal solicitor is assisting Papa with the matter. He will be in contact with my Uncle Phillips. Mr Darcy has generously pledged to assist in whatever is needed to break the entail, protecting our family. Is this not wonderful news?"

Within a moment, Mrs Bennet was out of bed and calling for Hill to help her dress. "I must go to my sister Phillips, and learn what her husband has to say on the matter. Oh, but Mr Darcy, that loathsome man, why is it he who is attempting to aid us? What could our troubles matter to him?"

"Mamma, remember, he is Lady Catherine and Lord Matlock's nephew. He was the one who discovered that Lizzy was injured and notified Papa. Jane said, in her last letter, that Mr Darcy is doing everything he can to see Lizzy is given the best care possible. Do not condemn him, when he is doing so much to aid us."

"Very well, though I wish it had been Mr Bingley. How I wish Mr Bingley could be found and that he would marry Jane. All would be well if Jane was the Mistress of Netherfield." Mrs Bennet continued to rant as she began to ready herself to leave the house.

A sly smile grew on Mary's lips, as she knew the truth of Jane and Mr Bingley's engagement. Jane had written to her middle sister, informing her of their desire of not having Mrs Bennet know until a later date. Mary was overjoyed at her sister's news, and pleased to keep the secret from her mother, for she knew Mrs Bennet would demand on being at Rosings to ensure Bingley married Jane, even if she had to ride horseback to get there.

Walking downstairs, Mary found her next eldest sister, Kitty, sitting in the front parlor. "Papa sent an express, Lizzy is awake and improving."

"Thank the heavens." Kitty said.

"Why are you here, all alone? Where is Lydia?"

Kitty looked sheepishly at her sister. "She went for a walk. I believe she was heading towards Lucas Lodge, to see Maria."

"Kitty, Maria and Charlotte are visiting their aunt in Salisbury. They will not be back until next week. Where is Lydia?" Mary demanded.

"She went for a walk, towards Meryton. She was planning to meet one of the militia, the new one who just arrived last month, Lieutenant Wickham."

"Kitty, why would you not stop her? Such behavior is highly improper and will ruin us all?"

"But they are in love. They have been meeting for

a fortnight, and nothing bad has happened. Lydia promised me that she was behaving, she swore that all she has allowed him to do is kiss her cheek. Mr Wickham has told her that he is to come into some money, an inheritance from his godfather, and then he will marry her."

Mary was disgusted with her youngest sister's behavior. "This must come to a stop. Do you know where they meet?"

Kitty shook her head. "No, whenever I have been with her, Lydia sends me off. She has been quite secretive about where they go."

"I must go look for her. She has to be made to stop her behavior immediately. With Papa and our elder sisters away, and Mamma allowing Lydia to run amok, it is up to you and me to correct our sister. If anyone were to discover them, or worse, Lydia was to lose her virtue to him, we would all bear the consequences of her ruination."

"It cannot be so bad, Mary. They are planning to wed as soon as Mr Wickham is given his inheritance. If they are engaged, such things are overlooked."

"But they are not officially engaged. Mr Wickham has not asked for Lydia's hand properly, by speaking to Papa. She is a young and silly girl, willing to behave so without thinking of the truth."

"Papa has been away, with Lizzy and Jane. How is

Mr Wickham to ask for his permission?"

Mary was growing frustrated. "If he truly wishes to marry Lydia, he could request a day of leave to journey to Hunsford. It is not as if he were having to travel to France to ask permission for Papa. No, we need to keep Lydia in check and not allow any further clandestine meetings with Mr Wickham, and I will write to Papa and inform him of the situation."

~~ ** ~~

Richard returned from Town, after several days of seeing to his aunt's being settled in the sanitarium and business with the solicitor. With him, the special licenses for both Bingley and Jane, as well as Richard and Anne, and it was decided to hold the wedding two days later. Mr Lowe was impressed with Elizabeth's improved health, and the decision had been made to transport her to Rosings to continue to heal. The parsonage was far too small for everyone wishing to remain near Elizabeth, and it was decided to have the cottage cleared of Mr Collins' belongings as well as to have Mrs Johnston's family collect her belongings. Anne declared that chapter of life over and in need to be readied to move forward.

With Elizabeth being moved to the grand house, she was able to recline on a sofa in the drawing room, enjoying her sister's wedding. A small wedding breakfast was enjoyed by those in attendance, which was a small group of family. Though Elizabeth was technically her sister's witness, as well as Anne's, she could not stand by her side. Darcy stood beside the sofa, as he wished to keep Elizabeth from feeling melancholy at having to be reclining. He was witness for both Richard and Bingley. Lord Matlock had given his niece away, as Mr Bennet gave Jane in marriage. Though not the ideal wedding of childhood dreams, both brides could not look any happier with the result. Anne and Richard soon removed to their rooms, where they remained until the following day.

The Bingleys, though wishing for some time alone, decided to remain with their family instead. "Now, Lizzy, as you are my sister, you must know you are welcome to live with Jane and me." Bingley said as he kissed Elizabeth's cheek.

"I am still thinking over your offer, Mr Bingley."

"I told you to call me Charles, my dear sister."

Elizabeth smiled. "Very well, Charles. I am still trying to decide what will be best. I do not wish to intrude upon you as you are newlyweds."

"I cannot see how it would be an intrusion." Jane declared. "And Mr Darcy and his sister will be joining us as well."

"Jane, we have discussed the reasons for me to return to Longbourn. I will decide before we return to Hertfordshire, have no fear."

"Very well, Lizzy. I would dearly love having you

at Netherfield with us, as you know."

~~ ** ~~

An express arrived for Mr Bennet from Mary. When he read it, he nearly collapsed from the strain.

Dearest Papa,

I am in a quandary as to what to do. I learned only today that Lydia has been secretly been meeting with one of the militia, a Lieutenant Wickham, who arrived near the time you left for Hunsford.

With Mamma unwilling to speak with my sister about her behavior, and Lydia's refusal to listen to me, I fear that I am in need of assistance. According to Kitty, who had been hiding the truth from me for weeks, Lydia believes Mr Wickham plans to marry her, allegedly after he receives an inheritance from his godfather. Believing she is engaged, Lydia has allowed him a few kisses, or so she has told Kitty. I fear she will risk her virtue foolishly, with no true promise of marriage.

Please give my love to Lizzy and tell her how happy I am she is recovering. Give Jane my love as well. I know you are worried about my sister, but I know no one else to help me with Lydia.

Write and tell me what you wish to have me do.

Your devoted daughter,

Mary

Bingley took the letter from Mr Bennet's hand, as Mr Lowe came forward to tend to the elder man. After reading the letter, Bingley gasped. "Good God, what is that girl thinking?"

Darcy heard the commotion coming from the drawing room, as he had just come downstairs from visiting Elizabeth. "What has happened?" Bingley held out the letter, which Darcy took. As he read, his stomach clinched as he read the name of Wickham. *Could it be George Wickham?*

"What is to be done?" Darcy asked. "Who will be traveling to Longbourn?"

Mr Lowe shook his head. "I do not believe it wise for Mr Bennet to make the journey today. The strain has done him great harm. With everything which has occurred here, it is amazing he has been in as good health as he is. Perhaps in a few days, he would be strong enough to make the journey in a slow manner."

"When do you believe Elizabeth will be able to travel?" Mr Bennet asked.

"Her broken bones are nearly healed, as are most of her cuts. She is growing stronger every day, but I am not certain when she would be able to sit in a carriage for so long a time." Mr Lowe stated.

"What if we were to rig a carriage with a bed inside it, along one side, so Elizabeth could rest as much as possible?" Darcy asked. "The carriage would also carry you and Mr Bennet, while Bingley, Mrs Bingley and I could leave immediately to intercede upon Mr Bennet's behalf."

Mr Lowe thought for a moment. "I believe it is possible to do so. If Mr Bennet approves, that is."

"If you do not feel my Lizzy would be further at risk from such a journey, then I agree." Mr Bennet announced. "But I cannot ask you to make such a journey, Mr Darcy. It is far too much for you to have to contend with."

"Mr Bennet, first and foremost, I hope to one day be a member of your family. Elizabeth has given me permission to court her, and I am determined it will lead to marriage. Secondly, I grew up with a young man named George Wickham. If it is he who is mistreating your daughter, you will require me to persuade him otherwise. He is not a man to be trusted, as he has ruined any number of young ladies and left debts wherever he goes. If it is the Wickham I know, the inheritance he has referred to would have been from my father, who was his godfather. But he has already received his inheritance, in the amount of four thousand pounds. I hold many of Wickham's debts, which I have paid off and hold the paperwork. If I need to, I can have him placed in debtor's prison."

Jane looked from Darcy, to Bingley, and then to her father. "I agree with Mr Darcy, Papa. It may be the best solution, if it is, indeed, the same man Mr Darcy knows. I will accompany my husband and Mr Darcy, to make certain Lydia and Mamma know the men act on your word."

Mr Bennet finally nodded his head. "Very well. We will leave here in two days' time, and I pray that my foolish daughter has not gone off and ruined our family."

"Have hope, Papa." Jane said, attempting to calm him.

Darcy stepped closer to Mr Bennet. "Sir, if you do not mind, perhaps I will have my cousin, Richard, accompany you. He has served in the military for many years now, and has resources which may be considered unsavory. In dealing with Wickham, we might just need such assistance."

"Yes, yes, whatever you think is best." Mr Bennet replied. "Though Jane is safely married, my other daughters could be ruined due to their youngest sister behaving so irrationally."

~~ ** ~~

After sending word to Rosings for his cousin, and receiving Richard's reply, stating he would be willing to travel with Mr Bennet and Elizabeth, ensuring they arrived at Longbourn as comfortable as possible.

Darcy and Bingley had prepared to leave with Jane. Before he could leave, Darcy felt it was vital for him to explain what was happening to Elizabeth, as he did not wish for her to believe he had abandoned her.

Sitting in the chair next to her bed, Darcy took hold of her hand. Elizabeth smiled as she felt his touch. "Mr Darcy. I am pleased to have you return."

A chuckle escaped Darcy's lips. "How is it that you knew it was me?"

"Several things, to be honest. First, your way of walking. I am able to distinguish some of the unique footsteps, and yours is definitely masculine, with a long stride. Secondly, the touch of your hand, I have come to recognize. You have a scar on the palm of your hand."

"Ahh, yes, from when I was a child. I fell onto a very sharp stone. It was a severe wound. The physician had to stitch it together."

"And finally, the most obvious way to discern as to you rather than someone else is your scent. You smell of lemon and spices." Elizabeth had a faint smile on her face as she declared what she had come to learn of Darcy.

"I am delighted to see you are adapting so well. Though I am certain it is only temporary, it will make the time more pleasant until your sight returns. You will not feel as helpless if you are able to determine some things for yourself. Now, I must inform you that an emergency has come about, one that forces me from your side."

Elizabeth was suddenly nervous. Though she was still not certain of who Mr Darcy truly was, she had grown accustomed to having him nearby. His soothing voice was of such comfort, she was loath to lose him so soon.

"I can see by your expression, you are not pleased. Believe me, I am not pleased to leave you. If it were not of the greatest urgency, I would remain here. But you will soon be traveling to Longbourn, as your father and Mr Lowe will be taking you there in two days. My cousin, Richard Fitzwilliam, will also see to your journey being a safe one. Once you arrive at Longbourn, I will be there. So it is only a few short days before I am at your side once again."

"What sort of matter could take you away from here, yet, you will be at my father's house in two days? Has something happened at Netherfield or Longbourn?" Elizabeth became nervous.

"I will be honest with you, though I insist you remain calm. Your sister, Miss Mary, has written to your father. One of the new militia is paying far too much attention to your youngest sister, Miss Lydia. Miss Mary is afraid, with no male family member close enough to put a halt to the behavior, Miss Lydia may place the family in jeopardy with her actions. I will travel with Mr and Mrs Bingley, to assist them, as I am acquainted with the young man involved."

"Please, Mr Darcy, use caution. I am fearful for you."

Darcy shook his head as he picked up her hand in his. "Have no fear, dearest Elizabeth. I only wish to protect your family, and we will ensure your sister is made to behave herself. Then, when you and your father arrive, Mr Bennet can take charge of Miss Lydia."

Elizabeth was in tears. "Papa, he is delicate. The strain this must be causing him. Please, Mr Darcy, my father is not well."

"Do not fret, Mr Bennet has been quite open with all of us of his condition, and Mr Lowe is seeing to your father as well as you. That is another reason for Mr Lowe to travel with you. He will see to the welfare of both you and your father." Darcy placed a gentle kiss on the back of Elizabeth's hand. "I go with your sister and her husband to protect your father as much as possible."

"I will be in your debt for your kindness, Mr Darcy. Though I know my time with Papa is limited, I wish to keep him with us as long as possible."

"Having lost my own father, I can understand your feelings. I will do whatever I can to make that possible."

Chapter 10

Darcy arrived at Longbourn with the newlywed Bingleys. Mary Bennet welcomed home her sister with a tearful expression. "Oh, Jane, it is horrible. We are in an uproar over the situation."

"Mary, calm yourself and tell me what has happened." Jane replied, concerned for her sister.

"This morning, we could not find Lydia. When we searched for her, she could not be found. Mamma is in her rooms, taken to her bed with her nerves. I sent Mr Hill to Lucas Lodge, for Sir William. He has taken charge of the search for Lydia, though no one is certain as to where to look for our sister. I suggested to him that he should speak to Colonel Forster of the militia. Sir William returned to inform us that not only is Lydia missing, Lieutenant Wickham and Captain Denny are also missing. If they cannot be found in the next day, the two men will be thought to have deserted. Colonel Forster's men are searching the area, though it is believed that they have fled during the night and are far from here."

Jane nearly collapsed from the news. "Mary, my poor sister, you have had so much with which to contend. Now, I must shock you even greater, as I must inform you that I have recently married. Mr Bingley is now your brother."

"Mr Bingley?" Mary questioned her hearing properly. "When were you married? Does Papa know of this?"

"Papa gave me away at my wedding. It was at Rosings Park, just a few days ago. Mary, I must also enlighten you on a few more issues. Papa is very weak. He is dying, my dear sister. And there is nothing which can be done for him. This is the reason Charles and I have come, so we can take care of the situation with Lydia. We did not know of her disappearing, though. Pray, tell me you did not send an express to Hunsford."

Mary nodded her head. "I did after learning of Wickham and Denny having disappeared as well. You did not receive it?"

"No, and if Papa does, I am certain it will do him more harm than good." Jane was deeply concerned.

"How is Lizzy? We have not received any word from Papa in a few days, so I was concerned as to our sister's welfare."

"Lizzy is improving, though she cannot see. We are not certain as to why, and we do not know if it is permanent, but we will concern ourselves with that later. The most pressing matter is to bring Lydia home as quickly as possible."

"Kitty will not speak to me on the matter, but I am certain she knows more, as Lydia tells her everything." Mary said as she wiped the tears from her cheeks.

Jane agreed. "I will question Kitty of what she is aware. Now, I wish you to go upstairs, take some rest and refresh yourself. Charles and I will discuss the situation with Mr Darcy."

"Mr Darcy? Why would Mr Darcy wish to be involved with our mess?"

"First, he has known Mr Wickham since they were boys, he may be able to help us find people who have aided Mr Wickham. And the second reason is that Mr Darcy loves our dear sister, Elizabeth. He wishes to do anything he can to protect our family."

Mary was amazed at the news, though she immediately did as her eldest sister had requested, and went up to her rooms to rest. Jane, Bingley and Darcy all went to Mr Bennet's study, asking Mrs Hill to join them.

Mrs Hill informed the newly arrived people that Sir William would be returning to Longbourn by four that afternoon. The men were still searching the area, though no one held any hope of discovering the three missing in the neighborhood. All were certain they would be found far away from Hertfordshire.

Bingley and Darcy discussed where Wickham could have gone. Darcy knew enough of Wickham's past behavior to know the man would be hold up in some seedy area of London, in an area where a man could become lost from all who search for him. The first person Wickham would run to for assistance would be Georgiana Darcy's former companion, Mrs Younge. It was learned, through painful experience, that Mrs Younge could not be trusted. She had been Wickham's lover for many years, and the two had concocted a plan the previous year to take Georgiana's dowry from her by Wickham's marrying the young girl. Fortunately, Darcy arrived before Wickham could convince Georgiana to elope with him, and sent Mrs Younge on her way without reference. Unfortunately, Wickham had been able to escape justice, fleeing the area before Darcy could exact any revenge.

Before they could leave for London, Darcy and Bingley wished to speak with Sir William Lucas and Colonel Forster. They needed to have all the information they could gather before rushing off after the trio.

~~ ** ~~

Colonel Forster was fit to be tied. Two of his officers had deserted their posts, leaving the neighborhood with the daughter of a gentleman. This was disturbing, and he knew there would be repercussions from this situation. He would have to be involved with the search and capture of the men, as well as the recovery of Miss Lydia Bennet to her family.

A knock alerted him to someone at his door. "Enter."

Captain Saunders entered the room. "Colonel, I have some information to report."

"Yes, go ahead."

"Sir, I believe Wickham and Denny are in London. Three days ago, I overheard their speaking of meeting with some friends of Wickham's, as they had a job planned which would make them wealthy. It is my belief they took the Bennet girl along to bring them some pleasure while they worked out the details of their plans."

"There was no intent on either man's behalf for a marriage to Miss Bennet?" Colonel Forster was appalled at the news. "What do they plan to do with the girl after they accomplish their goal?"

"I believe they will leave her in some gutter, ruined and destitute." Saunders said, his head bowed.

"Good God, how could these men fool so many people into believing they were decent? Do you know who they would contact in London? Do you know who they are working with?"

"No, Sir, but I will continue to investigate amongst the men and inform you of anything I learn."

"Thank you, Captain. You are dismissed." Colonel Forster was devastated.

After a few moments, Colonel Forster strode out of his quarters and called for his horse. He rode swiftly towards Lucas Lodge, wishing to confer with Sir William.

Arriving as Sir William was preparing to make his way to Longbourn, Colonel Forster decided to wait to speak until they were both at the Bennet house. Both men were surprised to learn of that Bingley and Darcy were at Longbourn, and surprised to learn of Jane's marriage to Bingley.

"Mrs Bingley, have you word as to when your father will be returning? Is Mrs Collins recovering from her injuries?" Sir William inquired.

"Papa will be returning the day after tomorrow. We were concerned for his health, and came ahead of him. He and my sister will be traveling with the physician who has been tending Lizzy." Jane replied. "In the meantime, my husband and his dear friend, Mr Darcy, will be in charge of the search for my youngest sister. Have you men learned any new information?"

Sir William shook his head no, but Colonel Forster nodded. "I pray that the news I have will not shock you, Mrs Bingley. It appears Wickham and Denny have, indeed, deserted their posts, and it is to be believed that they have journeyed to London. One of my captains admitted overhearing the men speaking of meeting up with some of Wickham's friends. They are supposedly planning some sort of venture which would bring them a considerable fortune."

"Whatever could they be planning?" Bingley wondered aloud. "I am certain it could not be anything legal, from what Darcy has informed me of Wickham's past behavior."

"Mr Darcy, you know Wickham?" Sir William asked.

"He is the son of my father's steward. When Wickham was a boy, we were friends. It was not long before I learned the sort of young man he truly was. He has caused my family many harms over the years." Darcy walked over to the sideboard, pouring himself a glass of port, and downed the drink quickly. After pouring a second drink, Darcy turned to offer the other men refreshment.

"Where would Wickham go in Town?" Colonel Forster began to hope he would be able to capture these two men and save himself from losing his position in the militia.

"I have a few ideas. One of which is a lady who has been a long-time lover of Wickham's, and who is very willing to do his bidding without question. Her name is Mrs Dorothy Younge. I have a report in my townhouse in Town, which gives me her address as of six months ago. Bingley and I will travel tomorrow morning to Town. My cousin, Colonel Fitzwilliam, recently resigned from the regulars, will be arriving with Mr Bennet. I will leave word for him to join us in

Town. He has contacts who will be vital to our search."

"I know of Colonel Fitzwilliam, though I was unaware he had resigned his commission." Colonel Forster announced.

"He recently married and has a future with his bride at their estate. He married my cousin, the former Miss Anne de Bourgh." Darcy stated. "Richard has many contacts with the seedier side of Town, ones I would never be able to utilize. Bingley and I can begin the search, and, once Richard arrives, we can further the investigation. Hopefully, we will be able to return Miss Lydia Bennet to her family within the week, and have dealt with your wayward deserters. I am interested in learning what their plans are, hopefully they will be thwarted from any illegal activities."

~~ ** ~~

Wickham and Denny sat at the table in the furthest corner of the pub. Above stairs, he had left Lydia Bennet, securely tied to the bed and gagged. She was to be their protection, if anyone should attempt to stop them. No one would wish to harm the daughter of a country gentleman. Wickham was willing to use Lydia as a shield or to barter her safety to allow him a safe escape from the law.

They were to meet with two other men from the docks. The men were burly and strong, and extremely thick headed. If anything went wrong, they would be sacrificed easily.

The plan was to break into Darcy's house and rob it. Wickham's intelligence was that Darcy was at Hunsford, as Lydia Bennet had commented on the express her father had received from the man. If Darcy was away from his townhouse, there would be minimal staffing. Darcy never left his younger sister alone at their townhouse, so Wickham knew there would not be any danger in robbing the place.

Wickham remembered his late godfather, Gerald Darcy, and his many collections. There was a coin collection which, Wickham knew, had been valued at twenty thousand pounds, as well as jewels and silver candlesticks. Also, hidden in the study of the townhouse, was a collection of gold snuff boxes. All in all, Wickham was certain he would be able to walk away with more than fifty thousand pounds in items he could pawn. And he was certain there would be cash kept in the study, and Wickham would make sure he took everything of value from Darcy's home.

Knowing his childhood friend, he was sure Darcy had spent most of his time, since his father's death, at Pemberley. Darcy disliked Town, and it was not unfathomable that Darcy had not discovered the many hiding places within the townhouse. Gerald Darcy had shown his godson several of these hiding places, swearing the young man into secrecy. But Wickham was never good at keeping secrets, especially if he could make a profit from his knowledge.

Wickham also wished to avenge himself on Darcy. Since his childhood friend had destroyed Wickham's attempts to convince Georgiana to elope with him, forcing him to give up the hopes to gain her dowry, Wickham's hate for Darcy had only grown.

The men Wickham had been waiting from arrived at the pub. The taller man, Floyd, spoke. "My brother and me been checking around, as you said. No one has seen the family at the grand house in weeks. The cook's girl was sayin' the housekeep be tellin' them it will be some time for the rich ones return."

"Good, good." Wickham said with a smile. "Today is Tuesday. They usually have more cash on hand on Thursday, as that is when they pay the staff. The housekeeper goes to the bank on Thursdays to withdraw the funds."

"So we will rob the place, then we will go to Wilbur's to pawn all the stuff, right?" Denny asked. "You already spoke with Wilbur about what we might be bringing?"

"I have. He will be prepared to handle whatever we bring him." Wickham had spoken to one of his longtime cohorts, one who had no love for Darcy and was pleased with the thought of making a bit off the grand man.

"Then let us drink up." Floyd declared.

Denny was concerned with another matter. "What do we do with that bit of fluff upstairs? Are we going to turn her loose or what?"

Wickham took a long sip of his drink. "I was thinking I should show that little fool just what to expect when she flirts with a real man. She thinks she is ready for the real world, but she is such a child."

"I thought we were going to just hold onto her until we were safe. There is no reason to butter that bun. She is a gentleman's daughter, and a young one at that. We could hang if we are caught, raping is never a good idea. Especially since there are so many willing ones to be had." Denny was fearful of what would come of them if Wickham had his way.

"The chit is already ruined, in the eyes of her family and society. Might just as well make her ruin complete." Wickham laughed. "And she is a fetching piece as well, so it would not be a hardship."

"I think we would be running too great a risk if we spoilt her. Best turn her loose as soon as we are safe from the grand house."

Floyd and his brother would never turn down a turn with a pretty young thing. "If you be not wishing for a turn, I be glad to taken an extra go at 'er." Floyd smiled as he elbowed his brother, Jack. "Me brother and me, we would take a poke at 'er iffen she be offered."

"We will see." Wickham began to think over the situation. If it were only he and Denny having a go at Lydia Bennet, it would be easy enough to cover their escape. But the brothers were low on intelligence and would be easily discovered. And Wickham was certain Floyd knew enough of Wickham's plans to hinder his freedom.

~~ ** ~~

Darcy and Bingley were having a late start the following morning. Darcy's horse had a loose shoe and another horse had to be made ready for the trip to Town. The delay was a blessing in disguise, as they were still at Longbourn when the carriage arrived with Mr Bennet, Mr Lowe and Elizabeth. Richard Fitzwilliam rode on horseback beside the carriage.

"Richard, we were not expecting you until tomorrow." Darcy exclaimed to his cousin. "Is everything well?"

"Mr Bennet received the express explaining his daughter's disappearance. He could not tolerate the delay of another day, so he demanded to make the journey as quickly as possible. We left near five this morning, before the sun had a chance to rise. Mr Bennet, he is not feeling well."

Darcy shook his head. He should have known the Master of Longbourn would demand to travel rather than remain an extra day at Rosings. Walking over to the opened door of the carriage, Darcy leaned his head inside. Mr Lowe was assisting Mr Bennet to exit the carriage, and Darcy stepped forward, his hands steadying the elder man. Next Lowe instructed Darcy on how they would aid Elizabeth into the house. After Lowe spoke of needing the stretcher on top of the carriage, Darcy shook his head. "I will carry her." Darcy stated. "If Miss Elizabeth agrees, that is."

Hearing the voice she had come to find peace in, Elizabeth declared her approval. Leaning inside the carriage, Darcy scooped the delicate frame of the woman he loved, into his embrace. Holding her firmly to his chest, Darcy exited the carriage. "I have missed you, Miss Elizabeth."

"I have missed your reading to me and hearing your voice." Elizabeth said, as she leaned into his body and placing her head on his shoulder. "What has been decided? Has my sister been found?"

"Not yet, though I would prefer to wait until we are inside to discuss the matter. Your father is, undoubtedly, wishing to be updated on the subject."

"Then take me to the parlor. I wish to learn more of what has happened to Lydia."

Darcy was concerned. "After such a trip as you have endured, it would be best if you rested."

"I could not rest comfortably, not knowing what

was happening with my sister."

Knowing he would feel the same, Darcy agreed to take her to the sofa in the parlor. Seeing that Darcy was not taking Elizabeth upstairs, to her room, Mr Bennet began to object. "Mr Bennet, forgive me, but it would be quickest to bring you up to speed with what has happened altogether. Miss Elizabeth is just as anxious as you are to learn more of her sister."

Not wishing to battle the young man, verbally or physically, Mr Bennet relented. "What have you learned of my youngest daughter? Has anyone been able to tell you where she is?"

"It is our belief that she is in London, with two men from the militia. We do not know if she went with them willingly or was abducted, but the men are not to be trusted. Wickham would have no qualms in violating Miss Lydia. From what we have learned, Wickham and a Mr Denny are preparing some sort of job which will make them very wealthy. It is my opinion that their scheme is illegal, and we must find them quickly, so Miss Lydia is not caught in the middle. After she is recovered, we will need to discuss what to do to save her reputation, and the reputations of your other daughters."

"Where is my wife?" Mr Bennet asked.

"The apothecary, Mr Jones, gave her a tonic to calm her nerves. She is in her rooms, resting." Bingley replied. "Jane is upstairs with her at the moment."

MRS COLLINS, AGAINST HER WISHES

"Are you men leaving for London then?" Mr Bennet could see by their clothing, they were prepared to travel.

"Indeed." Darcy said firmly. "Now that Richard is here, it will make things better. My cousin has many friends who know the...less than favorable side of Town. With his contacts, plus my knowledge of Wickham, it will be easier to find the trio."

"Once you find Lydia, I wish for you to take her to my brother's home. Edward Gardiner, who lives on Gracechurch Street, near Cheapside."

"We will do as you ask, Mr Bennet. Now, I wish to speak with you for a moment." Darcy asked the father of his beloved Elizabeth.

"Then let us step into my study. I am sure you wish to be off soon."

~~~~~~~ ** ~~~~~~~

Chapter 11

Shutting the door behind him, Darcy walked to the chair directly in front of Mr Bennet's desk and took his seat. "How are you fairing?" He asked Mr Bennet.

"I am as well as can be expected at this point." Came the reply from the worn and frail man. "I assume you wish to speak with me with regards to my daughter, Elizabeth."

"I do. I wish to come to some form of understanding before I leave for Town. I do not mean to offend you, but seeing you here, in this condition, it is clear that you are struggling."

Mr Bennet nodded his head. "I am weaker than I was, that is for sure. To be honest, I am amazed this whole episode has not killed me. Between my Lizzy nearly dying, my heir dead, and now Lydia missing, perhaps abducted, I do not know how much more I can take."

"I would like your permission to speak with Miss Elizabeth privately for a moment, before I leave Longbourn. I need her to understand that I will be returning to her as soon as possible, and that I love her."

"Mr Darcy, after spending so much time in your presence of late, I can honestly say you are one of the best men of my acquaintance. I would count myself fortunate to have you as a son in law, if Elizabeth should decide upon you. But I must ask you, are you willing to wait until there has been a proper mourning period for Lizzy's late husband? I do not wish for her to live through a scandal for marrying you too soon after Mr Collins' death."

"Of course, Mr Bennet. I do not wish to cause any harm to your daughter's reputation. And I promise to court her properly. You have my word of honor on that matter."

"I will write to my wife's brother and her brother in law, Mr Gardiner and Mr Phillips, and inform them of my approval. Most likely, I will not survive long enough to give my Elizabeth away to you."

Darcy glanced down at his hands. It was difficult for him to think of Elizabeth's father dying. Remembering the pain he endured with the death of his own father's passing, Darcy could not speak for several moments. Finally, he returned his vision to the Master of Longbourn. "Mr Bennet, I would like to inform you of something I have done. I sent a letter to my solicitor in Town. I have added Elizabeth to my will, so that she will be protected even if I were to perish before we are able to marry. As soon as I arrive in Town, I plan to sign the papers. And I wish to hire a master to work with Elizabeth. Her vision difficulty may continue for some time, so I wish to assist her in finding ways to do things for herself. She has been such an independent person, I would like to see her regain her confidence and some of her independence."

"I have sent a letter to Mr Gardiner, asking him to search for a teacher for the blind. He lives in Town, so has connections which will be beneficial in finding someone who can aid Lizzy." Mr Bennet spoke softly. "I, too, wish to see my dearest daughter return to her former vivacity. She has been a different person since I forced her to marry my cousin, and Lizzy deserves to be happy. I am grateful for your devotion to her."

"For the rest of my life, I will be devoted to her, and will do my best to earn her love." Darcy held his hand out, wishing to seal the deal he had just made with the father of his beloved. Mr Bennet accepted the young man's hand in his own, shaking it firmly in his approval. "It is best we be off, as I wish to make London as soon as possible. Please know I will do all I can to recover Miss Lydia. In my heart, she is my future sister, so she will be under my protection."

"You have my heartfelt gratitude, Mr Darcy."

~~ ** ~~

Elizabeth was still sitting on the sofa in the parlor, when Darcy returned to her. Fortunately, Jane and Bingley had stepped outside for a moment, leaving Elizabeth and Mary alone. Darcy walked quickly to his beloved's side and sat down.

"William...I told my sisters that you would return to speak with me before you left with the other men."

Elizabeth gave a weak smile. "I am so grateful for your assistance to my family. My father's health being what it is...I fear for him."

"As I have told you, my intentions are to marry you. That will make your family mine. I will do whatever I can to protect your family."

Hearing the sound of someone entering the room, Darcy's attention was turned. Mrs Hill was at the doorway of the parlor. "Miss Mary, your father wishes you to join him in his study. Miss Elizabeth and Mr Darcy will be fine without you for a few moments."

Once Mary had left the room, Elizabeth giggled. "That was not at all obvious."

Darcy smiled. "I asked your father for a few moments alone. He was kind enough to arrange a private audience for us."

"And of what did you wish to speak?"

"Dearest Elizabeth, you know of my devotion to you, do you not?"

Nervously, Elizabeth nodded her head. "I am aware."

"I could not leave you before declaring my intentions. When I return, I will remain in the neighborhood until the mourning period is over and you are free to marry. In that time, I intend to court you, discretely, and give you the chance to know me better. I love you, deeply, and I pray that, in time, you will come to love me as well."

"At the moment, I am quite confused. Part of me is frightened of what the future holds for me and my family, while the other part wishes to be loved as dearly as you claim."

"You deserve to be loved, and cherished. If you allow me, I intend to show you how precious you are to me, for the rest of your life. All I ask is for you to trust me, and trust my devotion to you."

Elizabeth held her lower lip between her teeth for a moment. Finally, she turned her head towards Darcy. "I believe I will place my trust in you, William."

"You have made me quite happy, Elizabeth. So very happy." Darcy lifted her hand to his lips, placing a gentle kiss on the back of her hand. "Now, I must leave, for my cousin and Bingley are waiting for me. While I am in Town, I wish to hire a companion to come here, to assist you in learning how to be more independent with your loss of vision. Will you permit such an indulgence on my part?"

A smile was gracing Elizabeth's lips. "That would be very generous, William. I would be grateful."

"Might I be so bold as to kiss you, before I leave?"

With a nod, Elizabeth nervously agreed. When their lips met, both were pleasantly rewarded with the excitement of the moment. They quickly lost themselves, as they took delight in each other. Only when they heard someone cough loudly from the hall, did they remember themselves and separate. Looking at her red and swollen lips, Darcy felt a sense of pride. "You look quite fetching, and it will be my pleasure to kiss those lips for the rest of my life."

A blush rose on Elizabeth's cheeks. "It was far more pleasant than I could ever have imagined."

"I will return, as soon as possible." Darcy said as his hand caressed her cheek. "Be safe, and remember, I love you."

"Please, William, be careful."

"You have my word on it." Darcy placed a gentle kiss on her forehead, before standing and leaving the room. Outside the parlor, Richard was waiting, a smirk on his lips. "We should be off, Richard."

Silently, Richard followed his cousin outside. Bingley was already on top of his horse, waiting for the other men to join him. Within a moment, the men were off.

~~ ** ~~

Mary and Jane returned to the parlor after the men had departed for Town. Mary was nervous, not knowing how to help Elizabeth with her disability. "Lizzy, is there anything I can get for you? Perhaps some water, or a glass of wine?"

Elizabeth pasted a smile on her face. "Mary, I thank you for your kindness, but there is nothing I need at the moment. I would much rather hear how you are, what you have been doing since I left here."

"I...I am so sorry about your accident. And I am sorry you have suffered. You were so brave, accepting Mr Collins as a husband. I know you did not love him, or even like him. But you married him to protect us."

"It was done, but now Mr Collins is dead." Elizabeth tried to make her voice sound saddened by the loss, but she could not make either of her sisters believe she was grief stricken. "We must now move forward in our lives. Jane is now Mrs Bingley and Mistress of Netherfield. So some good came from the accident, it brought Mr Bingley back to our dear sister."

"And Mr Darcy has declared his feelings for you, Lizzy." Jane stated. "How fortunate that he was Lady Catherine's nephew and she contacted him after the accident?"

"Yes, Mr Darcy has been very kind and caring to our family."

"Lizzy, do not try to fool me." Jane smiled. "You care for Mr Darcy, do you not?"

"Oh, Jane, I wish I knew exactly what I feel. One moment I feel as if I am being dishonorable for not mourning Mr Collins. He was, after all, my husband.

Whether I loved him, or even liked him, I made a vow to honor him. And yet, in my heart, I am grateful for his death, as it releases me from my vows to him. Is that not the most evil thought? How can I deserve the love and kindness of a good man, as Mr Darcy is?"

Mary leaned over to her sister and took hold of her hand. "Lizzy, you deserve to be cherished and loved. Mr Collins would understand, I am certain. You are young, beautiful, and one of the nicest people I know. It is only right for you to live your life as fully as possible."

"I agree with Mary." Jane replied. "You made the sacrifice for all of us, by marrying Mr Collins. As he is gone, you should reap the benefit of having sowed the seeds of generosity. Mr Darcy loves you, it is clearly written in his expression when he is with you. All the time you were so ill, and near death, Mr Darcy was distraught. I feared for his own welfare, especially when we thought you had died. I do not believe Mr Darcy could have survived your dying."

"Do I deserve such a man? From what I have come to know of him, since the accident, he is the sort of man I have always dreamed of marrying. But am I worthy of his love? My husband has only been dead for a little over a month. What will people think of me?"

"People will understand your desire to move forward. Most everyone knew the marriage was not one of affection. And if they do not approve, well, it is their problem. Besides, Pemberley is far enough from here to protect you from any cruel words anyone might say." Jane patted her sister's arm. "Now, I believe it is time for you to rest. Between the journey here and what we have told you of the situation with Lydia, you must be quite done in."

"It will be pleasant to sleep in my old room, I must admit to that." Elizabeth smiled. "I know that room so well, I do not need my eyes to move about that room."

"Mary, would you be kind enough to assist Lizzy to her room, while I ask Hill to send up some tea. Then I will check on Papa before joining you." Jane stood and made to leave her sisters.

"Thank you, Jane." Elizabeth said as she took Mary's arm.

~~ ** ~~

Mrs Bennet was awake when Jane entered her rooms. "Mamma, Lizzy and Papa have returned home."

"Oh, Jane, what will become of us, now that Mr Collins is dead? If Lizzy had married Mr Collins on a different day, or if they had stayed here after the wedding, Mr Collins would still be with us. But, no, that headstrong girl had to have her own way and now she is a widow. And not even a widow expecting her husband's heir. She will be the ruin of us all."

"Mamma, there is no need to fear. I was waiting for Papa to be with me when I told you, but I should tell you immediately. Mr Bingley joined us at Hunsford, and he asked permission to marry me. Papa agreed, and Mr Bingley was able to obtain a special license for us. So Mr Bingley, Charles, and I married at Rosings, in a double ceremony with Lady Catherine's daughter, Anne, and Anne's cousin, Richard Fitzwilliam. Mr Fitzwilliam is the second son of the Earl of Matlock, and a decorated colonel in the army."

"No, no, that cannot be. You are to be married from Longbourn, not some unknown estate, without your mother and sisters to be there. What was your father thinking?" Mrs Bennet was nearly hysterical.

"Please, Mamma, just think of it. I was married by special license, in the presence of the Earl of Matlock. Will that not be wonderful to tell our Aunt Phillips and Lady Lucas? They will be quite envious when they learn." Jane was desperate to calm her mother.

Kitty, who had been sitting in a chair in the far corner of her mother's bedchamber, moved forward. "Jane, how romantic. You were swept away by your prince charming and married by special license, in front of an earl. And in a double ceremony. Oh, I can imagine how special the wedding was."

Mrs Bennet began to consider her daughter's words. "Well, yes, no one else can claim to have had their child married by special license. And, since Sir

William Lucas is the highest member of society in the neighborhood, there have been no peers at any local weddings in our area."

"See, Mamma, it was better to marry as we did. With all that has happened with Lizzy and Mr Collins, Papa felt it would be wiser to not make us wait. And the Earl of Matlock has promised Papa to assist in breaking the entail on the estate. Then you would never have to leave Longbourn."

"The Earl, himself, has promised to assist our family?" Mrs Bennet began to be excited. "Is it possible for the entailment to be broken? Truly?"

"The Earl felt it would be possible. He has even spoken with his family solicitor to aid Uncle Phillips." Jane was pleased her plan was working. "I have asked Mrs Hill to send up some refreshments, Mamma. I will take some to Lizzy, then I will return to check on you."

"Very well, Jane, see to your sister. And tell her to remain indoors, as we cannot have the neighbors seeing her in her current condition. What will people think, our daughter being blind, and a widow on the day she married?"

"Our neighbors will feel sympathy for Lizzy's misfortune. Please, Mamma, you must be kind to my sister. She has been through a terrible ordeal."

"It would have been better had she died. It would have been easier for our friends and neighbors to accept. Now, they will think pity for Lizzy, and she will be fodder for gossips." Mrs Bennet began to wail loudly.

Realizing her mother would continue to carry on in such a manner, Jane took her leave of Mrs Bennet and made her way down the hall to Elizabeth's room. She found her sister sitting on the window seat, facing the window.

"Jane, have no fear. I could hear Mamma from here." Elizabeth continued to face the window as she spoke.

"You are becoming very well adapted at knowing who is around you." Jane chuckled.

"It is amazing, how your other senses become more important. Or, perhaps, it is that after being blinded, I have learned to appreciate my other senses." Elizabeth turned her head to face into her room. "I was enjoying the feel of the sun on my face. It was so warm and pleasant. I felt as if I were sitting on Oakham Mount on a warm summer day."

"Lizzy, please do not give Mamma's words any credence. She does care for you, in her own way. With the entail being in question, you can understand why she is nervous. Not to mention, Lydia being missing."

"I have no intention of exciting Mamma's nerves with my presence, Jane. I plan to keep to myself as much as possible. There are many things I need to learn to do for myself, and I would rather do so in private. I would feel foolish to be seen by anyone as I learn to adapt to my circumstances."

Jane shook her head. She knew her sister well enough to know there would be no arguing with her. "Lizzy, you know I will think no less of you if you ask for my aid, and I am sure that Mary would say the same. But I will leave you alone for the time being."

~~ ** ~~

It was Wednesday evening when Darcy, Bingley, and Richard arrived at Darcy House in Town. Darcy had sent a message to Mrs Maltby, the housekeeper, informing her of their arrival, and the fact that they wished to keep their presence quiet. They planned to enter and exit by the servant's door at the back of the house, as Darcy had no plans to socialize with his neighbors. He had also sent a letter to Matlock House, to Georgiana, explaining to her he would come by to visit her, but that he would be too busy for her to come to the townhouse.

The men were fatigued and hungry upon their arrival, and soon found their bellies satiated with cold meats, cheese, bread, and some biscuits the cook had made that day. While they ate, water was heated for them to bathe. After all had refreshed themselves, they met in Darcy's study to discuss their strategy.

"I will send word to Sergeant Timmons, as his brother is a Bow Street Runner. He will have connections to some of the low lifes we will need to flush out Wickham." Richard stated. "Timmons is a good man, and he knows Wickham. And Captain Chambers will wish to be involved, as Wickham ruined his young sister. Russell would also like a chance at Wickham. His father owned a shop in Lambton, and was cheated by Wickham. The strain from his dealings with Wickham caused Russell's father to have an apoplexy, which he succumbed to. Poor man."

Darcy was surprised. "I had not known of Wickham's dealings with Russell. If I had, I would have purchased the debts from Russell. I have enough to send Wickham to debtor's prison for the remainder of his days."

"We may use that as a way to deal with the scoundrel, but, for now, we must contend with locating him. Once we have found him, and we know the circumstances, then we can decide how best to deal with him."

"Send word to them to come here in the morning. I believe we all could use a good night's sleep before we begin the search of the dregs of London." Darcy stated, witnessing Bingley attempting to stifle a yawn.

Richard nodded his head and took the writing instruments his cousin handed him. Before they left the study, letters were ready to be dispatched to their recipients.

Bingley was the first to leave the room, bidding his friends a good night's sleep. Darcy and Richard made their way up the staircase, and parted ways as each went into their bedchambers. Darcy poured himself a glass of port and sat in the chair near the fireplace. Watching the flames hypnotized the Master of Pemberley, as his thoughts traveled to Longbourn, and the young lady who held his heart. Before returning to her, he would do all that he could to make her life as simple as possible. He would hire a companion, a master to train her in any field she wished to learn, whatever it took to make her feel complete. He could adjust to her lack of sight, and he wished for her to be able to feel her life was worthwhile.

Finally, near midnight, he climbed into his bed and succumbed to the blissful dreams of sharing the very same bed with Elizabeth.

~~ ** ~~

Wickham and Denny were near the mews at Darcy's townhouse, preparing to make their entry. Floyd and his brother were positioned nearby, and would come in just after Wickham, so they would be able to handle any potential problems with the staff who were in the dwelling. They were waiting for the housekeeper to return from the bank with the weekly funds, then they would make their assault on the home of the man Wickham hated most in life. There had been no sign of life inside, other than the movements of a handful of servants. The housekeeper was expected to return anytime, as she was a creature of habit. Every Thursday, she would leave the house precisely at nine, and return by ten. Wickham pulled out his pocket watch, the very watch he had stolen from Gerald Darcy years before, and learned the time was ten minutes before ten.

Unbeknownst to Wickham or the other men, Darcy and his guests had enjoyed breaking their fast with trays in their rooms. They had finished dressing for the day, and Richard and Bingley had already made their way to the game room to play a game of billiards while they waited for the others to arrive at Darcy House.

Mrs Maltby had just returned to the townhouse, though, unlike her usual habit of going to her private office, she made her way upstairs to meet her master in the sitting room connected to his bedchambers. He had asked her to collect some extra funds for him to have on hand, for he was certain he would be required to utilize coins to loosen some lips into speaking to him.

Placing the funds into the inside pocket of his coat, Darcy dismissed Mrs Maltby to go about her business. He walked down the stairs and opened the door of his study, only to find it occupied.

~~~~~~~ ** ~~~~~~~

Chapter 12

Wickham heard the doorknob moving, alerting him of someone entering the room. He motioned to Floyd to prepare to deal with the person who was about to intrude upon them, while pulling a pistol from his waistband. Leveling the pistol at the door, he awaited the person to enter. His jaw nearly fell as he viewed his nemesis enter the room.

"Darcy, how surprising to find you here. We have been watching the house, so you must have just arrived." Wickham stated boldly, holding the firearm firmly.

"Yes, I have." Darcy falsely agreed with Wickham. It was in Darcy's favor that the criminals knew nothing of his arrival, and that he had been joined by Richard and Bingley. If Wickham knew the former colonel was in the house, he would have shot Darcy and raced from the area as quickly as he could. Richard had left little question in Wickham's mind as to what he would do to the man if he ever had the opportunity. The one man who terrified George Wickham more than anyone else in the world was Richard Fitzwilliam.

"What are you doing here, Wickham? Robbing my home? Why am I not surprised?"

"I am taking what should have been mine all along,

Darcy. Your father had no love for you, it was his desire to name me as his heir, for he was quite disappointed in you." Wickham laughed. "Gerald Darcy was a foolish man. I was able to fool him into believing everything I told him. He thought me to be a better son, as he told me many times. I know he left me more in his will, I am sure of it. Gerald would never have left me a mere thousand pounds and a living as a clergyman. He would have seen to my being wealthy and well taken care of."

"You were not a Darcy, therefore you could not inherit my father's estate. No matter what you say, Wickham, I know what my father thought of you. You must accept the truth, as it will do you no good to continue in this deluded way. My father would have been disgusted with your behavior. What of the young lady who disappeared from her home in Hertfordshire? What have you done to Miss Lydia Bennet?"

"Ah, so you know of Lydia's running away with me. She is quite a tasty morsel, I must say. And so devoted to me. Lydia is willing to do whatever I ask of her." A smirk graced Wickham's lips.

Darcy looked at the other men in the room. Not recognizing any of them, he attempted to sum up their beings by their body language. The two men in the far corner were thugs, if Darcy read them correctly. No real intelligence, they would have been brought along for their brawn. The other man appeared to be near the size of Wickham, but seemed nervous. The man, from the description he had from Colonel Forster, was most likely Denny. Also from Colonel Forster, Darcy knew Denny was a follower, not an instigator. Being submissive, Denny was most likely only doing as he was told, which could be in Darcy's favor. If he could find a way to show Denny that his welfare was better served by helping Darcy, it would weaken Wickham's band of criminals.

"Darcy, since you are here, I would suggest you be a good chap and open the safe for us. I know many of the hiding places your father used to have in this room, but, with you here, I would have the contents of the safe as well."

"And, if I refuse?" Darcy stood straight and tall.

"Well, then we would send a message to your little sister to return home from your uncle's home. I would love to visit with dear Georgiana again." Wickham chuckled.

"You will never see Georgiana, nor will you ever speak with her again." Darcy spat out the words. "So you say you know all of my father's hiding spots in this room. Are you certain you will find what you are looking for? This has been my study, long before my father's death. Do you think, when I had it redecorated, I did not find those locations and have the items removed from them? Do you think I would leave everything where my father did? I was aware that my father had been carefree in front of you, and that you might know where some of his collections were kept. I also know your proclivity for taking things that do not belong to you. Remember, I knew you better than my father did. How many of my possessions came up missing when I was at school with you? How many of my possessions had to be reclaimed, by me, from those to whom you sold them? The man you frequently sold my belongings to, let me think, his name is…Wilbur, if I am not mistaken."

"I took from you, because you did not deserve so much. Your father wished me to be his son, I should have had all that was given to you!" Wickham was growing furious from Darcy's words. Little did he know, but his words carried outside the study's walls. The sound of his voice alerted Richard Fitzwilliam, who was walking with Bingley towards Darcy's study.

"Wickham, you are a fool. You were never grateful for what you were given, you always wanted more. I do not believe my father ever wished for you to be his son. You entertained him, after my mother died. You made him laugh at your hijinks. Like a court jester. That was all you were, a jester to lighten his heavy burden by making him laugh."

Fury was growing into insane hatred of the man before him, making Wickham wild. "I should kill you, and then console Georgiana. Once I marry her, I will have all that is yours."

Denny grew nervous as the conversation took such a turn. He was not one for killing another man, this was one of the reasons he decided to desert his post in the militia. When rumors had begun to spread that they may be sent to France, Denny knew it was time to escape. And now, Wickham was speaking, not of killing in a battle against the French, but cold blooded murder. No, Denny wanted no part of that.

"Wickham, we are here to rob the house, not murder anyone." Denny said softly. "I cannot be part of murder. We would be caught and hung for such."

This made the brothers begin to reconsider their options. Though they were dimwitted, they knew Denny was speaking the truth. Neither of them was ready to be a part of murdering a wealthy man. They did not wish to visit the hangman's noose.

Darcy could see the expressions of Wickham's party beginning to waiver. "Wickham, you will pay for your crimes against my family. You other men, I am willing to pay you to leave my home and never come back. I will tell the authorities that Wickham acted alone. Which would you prefer, dancing on the end of a rope, beside Wickham, or having some coins in your pocket and be on your way?"

"These men cannot be bought off so easily." Shouted Wickham. "They are loyal to me, and they can go home with an even larger profit if they aid me."

Denny looked at the brothers and they all seemed

MRS COLLINS, AGAINST HER WISHES

to come to the same conclusion. It was better to take their chances with Darcy. They would come out with less in their pockets, but their lives would be spared. "Just how much coin ya be thinkin'?" Floyd asked.

"I will give you each one hundred pounds to leave here and never come back." Darcy said, turning his eyes to the man who had spoken to him. "One hundred pounds and you are free from any prosecution. If Wickham attempts to implicate you in the crimes, I will soundly deny your ever being here."

Now, Wickham was nervous. Without his enforcers, his ability to come out of this unscathed was shrinking. "If you continue helping me, you will receive more than a thousand pounds each. Would you not prefer to have such a bounty? What he is offering you is pittance to what he has, locked away in this room."

Floyd looked at his brother. Without speaking a word, they came to the same conclusion. Simple as they were, a thousand pounds was something they could not fathom. One hundred pounds, they could comprehend such an amount and would consider themselves quite rich. As they were caring for an ailing mother, one hundred pounds each would take care of her needs nicely.

"Me brother and me, we be takin' the gent's offer." Floyd stated as he turned towards Wickham, pointing his pistol towards the ring leader.

"You fools. He will not make good on his promises; rich men never keep their promises. As soon as possible, he will send the authorities after you and you will be taken to the gaol."

Darcy was pleased he could mask his expressions on his face. While he wished to smile at the fact that these men were easily turned from Wickham, he knew he had to remain stoic. "You have my guarantee, I will do exactly as I have stated. I will give you each one hundred pounds and will do all in my power to protect you from any prosecution for this crime. I do not know your names, nor where you hail from, therefore, how can I send anyone after you? I wish no further dealings with you."

Those words were enough to finalize the decision for the brothers. Floyd kept his firearm pointed at Wickham while his brother walked to Darcy. After hearing the conversation from the hall, Richard and Bingley entered the study, weapons in hand. Darcy saw his friends and nodded his head. "Have no fear, gentlemen, the situation is under control. Bingley, would you ask my butler to send for the constable? Wickham will be in need of an escort to the gaol."

Bingley hurried from the room, leaving Darcy and Richard to contend with the intruders. Darcy turned his attention from Wickham, pulling the funds from his pocket. Rather than the hundred pounds for each of the brothers, Darcy felt generous enough to give them each an additional fifty pounds. By Darcy's way of thinking, the men had aided in capturing the two deserters and making fast work of the matter. "Now, I will give you an additional fifty pounds if you will tell me where Miss Lydia Bennet is to be found."

Floyd nodded his head. "She be in the Bull's End pub. They hav' rooms upstairs to rent. Wickham has 'er trussed up."

Darcy had a difficult time holding his fury. "Has she been harmed by any of you?"

Denny decided to speak. "I refused to allow them to harm Miss Lydia. She is the daughter of a gentleman, and a mere child at that. It was Wickham who took her from Longbourn. As we were preparing to quit the neighborhood, Miss Lydia was out for a stroll. Wickham thought it would be easier if we took her with us, as she was able to tell everyone which way we were heading. He forced her onto his horse, keeping his knife ready to tame her spirits if she misbehaved."

"So she has not been ruined?" Richard asked.

"No, Sir. She has not. I kept an eye out for her, making sure Wickham and the brothers made no attempts to ruin her."

Just then, Wickham turned on his cohort. "You traitorous scum...how dare you turn on me?" Wickham lunged at Denny, knife in hand, plunging it into Denny's gut.

Richard's reactions were in full military response, allowing him to rush forward before Wickham was able to do any further injury. Grabbing Wickham with his arm around his nemesis' neck, he pulled the scoundrel from Denny. The knife was still protruding from Denny's abdomen, with blood oozing from the wound.

Darcy moved to Denny's side, while shouting for assistance. Bingley was returning to the room, and called out to the butler to send for a physician. He then cried out for Mrs Maltby, telling her they needed water and bandaging. Richard still held Wickham in his arms, as the fiend struggled to break free.

"Damn you... Fitzwilliam... let me go. You are choking...the life out...of me." He gasped.

"Wickham, you just attempted a murder, while in the commission of a robbery. You will be lucky if you get transportation, most likely you will swing. I will hold you until the constable arrives to take custody of you, for I do not trust you, not in the slightest." Richard hissed in his prisoner's ear. "You will never cause harm to my family or our friends. You made a serious mistake in kidnapping Miss Lydia Bennet, not to mention the great mistake you made in coming to this house to rob it."

"I should have...plunged the knife...into Darcy's...heart." Wickham tried desperately tried to sound as dangerous as he wished. This was rewarded with Richard squeezing his arm around Wickham's throat even tighter.

"Richard, we have to turn him over to the constable. I will not have you murder him."

"Cousin, after all he has done, to so many people, he deserves nothing less than to die." Richard argued.

Hearing someone coming towards the study, Richard and Darcy turned their attention towards the doorway. There stood three soldiers and another man, dressed in regular clothing. The men who had been summoned to aid in the search had arrived. Russell, Chambers and Timmons, along with Timmon's brother, had all come, wishing for their pound of flesh from Wickham. Seeing Richard, his arm around Wickham's neck, the men moved closer.

With the arrival of the men, Richard knew it was safe to release his hold on Wickham. Though he wished nothing more than to end the life of the man who had been the cause of so much anguish, he knew it would be construed as murder. Now that he was married, he needed to think of Anne, and their life together. "Take custody of this deserter. He not only deserted the militia, he was attempting to rob my cousin's home and stabbed this young man. He is also guilty of many debts throughout many locations. My cousin has purchased a great many of them, enough to see him locked away for the rest of his life. And I believe you men also know of debts he has to your families."

"Timmons, you and your brother, keep hold of Wickham over in that corner." Chambers ordered. "Russell, perhaps you should compile a list of all the charges against the scum, so we will be ready for the constable when he arrives. Fitzwilliam, has a surgeon been sent for?"

"I believe one has. I believe I should assist my cousin in moving the injured man."

Looking around the room, Richard noticed that in all of the excitement, there were two men missing. Floyd and his brother had quickly fled when no one was paying attention to them. Having heard Darcy's promise to the men, Richard did not raise the subject in front of all who were present.

Darcy and Richard carefully lifted Denny, carrying him down the hall, to the sick room which was near the rear of the servant's rooms. Denny was unconscious, having lost copious amounts of blood. Darcy had removed the knife and feared the young man was not long for the world. Once Denny was placed on the bed, Darcy and Richard stepped to the hall. "We need to take Bingley and retrieve Miss Lydia from where Wickham stashed her."

"It would be best if Bingley and the officers went to retrieve Miss Bennet, as the pub in question is located in a very disrespectable part of Town. And the constable will require you and me here to answer questions on what happened. What are you going to say to him, with regards to the young man in there?" Richard motioned towards the sick room.

"I will state that Mr Denny was assisting us in finding Miss Lydia, and, when we found Wickham robbing the house, the scoundrel stabbed Denny due to Denny's attempting to protect me. It is the truth, in a way." Darcy shrugged his shoulders as he spoke.

"I will verify your statement, for this young man was responsible for protecting Miss Bennet, from what I heard of the conversation." Richard turned away, though a few moments later, turned back towards his cousin. "How will we handle his desertion from his post? The militia will still wish to punish him."

"Would it be too much of a stretch to claim Mr Denny had been forced to leave Meryton with Wickham? Perhaps he had been speaking with Miss Lydia when Wickham found them and forced both to come to Town with him."

Richard shook his head. "It will take speaking with Miss Bennet, convincing her to agree to the tale we are weaving."

"I believe we will be able to convince her." Darcy replied. "She is young, and I am certain she will verify what Denny has stated, with regards to his protecting her. The young man should be given a chance to redeem himself. He was foolish to desert with

Wickham, but he has learned a huge lesson from all of this. You did not see him when I first entered the room. I could tell he would be the weak link in Wickham's armor. The other two surprised me, they gave up without a fight and accepted what I gave them to leave. No, Wickham is the only one I wish to see punished in this matter. Have Bingley and the officers take Miss Lydia to her uncle's home. It is the Gardiner home on Gracechurch Street. Have Bingley tell her not to speak to anyone until after I have arrived. Between Bingley and I, and the Gardiners, we will, hopefully, be able to convince her to go along with our story."

Richard nodded his head and went in search of Bingley. Darcy began to pace the hall, wishing desperately that he could hold Elizabeth in his arms. The morning had been highly stressful, and he wished for some comfort in the arms of the woman he loved.

~~ ** ~~

The next two hours saw a flurry of activity at Darcy House. The constable arrived with two of his men, taking custody of Wickham. With their arrival, the officers and Bingley left for the pub to recover Lydia. They had yet to return to Darcy House, and Darcy was anxious to make his way to Gracechurch Street to ensure that the young girl was unharmed. He was pacing outside the sick room, waiting for the physician to come out and speak to them on Denny's condition. Richard was in Darcy's study, giving his statement to the constable and the magistrate, who had arrived a half of an hour previously. As soon as Richard was finished, it would be Darcy's turn to give his statement.

Darcy had sent an express to Longbourn, informing Mr Bennet of his daughter's recovery. At the time, he only knew what Denny had stated, that Lydia had been unharmed, only tied up. Once he learned more from seeing her first hand, and speaking to her, he would send another letter express. With a prayer in his heart, Darcy hoped Mr Bennet would survive the stress under which he had been. Knowing Elizabeth's close relationship with her father forced Darcy to be concerned for the elder man.

Bingley entered the house and was heading towards his friend. "Mr Gardiner has issued an open invitation for you and I to come to his home when we finish here."

"How was Miss Lydia?" Darcy asked.

"Frightened, angry, exhausted. She has not slept, for fear of what the men would do to her. And, the only food or drink she was given was by Denny. I truly do not believe him to be a bad sort of fellow."

"I agree with you. I knew from the moment I saw him in my study, he did not wish to be there. I am prepared to protect Denny, for I believe he protected Miss Lydia, as much as he could." Darcy turned and began to pace again.

"Have you spoken with the constable?" Bingley inquired.

"Not yet. Richard is in with the constable and magistrate, giving his statement. I will be next. They may wish to speak with you, but I doubt it."

"I will be ready, in case they need my statement. I did not see as much as you and Richard did."

Darcy turned back to his friend. "I wish I could say the same. But, at least now, Wickham will not be able to cause any further harm. He will be locked away, or even transported."

"You do not believe he will be sentenced to hang?" Bingley was surprised.

"To be honest, I am not sure. Where he kidnapped a gentleman's daughter, attempted to rob a member of society, threatened my life while attacking another man, nearly killing the man, the penalties will be stiff."

The door to the sick room opened and the surgeon stepped out into the hallway. "Ah, Mr Darcy, there you are."

"How is your patient?" Darcy asked.

"I believe he will pull through. It was a nasty wound, but he was fortunate that no vital organs were injured. So long as he does not take a fever, he should recover with no long term problems."

"Good, good. What does he require?"

The physician had known Darcy for many years, and was not shocked at the young Master's behavior. Fitzwilliam Darcy was well known for seeing to the care of all his servants and staff. "I left instructions with Mrs Maltby. Primarily, he needs peace and quiet. Rest, good food, and the medicines I have left with your housekeeper."

"You have my utmost thanks. When will you return?" Darcy inquired.

"I will drop by later today, and then, if there is no fever, I will come by once a day."

"Mr Owens, I appreciate your coming as soon as possible. Can I offer you some refreshments before you leave?"

Shaking his head, Mr Owens declined. "No, Darcy, my wife will have my luncheon ready for me by now, and I hate to disappoint her."

"Extend my wishes for her health, if you would be so kind."

"I will do so. I will speak with you later, Darcy."

~~~~~~~ ** ~~~~~~~

Chapter 13

Darcy entered his study, walking directly to the chair behind his desk. Once seated, he nodded to the two men before him. "Mr Weston, Mr Hammerly, I am sorry to see you under these circumstances."

Mr Hammerly, the constable, looked at the magistrate before speaking. "It is a sad state of affairs, Mr Darcy. I believe I speak for Mr Weston, when I say that I am grateful you were not harmed. Wickham seems like a brutal sort of scoundrel."

"He is. I have known him all his life, as his father was my father's steward. The father was a kind and devoted servant to my father, while the son was always cruel and abusive. Wickham has long felt that my family, as well as the world, owes him a life of leisure."

"Having spoken to him, briefly, it is clear that he is quite unstable." Mr Weston remarked. "He spoke of being the true heir to Pemberley, claiming your father was devoted to him and preferred Wickham over his own son. Mr Darcy, I was well acquainted with your father. I know how proud he was of you and your sister. Wickham's claims are falling on deaf ears, with all his nonsense."

"What are Wickham's claims with regards to what happened here?"

"He stated that he was accompanied by three men, the injured one included, and that the injured man is involved in the kidnapping of the young lady from Hertfordshire."

Darcy shook his head. "More of his lies. Mr Denny is a member of the militia which are staying in Meryton. He had been returning to the camp when he happened upon Miss Lydia Bennet. Her father is the master of Longbourn, an estate a few miles outside Meryton. While the two were speaking, Wickham rode up. Realizing Mr Denny would be able to report his desertion and the route of his travel, Wickham forced, at gunpoint, both Mr Denny and Miss Lydia onto Mr Denny's horse and brought them to Town. It was mistakenly believed that Mr Denny deserted his post, but I have come to believe his tale. And Wickham stabbing him only goes to reinforce my belief in Mr Denny's words."

"It is my understanding that Miss Bennet was tied up and gagged, left in a room above a pub." Mr Weston further explored the situation.

"Yes, and it was fortunate that Mr Denny was able to inform us where, just before he was stabbed by Wickham. I was certain Wickham would have harmed me, if Mr Denny had not drawn Wickham's attention from me by informing me where Miss Lydia was to be found." Darcy spoke plainly, his mask of indifference firmly in place.

Mr Hammerly agreed. "Well, Mr Weston and I have been discussing the matter. Seeing as the young man is a deserter from the militia, and it is a time of war, that penalty alone will be enough to be put to death. With the added charge of attempted murder of an officer, I believe Wickham's fate is sealed. I see no need to bring the young lady into this mess. I would prefer not to force her into testifying, as young ladies can be quite...delicate, in these matters."

"I am certain Mr Bennet would be grateful for your diligence. Will you be needing to speak with Mr Denny? It is my understanding, from the physician, that the man is sleeping due to medication he was given. It would most likely be best to wait until tomorrow to take his statement."

Both to the men nodded in agreement. "We will contact Wickham's commanding officer, and determine what will be needed to deal with the scoundrel." Mr Hammerly replied.

The men soon left the study, making their way to the front door of the townhouse. Darcy escorted them, bidding farewell to them. As soon as they were gone, Darcy called for his carriage to be brought around. He was in a hurry to arrive at Gracechurch Street, wishing to see for himself that Lydia Bennet was well.

Richard and Bingley joined Darcy in the carriage. Their arrival at the Gardiner home was expected, and

Mrs Gardiner was ready to welcome the young men. "Gentlemen, please, take a seat. I will ring for refreshments." She said as they entered the parlor. "My husband needed to resolve a problem at his warehouse, but he should be back any moment. I know he wishes to speak with all of you."

The men all sat down, with Darcy and Richard seated on the sofa, and Bingley on the chair nearby. Looking about the room, Darcy was pleased to see the décor of the home was tasteful and comfortable. He knew, from speaking with Elizabeth, the Gardiners were dear to his beloved. From the appearance of the house, and even Mrs Gardiner's clothing, they were not of the upper circle of society, but they could pass as quality.

"Mr Darcy, it is a pleasure to finally meet you. I remember your parents when they came to my father's shop." Mrs Gardiner stated.

"Your father's shop? Who is your father?" Darcy was curious.

"Mr Albert Tinker was my father. He passed away near the same time as your father." Mrs Gardiner said, a note of pride in her voice.

"I remember him well. It was a sad day in Lambton when Mr Tinker died. Your mother moved to Surrey, to live with her sister, did she not?"

"I am honored you remember them. Yes, Mother

moved to her sister's home. She joined my father a year ago. I miss them, both, very much." Mrs Gardiner smiled, though tears threatened to flow from her eyes.

"I remember your mother usually had fresh biscuits on hand to pass out to all who came into their shop. She was an incredible baker, the biscuits were always an enticement to make the trip to Lambton with my father."

Richard was curious. "Which shop was this?" he asked.

"Mr Tinker owned the bookshop in Lambton. We purchased many books from them, and also, most of our stationary supplies. Mrs Gardiner, I believe I now recognize you. If memory serves, you were fond of flowers and you worked in the gardens near the east side of the shop. Your family lived in the rooms above the shop."

"Yes, I had a green thumb for growing some of the finest blooms." Mrs Gardiner announced. "My father built a solarium on the back of the shop, so I could grow my flowers and my mother could grow her herbs."

"Your mother assisted the midwife, if I remember correctly." Darcy smiled.

"My mother was with the midwife when your sister was born. Mother declared she had never seen a baby girl with such sweetness clearly etched upon her face. We all knew your sister would be just like your mother, for Mrs Darcy was just the same."

"Thank you, Mrs Gardiner, for your kind words. I, too, miss my parents. Do you still keep in contact with anyone from Lambton?" Darcy inquired.

"I still exchange letters with Mrs Levison and Mrs Bennington. They are my age and we have known each other since we were quite young." Mrs Gardiner said. "We plan to take a holiday this summer, and my husband has been generous enough to declare we will journey to Derbyshire to visit my friends and take in the sights."

"I wish to extend an invitation to your family to stay at Pemberley while you are in the area. From my home, you can travel through the county easily." Darcy offered. "And, if your husband is fond of fishing, he would be welcome to utilize my streams and pond. My grounds keeper wrote to inform me there is an abundance of fish this year."

"Fishing?" Came a voice from the door of the parlor. "I am quite fond of fishing, though I seldom have an opportunity to enjoy myself."

Mr Gardiner entered the room, a smile on his face. "Welcome back, Mr Bingley. I assume that your friends are Mr Darcy and Mr Fitzwilliam."

Darcy and Richard stood, both exchanging greetings with the jovial man. "Mr Gardiner, I was just inviting you and your family to stay at my estate, when you are in the neighborhood. On my estate, you will be able to enjoy fishing until your heart's content. There are ample supplies that you are welcome to use for such an excursion."

"Mr Darcy, you are quite generous. It would be an honor to stay with you, if my wife agrees with me." Mr Gardiner turned towards his wife, noting the smile on her lips.

Soon, the refreshments were brought into the parlor, and everyone began discussing the situation with Lydia. All agreed to protect Denny, especially after Lydia joined the group. According to her, Denny had protected her from Wickham's advances during the night. She agreed to the story Darcy had come up with, that Denny had been kidnapped along with Lydia. As Lydia had not seen much of the brothers, she had no difficulty in forgetting they were involved.

Seeing the calm and sedate young girl in front of him, Darcy knew it had been a terrifying event for Lydia. Her normal behavior was quite wild and untamed. Lydia, now, sat beside her aunt on the settee, her hands folded in her lap, and she was leaning towards her aunt as if in need for support.

As the men prepared to take their leave, Mrs Gardiner invited them to return to dine with them that evening. The invitation extended to Georgiana, as well, and Darcy agreed. He felt that the two young girls would enjoy spending time together.

~~ ** ~~

Three days later, Darcy, Bingley, and Richard escorted Lydia and Georgiana to Longbourn. They had received word from Colonel Forster that Wickham would be dealt with by a military court, and Richard was certain the conviction would be swift, as would be the sentence. In Colonel Forster's letter, he informed Darcy of his hopes for the harshest sentence of his former officer.

Denny had recovered enough that he had been sent on a wagon, which had been prepared to give him as much comfort as possible, to Meryton. He was returning to his militia unit, where he would continue his recovery. Denny was grateful for the second chance he was being offered. Knowing he could be facing the same fate as Wickham was eye-opening, and Denny was looking forward to returning to his duties. When he woke, at Darcy House, after the physician had tended to him, Denny realized he could trust Darcy. No word had been discussed of the brothers who had worked with Wickham, and Darcy explained the story which had been given to the authorities by himself, his cousin and Lydia.

The journey to Longbourn was taking far longer than Darcy wished. His desire to see Elizabeth, to be in her presence, to reassure her that her youngest sister was well and whole, all made him desirous to arrive. At the inn where they would change horses for the final time before arriving at Longbourn, Darcy decided to ride his personal horse for the rest of the journey.

Georgiana giggled behind her hand, knowing her brother's desire to be with Elizabeth. She looked forward to meeting Elizabeth again, and to know the young lady, who had stolen her brother's heart. After all she had heard from her brother and Richard, both in person and through letters, Georgiana was thrilled to think she may soon have a sister. Though she loved her brother dearly, Georgiana had come to feel as if her brother was more like a father to her. The age difference of more than ten years, and Darcy being forced to take on so many responsibilities so soon in his life due to their father's death, had weighed heavily on his shoulders. Seeing the change in him, the lightness in his step, the smile on his face, Georgiana could not be happier.

Lydia was surprised when she had learned of Darcy's love for her second eldest sister. After learning Bingley had married Jane in a private ceremony in Kent, Lydia wondered if she had been missing for longer than a few days, for all the changes that had happened. Being around Darcy more, Lydia could see a difference in the taciturn and somber man they had all known the previous year. The two girls had spent time chatting about their siblings, and Lydia came to the same conclusion as Georgiana. Elizabeth and Darcy were made for each other.

Darcy arrived, well ahead of the others, and handed the reins of his horse to the stable hand who approached him. He quickly strode to the front door of the main house of Longbourn, knocking just as the door opened wide. Mrs Hill had heard the horse approaching quickly, and hurried to see who had come, nervous there had been another tragedy.

Seeing Mr Darcy, alone, made the devoted housekeeper worry even more. Noticing the fear in Mrs Hill's expression, Darcy smiled. "Fear not, Mrs Hill, the carriage is not far behind me. I needed to expel some energy, so I rode ahead. Is Miss Elizabeth in the parlor?"

"No, Mr Darcy, she is actually in the garden, enjoying the warm weather we are experiencing." The housekeeper sighed in relief. "I was planning to go escort her inside, as she wished to be in the parlor when you all arrived."

"I will assist her, Mrs Hill." Darcy said as he walked past the housekeeper.

The devotion for Elizabeth, which was clear in everything Darcy did, pleased Mrs Hill. The Hills were fond of Elizabeth, finding her and Jane to be the best of the Bennet daughters.

Darcy stopped at the rear corner of the house, as he had spotted Elizabeth sitting alone on a bench, in the garden. Though the garden was not in bloom yet, seeing his beloved outdoors, enjoying nature as was her custom, was the most beautiful sight to him.

"William, is that you?" Elizabeth turned her attention towards the house.

Shocked, Darcy moved forward. "How did you know I was here?"

"There is enough of a breeze, coming from behind you. I told you, I find your scent to be pleasant. And I can tell you rode horseback, and quickly, as your horse was perspiring." Elizabeth chuckled.

"You are a quick learner, Miss Elizabeth. You have learned to adapt rather quickly." Darcy said as he took her hands in his, placing a kiss on the back of each.

"How is my sister? Tell me the truth." Elizabeth said, a worried line furrowed in her forehead.

"Miss Lydia is well. Other than being tied up and gagged, the only other harm which was perpetrated was lack of food and drink. She has bounced back from that though. And she has become close friends with my sister. Georgiana has traveled with us, and will be staying at Netherfield with me and the Bingleys."

"I look forward to knowing Miss Darcy better." Elizabeth said. "I cannot thank you enough, William. You have now saved two of my sisters."

"How do you come to this conclusion? Was another of your sisters taken prisoner by Wickham?"

"You saved Jane by reuniting her with Charles, and now you have saved Lydia from the clutches of Wickham. You have my gratitude on behalf of my entire family."

Darcy's eyes smoldered with desire for the woman before him. "You must know, Elizabeth, your family may be grateful, but I admit I thought only of you. I do not wish for your gratitude, I wish for you to love me for the man I am."

"I have had time to think, while you were gone. Being here, in familiar surroundings, has allowed me to search my feelings. Though I cannot commit to a relationship at this moment, due to my recent widowhood, I must confess my feelings for you have become clearer. I do believe I am falling in love with you. We must take our time, learn more of each other, but, to be honest, I believe my future is meant to be with you."

The smile which broke across Darcy's face was dazzling. He scooped Elizabeth into his arms and twirled her about. "You have made me so very happy, Dearest Elizabeth."

"William, I have some news for you as well."

"Yes, dearest?"

"The reason I am enjoying spending the daytime

outside, as much as possible, is I can see the bright light. Nothing distinctly, no shapes or anything, but the bright light, I can see it."

Darcy placed a kiss on her forehead. "This is wonderful news, my love. Wonderful news, indeed."

~~ ** ~~

Caroline Bingley was beside herself with frustration. She had learned from her sister, Louisa Hurst, their brother was re-opening Netherfield Park. After all the effort they had put into keeping their brother away from the Bennet family, especially Jane Bennet, and now he was returning to the estate. She was determined to force him away from the neighborhood, before it was too late.

Borrowing the Hursts' carriage, Caroline was traveling to Netherfield as quickly as possible. Determined, she would do whatever was necessary to protect her brother.

I will arrive at Netherfield on the morrow, and, hopefully, will have Charles back to Town, or better yet, take him to Scarborough, within a day or two. The less time in the company of those country nobodies, the better. And it is time to put my plan into action. We must spend more time with Mr Darcy and Georgiana. My brother must marry Georgiana, for it will then make Fitzwilliam more favorable towards taking me as his wife.

~~ ** ~~

The arrival, at Longbourn, of Charles, Richard, Lydia, and Georgiana was met with joy. Mr Bennet was grateful for the return of his daughter, and embraced his youngest to his chest within moments of seeing her again. This was highly unusual behavior, as the only daughters who had been embraced by Thomas Bennet were Jane and Lizzy. The uniqueness of the situation broke through Lydia's defenses and the girl broke down in tears.

"Papa, please forgive me for causing so much worry." Lydia sobbed.

"My dear girl, Mr Darcy has informed me of the circumstances surrounding your abduction. I am pleased to know you are safe and returned to us." Mr Bennet pulled back from the embrace, a loving look bestowed upon the girl. "I will never be able to repay these men for restoring our family."

Lydia stretched out her hand towards Georgiana. "Papa, this is Miss Georgiana Darcy. I met her after I was rescued, and we have become the best of friends. Georgiana, this is my father, Thomas Bennet."

Georgiana curtsied to Mr Bennet. "It is a pleasure to meet you, Sir."

"The pleasure is mine, Miss Darcy. I have heard many wonderful things about you from your brother." Mr Bennet bowed over Georgiana's hand.

"My brother would have the world believe I am perfect, though I am hardly so." Georgiana blushed. "He is far too kind to me."

"A perfect elder brother?" Elizabeth inquired as she stepped forward in the direction of the voices.

Darcy was quick to take hold of Elizabeth's hand and wrap it gently around his arm. Seeing the tenderness in her brother's actions, Georgiana could not contain her smile. "Miss Elizabeth, I am so pleased to see you again."

"Miss Darcy, it is a pleasure to be in your company. I am afraid, when we met at the theater, I was not in the best of moods."

"I understand, as my brother has explained to me what happened. And, please, would you call me Georgiana? I can sense we are to be the very best of friends."

Elizabeth smiled. "Only if you call me Elizabeth, or Lizzy."

Darcy was pleased to watch the interaction between his sister and the woman he loved. "Oh, dearest, Georgiana and I have brought you gifts."

"Mr Darcy, it was highly unnecessary for you to purchase gifts for me, not to mention improper." Elizabeth teased.

"Propriety be blown out the window, for I care

nothing for what propriety declares when it comes to spoiling you. But some of the gifts are practical ones." Darcy turned and asked for one of his trunks to be brought inside the house. Once inside the parlor, the trunk was opened.

The first item he brought out was a beautifully carved, slender, wooden cane. "I have spoken with a Mr Butters, at a school for the blind in Town. He stated that use of a cane can be helpful to a blind person, as it gives them more stability when walking. I found this one, which has roses carved along the length. It reminded me of the rosewater you use."

Elizabeth allowed her hand to caress the cane's carvings. "If it is half as beautiful looking as it feels, it is truly a work of art."

"Not nearly as beautiful as the young lady who will use it." Darcy exclaimed as he smiled at her. Georgiana's eyes sparkled at the sight before her. It pleased her to no end to witness such love.

More items were removed from the trunk. There were items for everyone, including books and cigars for Mr Bennet, a shawl for Mrs Bennet and Elizabeth, bonnets for all of the sisters, sheet music for Mary, hair pins for Kitty, and a set of hair combs for Jane. There were also treats from the confectioners for everyone, bottles of the finest brandy for Mr Bennet and Bingley, and other trinkets. With each oohs and ahhs Elizabeth heard from her family, her smile grew.

"I feel as if it were Christmas all over again."

"As Bingley and I were unable to spend Christmas with you, we are making up for it." Darcy responded. "Bingley has a surprise for you as well, Elizabeth."

Jane looked at her husband with surprise. Bingley squeezed his wife's hand as he looked at her sister. "Lizzy, I insisted that Jane and I be the ones to hire a companion for you. Darcy and I interviewed several ladies while we were in Town, and we believe we have found the perfect young lady to serve as your companion. Her name is Hannah Loft, and she will be arriving tomorrow. Her father is blind, so Hannah grew up with the disability. She is compassionate, but realizes there is a need for some independence in the person who is blind. She is well read and kind."

"Charles, Jane, this is far too generous of you. I am certain I will not require a companion for long." Elizabeth stated.

"As long as you have need of her, she will be your companion." Bingley declared.

Seeing the look of pride on Darcy's face, as well as the beaming smile on Elizabeth's, everyone in the room could see there was more that had not been said. Finally Mr Bennet inquired as to what news Elizabeth had to share.

~~~~~~~ ** ~~~~~~~

Chapter 14

"Elizabeth, you appear to be ready to burst with information. Is there something you wish to tell us?" Her father inquired.

"Yesterday, when I woke, I could see light. No objects or people, but bright light, from the window, could be seen. When the sun went down, everything was dark again, but, again this morning, with the sun in the sky, I can see light."

Mr Lowe had remained at Longbourn, to look after his patients, though he was in Meryton at present. He was speaking to the apothecary, to order some tonics and medicines for Mr Bennet and Elizabeth.

Everyone was silent for a moment, looking at Elizabeth with great joy. Then suddenly, everyone was at Elizabeth's side, embracing her and chattering all at once. The joy in Longbourn was tremendous, as Mr Lowe returned. Entering the house, the physician made his way into the parlor.

"Have I missed something while I was in Meryton?" Mr Lowe inquired.

Darcy draped his arm on his beloved's shoulder. "Elizabeth can see light, bright light from the sun."

Lowe was quite pleased. "This is, indeed, wonderful news. Miss Elizabeth, may I examine your eyes?"

With a nod of her head, Lowe approached her. "Darcy, would you light a candle and bring it close?" When Darcy did, Lowe could see the dilation of Elizabeth's pupils. "This is wonderful. It may take some time, but I believe that your sight will return. There may be difficulties with it, but, knowing you, I would not doubt a complete recovery."

"I have been enjoying time outside, during the daylight. I can feel the warmth on my skin and everything is bright rather than black."

"I must caution you not to spend too much time with your eyes directly towards the sun, for too much sunlight may cause harm as well. I would suggest you keep your bonnet on and keep your eyes closed if you tilt your head towards the sun."

"She will obey your directions, Lowe." Darcy declared. "I plan on making sure she follows your orders completely."

Everyone in the room laughed. Lowe turned to his other patient. "And, Mr Bennet, how are you fairing? Your continence is showing some color and you appear to be in less pain."

"Knowing my daughters are safe, especially Lydia being returned to us and Lizzy improving, has lightened my burdens and I feel somewhat stronger." Mr Bennet responded.

"Very well, but I insist you rest the remainder of the afternoon. I do not wish to ruin all the improvement with a setback."

Mrs Bennet had finally brought herself to join her family in the parlor, only due to the return of her favorite daughter. Ignoring her second daughter completely, Mrs Bennet embraced her youngest to her chest, causing Lydia to struggle against her mother's crushing the wind from her lungs. "Mamma, please, I cannot breathe."

"Oh, Lydia, I could not tolerate the thought I might lose you forever. It caused me so much pain and flutterings about my chest. But you are returned to us and all will be well again." Mrs Bennet waved her handkerchief about as she spoke, the dramatic flair was well known to her family.

"Mamma, have you heard Lizzy's wonderful news?" Jane asked.

"Jane, I am busy with Lydia, I have no time to deal with Lizzy's nonsense."

Mr Bennet and Darcy both stood, fury apparent on their faces. "Mrs Bennet, I insist you come down the hall to my study." Mr Bennet declared harshly.

"Mr Bennet, I am not moving from my dear Lydia's side for some time to come. If you have something to say, then say it now. But I am not joining you down the hall to have you dictate to me how to treat your favorite daughter. She has brought shame to our family by allowing her husband to perish before she could conceive a child. As far as I am concerned, I wish she had never returned to my home."

Before Mr Bennet or Darcy could react, Jane stepped closer to her mother and let loose her fury with a swing of her hand which connected to Mrs Bennet's cheek. "How dare you speak so of my sister? My dear sister, who nearly died from her own injuries. You have no right to be in the same room with her." Turning her attention to her father, Jane continued. "Papa, Charles and I have spoken on the matter of inheritance of the estate. Charles agrees with me, the estate should be left to Lizzy. Though I am the eldest, it is Lizzy who has devoted so much of herself to protecting our lives. It should be Lizzy's inheritance."

"You cannot give the estate to that ungrateful child." Mrs Bennet screeched. "She cannot be the next Mistress of Longbourn...why, she is crippled and cannot be a proper mistress."

"My sister has given so much to protect us all." Mary stepped to Jane's side to show solidarity. "I agree with Jane, Lizzy should inherit the estate."

Lydia pulled away from her mother's embrace. "Mamma, I agree with Jane and Mary. I have learned all that Lizzy has done for our family, and I agree that Lizzy should inherit the estate."

Kitty had followed her mother into the parlor, though she kept to the back of the room, blending into the background. When she spoke, everyone was startled to hear her. "For what it is worth, I also believe Lizzy should have the estate. She has nearly died in an attempt to protect us, after being forced to marry that awful toad of a man. If I had been in Lizzy's place, I would have ran away from home."

"None of you know what it takes to run a household." Mrs Bennet was angry by the behavior of her daughters. "Your sister is a cripple, and she will never be able to run a household. And she would be fodder for all the gossips. How could you expect me to accept being ousted by such an incompetent cripple?"

"Mrs Bennet, your daughter is not crippled." Darcy stepped closer to the elder lady. "You will refrain from speaking so of the woman I love."

"You will be a laughing stock if you show such dedication to her. She is damaged goods, blind, widowed with no child, and worthless. Mark my words, she will destroy our family."

"As I said, YOU WILL REFRAIN FROM SPEAKING OF ELIZABETH IN SUCH A MANNER!" Darcy stood his full height, moving to stand mere inches from Mrs Bennet. "I will not warn you again. If you will not control your tongue, I will make certain you are homeless when your husband is gone."

"You have no right to tell me how to behave." Mrs

Bennet placed her hands on her hips. "I demand you remove yourself from my home."

"HOW DARE YOU SPEAK SO?" Elizabeth had had enough of her mother's behavior. Moving towards the sound of Darcy's voice, Elizabeth made her way towards the conflict, without aid from anyone else. "You are a selfish, petty woman. I am damaged goods? I am bringing shame to you? I will not say what I feel towards you at the moment, as I am a lady, gently raised."

Mrs Bennet was shocked to watch her least favorite daughter stepping towards her without assistance. "Do not come near me. I do not wish to be contaminated with your curse. You have always been the shame of this family, and now look at what you have done. You have destroyed our family's future by not submitting to your husband before he died, you should be carrying his child, the next heir of Longbourn, to protect us all. But you return here, barren and widowed, not to mention severely ruined in the process. My poor nerves, how I have suffered, fearing what our friends and neighbors will say."

"You are a bigger fool than I thought all these years." Elizabeth said. "Jane, is the offer to stay at Netherfield still available?"

"You are always welcome, Elizabeth." Bingley stepped behind his new sister, placing a hand on her shoulder. "You are a part of my family, and you will always have a place to stay with Jane and me."

"Would someone ask Mrs Hill to have my belongings packed and sent to Netherfield? I will not remain in this house a moment longer." With that, Elizabeth held her cane in one hand and turned towards the door of the parlor. Her familiarity with the house allowed her to know which direction to turn. Before she was able to take two steps, Darcy had hold of her arm, leading her outside. Georgiana was fast following her brother and the woman he loved.

Bingley turned back towards his mother in law. "Mrs Bennet, I have tolerated your rudeness long enough. I am a tolerant man, but you have pushed me to my limits. You will find no entrance into my home, if you cannot control your appalling behavior and speak with kindness towards my sister, Elizabeth."

Mr Bennet was forced to sit down, pain coursing through his chest. Richard was seated closest to Mr Bennet, calling attention to the elderly man's condition. "Mr Lowe, your assistance please."

Mr Lowe called out for some wine and water to be brought immediately. "And remove that woman from this room, immediately. She is not to come near my patient again."

"Your patient?" Mrs Bennet shrieked. "I am the one who is suffering. I am the one who is always treated so poorly, as you have just witnessed. My husband has no need of a physician, I do. My poor nerves, and the flutterings and pains I am suffering are such a burden.

Surprisingly, it was her favorite child who solved the problem. "Mamma, it is best if you return to your rooms. I will bring you some tonic to make you better, but you have to go and lie down on your bed."

"Oh, Lydia, you are so kind to your poor mamma, unlike everyone else. Thank you, my dear girl. Thank you." Mrs Bennet hurried from the parlor, with Lydia holding on to her arm, to guide her and keep her from turning back towards the parlor.

With Mrs Bennet gone from the room, everyone turned their attention to Mr Bennet. The Master of Longbourn gasped out his request. "Jane...send for your Uncle Phillips...and send for...Mr Morton. Quickly. They must come...quickly."

Jane nodded her head as she wiped tears from her eyes. She stepped out of the room, speaking with Mrs Hill. Lizzy had taken hold of her father's hand, holding it to her cheek. "Papa, please, do not leave us."

"I thought I was... growing stronger. The pain...it is severe. Never this bad...before." Mr Bennet held his other hand to his chest, as if he could hold the pain at bay.

"Calm yourself, Papa." Elizabeth pleaded. "We need you here."

"I wish I could stay here... my dearest girl. I wish I

could... watch you marry Mr Darcy... and have your own children. But I will... have to watch my grandchildren... from heaven. I know my time... in this world is short." Mr Bennet placed a kiss on his daughter's hand. "Mr Darcy...please step nearer."

Darcy stepped to his beloved's side. "What can I do to ease your pain, Mr Bennet?"

"Lizzy, do you...love this man?" Her father asked.

Elizabeth had a look of question on her face. "I believe I do, Papa."

"Then I wish to see...you married...to him. Today."

"Papa, it would not be legal. We have not had time to have the banns read, nor would it be proper, given Mr Collins' death being not so long ago."

"Special circumstances...require special...exceptions."

"Mr Bennet, if I may, I think I have the perfect solution to the problem." Richard said as he stood behind his cousin. Everyone turned their attention to him. "While I was in Town previously, and obtained special licenses for Bingley and myself, I was able to obtain another license. It is for my cousin and Miss Elizabeth."

Elizabeth gasped at the news. "How did you know I would accept Mr Darcy?"

"Miss Elizabeth, anyone who could see how dearly my cousin loves you could be in no doubt that he would be able to win your heart. You have owned his for some time now. And, if you chose to deny your heart, I could always destroy the document. It is in my saddlebag."

"Papa, it will only cause speculation, marrying so soon, while still in mourning period for Mr Collins."

Mr Bennet smiled. "Anyone who knew Mr Collins…would not fret over you…remarrying so soon. And if anyone cares…to seek the truth…they will understand…I wish to see…my dear daughter…married. I wish you…to be secure…especially after…your mother's…behavior. Please…indulge me this…last request."

"William, what do you say?" Elizabeth held out a hand for him to take. Darcy took hold, squeezing lightly.

"My dearest, you know that I love you. You are dear to me, and I will cherish you for the rest of my life. Of course I wish to marry you, but I do not wish to rush you. You have suffered so much, and then, to have your mother behave so abominably. I will stand by your decision."

Elizabeth sat for a moment, before a smile grew on her lips. "Very well. I wish to have Papa at my wedding. Now I will have him at both of my weddings. And, just for your information, this will be my last wedding, for I am determined to be Mrs Darcy for many, many years to come."

~~ ** ~~

Everything happened in a flurry of activity. Mr Morton, the clergyman from Meryton, arrived with Mr Phillips. Matthew Phillips knew his brother in law was not long for the world, and he had prepared some paperwork, at Mr Bennet's request. He now brought the papers to have the Master of Longbourn sign. Upon arriving, Mr Morton was enlightened of the service he would be performing that day. Though he was hesitant, at first, witnessing the obvious love which flowed from Darcy and Elizabeth eliminated all doubts of what he should do.

Mrs Hill scurried about, assisting the Bennet sisters prepare for the impromptu wedding. While the ladies were busy, the young men stepped outside, giving Mr Bennet a moment of peace and quiet.

Darcy slapped his hand on his cousin's shoulder. "So, when were you planning to share with me the knowledge that you had brought a special license for me to marry Elizabeth?"

"I was waiting, for the perfect moment. But then, everything went insane. Miss Lydia's disappearance, Wickham's attempt to rob you. I believe we have all had a lot to contend with." Richard laughed.

"William, we will be brothers today." Bingley

smiled as he nearly jumped with joy.

"Are you comfortable with Lizzy and I staying at Netherfield for a while? If Mr Bennet's time is limited, as I believe it is, I do not wish to remove Elizabeth from what comfort she will derive from being near him."

"You are both welcome to stay at Netherfield, for as long as you wish." Bingley smiled. "I know my dear wife will be pleased to have you both stay with us."

"We are grateful, Bingley. Richard, I am pleased you are here with us as well. I only wish your parents and Anne could be here too."

Richard laughed. "Anne will be delighted to learn of the wedding. We had a bet on how soon you would marry. I said you would wait for the mourning period to be over, and the following day you would marry. Anne said the mourning period would be ignored and you would marry within two months. I have lost the bet."

"And what is your penalty?" Darcy inquired.

"I must purchase a new horse and teach Anne to ride."

The paperwork was signed by Mr Bennet, making his beloved daughter, Elizabeth, his heir. In the papers, which had been re-written at Longbourn, Mrs

Bennet was given the use of a cabin, located at the southern edge of Longbourn's property, to use as the dower cottage. There was very little room in the cabin, but it would be satisfactory for Mrs Bennet alone. The younger three daughters would remain at Longbourn, as Elizabeth insisted they not leave their home until they wished to begin their own lives.

Darcy had written a makeshift contract, listing his plans for the settlement he planned to bestow on Elizabeth. Besides fifty thousand pounds being allocated for her when he died, Darcy gave her a generous monthly allowance which was separate from the house accounts. He planned to take her to Town soon to have a new wardrobe made for her, though it would most likely be delayed when her father died. She would be in mourning weeds for months.

Included in the contract, Darcy planned to set up dowries for his new sisters. Lydia, Kitty and Mary would each have a ten thousand pound dowry, giving them a better chance at marrying well.

~~ ** ~~

Mr Bennet was weak, but he was aided to stand next to his daughter outside the parlor door. "My dear girl...I am pleased...to be able to correct a... mistake I made in forcing...you to marry Collins. I know you will have...a wonderful life...with Mr Darcy."

"I love you, Papa. I will always love you." Elizabeth

entwined her arm about his. "Let us meet my future husband now, so you can rest."

"I will rest soon enough, Lizzy. Soon enough. First, I wish to enjoy this moment." Mr Bennet nodded his head towards Jane, who opened the door. Mr Phillips followed closely behind his brother in law, incase Mr Bennet required his assistance.

The sisters had spent what little time they had to making Elizabeth into a beautiful bride. Though Darcy would not have cared if she was wearing a flour sack and her hair tangled with leaves and twigs, the sight of his beloved walking towards him, ready to become his wife, was breathtaking.

The gown Elizabeth wore was pale yellow, with golden stitch work on the bodice. The cut of the gown was perfect, modest with just a touch of daring. Her hair had been arranged on top, with curls winding their way down, a few hanging down upon her neck. There were flowers pinned into the curls on top, making her appear to be a beautiful nymph. And her eyes, the eyes which were beginning to heal, the eyes Darcy loved to lose himself in, sparkled with life. Though the specter of death loomed nearby to claim Mr Bennet, the moment Darcy saw his dearest love walking towards him, prepared to become his wife, no other thoughts mattered.

Mr Bennet placed his daughter's hand into the strong grasp of Darcy. "Be good to her, my son."

Darcy nodded, unable to speak. His eyes were fixed upon the vision before him, unwavering for even a moment.

Anyone who witnessed the ceremony would have declared Elizabeth was able to see, as her eyes were trained upon Darcy's face the entire time. Her lack of vision had been compensated by her other senses, especially in her hearing. The first words from his lips told her where he was, and knowing how tall he was, allowed Elizabeth to know where to turn her gaze.

The service was over quickly, with everyone pleased with the outcome. The register had been brought to Longbourn, allowing the newlyweds to sign, and not a moment later, Elizabeth was securely wrapped in her husband's embrace. "I love you, Elizabeth Darcy." He exclaimed, kissing her cheek as he spun her around in his arms.

"I love you, to, William." A moment later, Mr Lowe called for the couple to come to Mr Bennet's side.

Looking at Darcy, Mr Lowe gave a whisper of a shake of his head. Elizabeth knelt beside her father, slumped in his chair. He had died, just a moment after Mr Morton declared Elizabeth and Darcy as husband and wife.

"My love, your father is gone." Darcy knelt at her side. "He was able to fulfill his final request, he saw you married to a man you loved."

Tears streamed down the cheeks of everyone in the room. Jane and Charles embraced, pulling Kitty into their arms. Lydia was beside Elizabeth, her hand on her elder sister's shoulder. Mary had been pulled into her uncle's arms. Richard stepped into the hall, quietly announcing to Mr and Mrs Hill the loss of Mr Bennet.

After what seemed like an eternity, Darcy assisted Elizabeth in rising from her place beside her father. Mr Hill and Richard came forward. Between the men, Mr Bennet was laid down on the nearby sofa, gently given the respect they could afford him. Mr Phillips stepped forward, with a rug he had been handed by Mrs Hill. The rug was placed over the Master of Longbourn, with only his peaceful countenance visable.

Darcy moved to the settee, sitting Elizabeth beside him. Georgiana joined them, handing a handkerchief to her brother and feeling quite distraught at the suffering surrounding her.

Mr Hill stepped closer to Jane and Elizabeth. "I have sent my son to Meryton to have a casket brought here. It is my belief that Mr Bennet had already made arrangements with Mr Oliver, the casket was made for him a few months ago."

The news did not shock any of Mr Bennet's loved ones. Jane smiled. "Papa told me, while we were at Hunsford, he wished to be buried in walnut. He said he had loved the nuts, and he wished to have his remains entombed in something which had brought him pleasure in life."

Elizabeth gave a half strangled chuckle. "And the lining has to be blue. Papa said he hated black linings for caskets. He said it would make him appear pale, where light blue would make his grey hair stand out."

A half-hearted laugh made its way through those who were present.

~~~~~~~ ** ~~~~~~~

Chapter 15

The carriage arrived in front of Netherfield, and a footman moved forward to assist the occupant down. Caroline looked around the house, a sneer on her face. *How I despise this retched place. I wish my brother had never come here.*

Entering the foyer, Caroline was greeted by the housekeeper, Mrs Blaine. "Oh, dear me, Mr Bingley did not inform me of your arrival. It will be a delay in having a room prepared for you."

"Can you tell me where my brother can be found?" Caroline inquired with an undisguised dislike voice.

"The master left for Town a few days ago, and the mistress is staying with her family at the moment."

Shocked, Caroline looked at the housekeeper. "Of what are you speaking? My brother is in Town? And who is this mistress you speak of? My brother is not married."

"Oh, my, well…um…I am not certain what is happening. I received a missive from Mr Bingley just yesterday, asking for everything to be made ready for his arrival this afternoon. He will be arriving with several friends."

"And who is this mistress of whom you spoke? Who is claiming to be my brother's wife? I am the mistress, as I was last year."

Mrs Blaine knew not what to say. "I think it would be best if you spoke with your brother when he arrives."

"Do you know who is coming with him? Did my brother give you any hint?" Caroline grilled the housekeeper mercilessly.

"He asked that the master and mistress suite be prepared, as well as three to four other bedchambers. He was not certain how many would be staying at Netherfield."

As Caroline was steaming from lack of information, she heard the sound of another carriage pulling to a halt in front of the house. She walked out the front door, waiting at the top of the stairs.

A gasp escaped Caroline as she witnessed her brother hand down Georgiana Darcy. *Finally, my brother has come to his senses with regards to his wife. If only I can convince him to leave this horrid place.* A moment after Georgiana stepped down, Caroline was furious to see Jane Bennet exit the carriage.

"Caroline, what are you doing here?" Bingley inquired. "I did not expect you to come until I sent for you."

"I see we have many things to discuss, Brother. I was informed by your housekeeper that I am to wish you joy." Caroline nearly hissed with her disapproval.

"My dear Jane has made me the happiest of men. She and I married while we were in Hunsford. With everything we have had to deal, I thought it wise to wait to notify you and Louisa."

"You married Miss Bennet? Charles, you know what we told you of her lack of esteem for you. With no dowry or connections, it is clear that she is a fortune hunter."

"I have had enough of people disparaging my beloved and her family. If you plan to remain here, you will control yourself and treat my Jane with respect." Bingley's face became red with fury.

Seeing Darcy dismount his horse, along with his cousin, Caroline realized she would have to change her tactics. "Mr Darcy, what a pleasure to see you again. And dear Georgiana, welcome to Netherfield. I know you will not find the neighborhood to be to what you are accustomed, but I pray it is not too rugged for your tastes."

"Miss Bingley, I thank you for welcoming my guests." Jane stated, attempting to prove to Caroline just who was the Mistress of Netherfield. "Ah, Mrs Blaine, would you please have refreshments brought into the blue drawing room?"

The housekeeper nodded her head and went towards the kitchen. As Caroline was attempting to calm her anger at being treated as an inferior to Jane Bennet, she turned around to witness Darcy assisting a young lady down from the carriage. It took a moment to recognize her, as Elizabeth had lost weight and was obviously distraught. But when Caroline realized that Mr Darcy was holding Eliza Bennet close to his side, the harridan nearly yanked her nemesis from Darcy's side.

"Mr Darcy, sir, I believe Miss Elizabeth is fatigued. Perhaps she would prefer to return to Longbourn to rest." Caroline attempted to speak sweetly to the object of her obsession.

"Dearest, Miss Bingley is correct. You do appear to be fatigued. Would you like to rest for a while?" Darcy asked his wife.

"Perhaps I should." Elizabeth decided.

Mrs Blaine returned from requesting refreshments. Bingley stepped to her and quietly requested new accommodations for Darcy and Elizabeth, rooms which would connect for the newlyweds. The housekeeper was excited to hear the news, though she did not show any change in her expression. "Mr Darcy, if you would follow me, I will take you and Miss Elizabeth to your rooms."

"To their rooms?" Caroline was confused. "Miss Elizabeth is to return to Longbourn, is she not?"

"Caroline, Elizabeth and Darcy were married today. They will be staying here until they leave for London. The family is in mourning, as Mr Bennet died a few hours ago. Now, I would ask that you go to the drawing room and have some refreshments. I must see to my family and friends."

Caroline could not move. She stood, facing Darcy and Elizabeth, with her jaw hanging down. "This cannot be. No, this cannot be. Mr Darcy cannot be married to Eliza Bennet. If anyone else than me, he was to marry his cousin, Miss de Bourgh."

"Miss Bingley, Miss de Bourgh is now Mrs Richard Fitzwilliam." The former colonel stated, as he entered the foyer, glaring at the woman in front of him. "My wife is at Rosings, awaiting my return."

"Has the world gone mad?" Caroline said softly as she watched everyone climbing the stairs to the second floor. "I must be having the worst nightmare ever, for these things cannot be true."

~~ ** ~~

Elizabeth laid on the bed, curled up as she had done when she was a small child. The wonder of the day had also become the pain, as she had become a wife, for the second time in a few months, only to lose her father moments later. Darcy had excused himself to check on the arrival of Elizabeth's belongings from Longbourn. He knew she wished for some time to herself, to grieve as she needed.

Papa, how I wish you had been able to stay with us. I wish you could have had a better lot in life. Mamma was forced upon you, and you had no recourse but to marry her. I will not share your secret, of Mamma's forcing a compromising situation to trap you. Unlike your marriage, the one I entered today will be filled with love and respect.

I do not hold you responsible for my first marriage. I could never hate you for making me go through with such a miserable union. Thankfully, I will not have to endure his attentions any longer. I know it sounds selfish, the man did die. But I can feel no remorse for the loss. Nothing at all.

It is William who holds my heart. Now that I look back, I believe I have had feelings for him for some time. Perhaps my feelings were blackened by his statement at the Meryton Assembly, but he has explained his words to me. If only I had not heard those words, it might not have been necessary to marry Mr Collins. But what is done is done. And the wrong has been made right. My hopes are for a long life together with William, even if I never regain my sight.

What will we do with Mamma? Why does she hate me so? How I wish she could show me even a sliver of the love she shows Jane. But she is so hateful towards me. Her anger and hurtful words tear at my very soul. I am certain she will be angrier at me, now that Papa has died. Mamma will make sure she tells everyone that the blame for his death lays at my feet.

William has promised to protect Mary, Kitty and

Lydia. He will see they have dowries, and they will remain at Longbourn. Jane and Charles suggested hiring a governess to stay at Longbourn to watch over our sisters, since Mamma will be forced to move to the cottage. Her forced move will infuriate Mamma further. I should have insisted on her remaining at the main house. I should tell William to allow Mamma to remain as she is.

No, William and Charles were furious with Mamma's behavior, as was Uncle Phillips. Uncle Gardiner will feel the same when he arrives. Mamma has always been so different from her brother and sister, sometimes I wonder if she was a foundling, as Mrs Phillips and Mr Gardiner are so different from her.

Oh, William, I wish I could remain here, in this room, with you at my side. I wish for us to be on a private island where we would be alone. I love you, William...I love...

Elizabeth finally succumbed to blissful sleep.

~~ ** ~~

Jane and Bingley retired to their rooms, as Jane was quite fatigued. She had tried to remain strong for everyone else, but she was in need of the loving strength of her husband.

"Charles, you have my gratitude for how you acted today with Mamma. I have never understood her anger towards Lizzy, and now, now that Papa is gone, it will only be worse."

Wrapping one arm around his wife's waist and the other around her shoulders, Bingley held his wife firmly against his chest. "Have no fear, my love. Now, Lizzy is safe from your mother. Darcy will watch over her and never allow any harm to come to her. Once all is settled, Lizzy and Darcy will make their way to Pemberley. Your mother will not be able to cause them harm."

"Your strength and kindness kept me going through this day." Jane wrapped her arms about her husband's waist. "It is difficult to believe, Papa is gone from us."

"Though I was shocked, it pleased me to know he was able to witness Lizzy's wedding to Darcy. He entrusted her into Darcy's keeping."

"Papa loved Lizzy dearly, she was always his favorite. It nearly killed him when he insisted she marry Mr Collins. And then, the accident. Seeing Lizzy in such a state, knowing she was a breath away from death, Papa was devastated. He told me that had Lizzy died, he would have been to blame. He had forced her to marry our cousin, which placed her in the carriage."

"Your father was attempting to protect all of you. If only I had returned to Netherfield sooner, but I cannot change that now. We must look forward, rather than back."

"Lizzy has always said to think of the past, only as it brings you pleasure." Jane smiled. "I will remember Papa's goodness and his love for us girls."

"Mr Phillips sent an express to Town, to your uncle, Mr Gardiner. We should expect your aunt and uncle to arrive at Longbourn within a day or two. Between Mr Gardiner and Mrs Phillips, they should be able to handle your mother."

A small chuckle was heard from Jane. "Mamma, being handled by anyone, would be a miracle. Aunt Phillips can usually convince Mamma to behave better, but it is Uncle Gardiner, who has the authority as the head of the family, who can make a real difference in Mamma's behavior."

"Come, now, my love. You should rest. There is time to dwell on what has happened today, but you must take care of yourself." Bingley placed a kiss on the top of his wife's head.

Jane nodded, turning from his embrace. "Would you stay with me, until I fall asleep?"

"Of course, dearest. I will be at your side forever."

Caroline was pacing in the bedchamber of her rooms. *How had all of my worst nightmares come to be? My brother married to that chit, Jane Bennet, Colonel Fitzwilliam married Miss de Bourgh, and, worst of all, Mr Darcy married to Eliza Bennet. No, this*

cannot be. I must write to Louisa and beg her to come immediately. We must remove Charles and Mr Darcy from this hideous place as soon as can be.

And what is wrong with Eliza? She seemed to be quite ill, and her eyes are not near what Mr Darcy had referred to as fine. Perhaps she will perish soon as well, then I will have Mr Darcy as my husband. Yes, while he grieves her death, I will be kind and compassionate, which will open his eyes to the benefits of having me as a wife.

What happened in Hunsford, to have brought Charles there as well as Jane? Obviously it was not the wedding of Mr Darcy to his sickly cousin. There has to be more to the tale than what I know. I will approach Charles and demand he tell me what has happened. I deserve to know the truth, as I am his sister.

Yes, I will find Charles this moment and insist he tell me what is going on.

With that thought in mind, Caroline left her rooms, in search of her brother.

Bingley was sitting behind his desk in his study, his thoughts lost to the world. So much had happened in the course of two months, so many changes in the world as Bingley knew it. He was married to the woman he loved, his dearest friend was now married to Elizabeth, the deaths of Mr Collins and Mr Bennet had made such a difference in all their lives. Darcy had been forced to watch as Elizabeth was near death, anquish was etched in his expression every time Bingley had seen him during their stay at Hunsford. Then his friend had to contend with the difficulties of his aunt. Elizabeth was blind, but there was improvement in her sight. Mrs Bennet was ashamed of Elizabeth and wished her daughter had died in the accident. *How has everything become so upended, so quickly?*

A knock on the door of his study brought Bingley back to the present. "Enter." He called out.

The door opened to admit Caroline. "What brings you to Netherfield, Caroline?"

"You are here, Charles. I thought it was wise for me to come. I know you fancy the notion that Jane esteems you, but she does not. Mr Darcy even acknowledged it."

"Darcy was wrong. When he learned the truth, while he was at Hunsford, he sent word to me to come there. As soon as I renewed my acquaintance with Jane, I knew I was correct. Jane loves me, as dearly as I love her. That is the reason we married as we did. We wished for no one to interfere in our decision."

"What happened in Hunsford? I assumed you were going there to stand up with Darcy as he married his cousin, as his aunt had declared for so long would happen. But he did not marry Miss de

Bourgh."

"No, Richard and Anne married in a double ceremony with Jane and me. Lady Catherine has been ill for some time and she is now under constant care of a physician."

"But you have not answered my question, Charles. What happened at Hunsford?"

Taking a deep breath, Bingley turned towards his sister. "Just after New Year's, Miss Elizabeth had married her father's cousin, Mr Collins."

Caroline gasped. "She is a bigamist? How can she be married to Mr Darcy?"

"On their way to Hunsford, after the wedding, there was a carriage accident. Mr Collins was killed. Elizabeth nearly died as well. She suffered greatly from her injuries, and took ill. Lady Catherine knew not of her nephew's prior acquaintance with Elizabeth, and she sent for him to attend business for her at Rosings. When Darcy arrived, and learned of the situation, he sent for his family physician to tend to Elizabeth."

"That explains why she looks so different, so weak. Is she dying?"

Bingley was disturbed at his sister's thinking. "Elizabeth is not dying, she is recovering. You saw her shortly after her father's death, and she is quite distraught."

"And now, you and Mr Darcy have committed yourself to take care of the remaining Bennet family members? Is the mother to move in here with you? And the youngest sisters? My, what a merry time it will be at Netherfield." Caroline snorted.

"ENOUGH!" Bingley stood as he made his declaration. "I have had my fill of rudeness today. No more. You will either control your tongue or you will leave. I will not have it in my home. And, for your information, Mrs Bennet will be moving to a cottage on Longbourn's property and the sisters will be living at Longbourn's main house."

This news peaked Caroline's interest. Why would the mother be moved from the home? Removed from her youngest daughters' spoke of problems within the family.

"Now, can you be civil to my family or will you be leaving Netherfield?" Bingley's words brought his sister from her woolgathering.

"I will remain here for some time. Louisa and Mr Hurst were planning to journey here soon, so I might as well wait for them."

Bingley sighed. He had hoped his sister would leave. "Very well. You will abide my rules or you will be shipped off. And you will respect Jane, as she is the Mistress of Netherfield."

"Of course, Brother."

"And, just so you know, Elizabeth cannot see. Her vision is beginning to recover, but at the moment, she is blind. I have a companion arriving soon to assist her."

Caroline was shocked. *So there is something wrong with Eliza. Oh, this will be delightful to prove to Mr Darcy of her unworthiness to be his wife.*

"If you will excuse me, Brother, I wish to rest until dinner."

Bingley nodded his head. "Very well, I look forward to dining with you later."

~~ ** ~~

Colonel Forster received word of Wickham's arrival for court martial the following day. He looked forward to seeing the man pay for his betrayal of his command. Since the desertion of Wickham, and the disappearance of Lydia Bennet and Denny, Forster had suffered from a lack of respect from his men. Though he was suspicious of the tale he was told, by Richard Fitzwilliam, of Denny's abduction rather than desertion, Forster accepted the young man's return.

Since his return to the unit, Denny had been tended by the local apothecary. He had kept to himself as much as possible, not speaking with the other men as he had in the past. When anyone asked him questions as to what had happened, Denny would change the subject.

Colonel Forster would have two of his captains and several officers from London hold the trial, though he was certain it would not take much effort to see Wickham found guilty. The blackguard had proved himself unworthy of being a soldier, leaving his post and taking hostages with him to protect himself from being caught.

The talk around Meryton spoke of Lydia Bennet's ruined reputation at the hands of her captor. Colonel Forster knew it would be natural for the Bennet family to wish justice against the vile perpetrator, as the reputation of the entire family was damaged. When he questioned Denny with regards to the youngest Bennet, Denny was adamant that no harm was brought to Lydia, due to his protection. Knowing from what Denny would be protecting a young maiden made the colonel's hair stand on end. *The world will be a much better place when it is rid of George Wickham.*

Captain Carter knocked on the door of Colonel Forster's room. "Sir, we just received word from Sir William Lucas. Mr Bennet has died. According to Sir William, Mr Bennet was suffering from a heart condition, and the strain that he was under while his daughter was missing, and his other daughter having been injured in an accident before, all became too much to bear."

"Thank you, Captain. By the way, I received a letter stating that the escort detail will be bringing

Wickham here tomorrow. We will convene a court martial the following morning. Would you be available to serve on the board?"

"W...Well, I...you know, I was friends with Wickham, until all of this happened. I do not wish to cause you any hardship, and I pray you know that I am not like Wickham. I hold my duty to be sacred."

"Yes, yes, I am well aware. We all thought Wickham to be a pleasant sort of chap, and enjoyed his tales. But we were all deceived. If I thought you would bring me further hardship from being involved in the court martial, I would never have mentioned it. Officers from other units can always be brought in."

"No, Colonel, I am more than willing to do my duty in this matter. It brings shame to all of us who wear the red coat proudly." Carter stated as he puffed out his chest.

"Captain, you will go far in the militia. Now, off with you. I will discuss the issue more tomorrow, when we know when we will conduct the trial. I will have a letter ready for you to take to Netherfield later. I am certain Mr Bingley and Mr Darcy will wish to know what is happening, as they will most likely be called as witnesses."

~~~~~~~ ** ~~~~~~~

Chapter 16

Waking with a start, Elizabeth was unfamiliar with her surroundings. At Longbourn, her bedroom held a window on the west wall, giving her the warmth of light until the sun had bid farewell to another day. Her bed was situated so that the window was near the left side of her bed. What sunlight Elizabeth could now feel warming her skin was coming from the right side of the bed. Also, this bed was far bigger than her bed in her childhood home.

After a few moments, realization settled in on Elizabeth's mind. *Netherfield. I am at Netherfield. I was married today. Mr Darcy is my husband now. Oh, Papa, you have left us.* Tears welled in her eyes at the thought of her father's death.

"My love, are you well?" The baritone voice she had come to know so well asked.

"William, I was disoriented. What time is it?"

Darcy came to the bed, sitting on the side of it. Reaching out his hand, he grasped Elizabeth's hand with it. "Nearly time to dress for dinner. Would you prefer to have a tray sent up instead? You have had much to take in for one day."

"No, I wish to be with Jane, as I know she is suffering. My sister may not be as demonstrative as I, but she holds her feelings to her heart."

"Very well, my love, I will ring for a maid to come assist you." Darcy leaned towards her, claiming her lips with his own. "I love you, Elizabeth Darcy."

Smiling at the sound of her new name, Elizabeth could not help but give a slight giggle. "I love you, my handsome knight. You continue to rescue me from all sorts of harm. And all I can do in return is to give you my heart and my love."

"No man could want more from the woman they love." Darcy placed another kiss on her lips. "Your love is worth a mountain of gold, and your heart is the most precious gemstone in the world."

"Fitzwilliam Darcy, has anyone ever told you that you are a silly man?"

"No one knows this side of me, except you." He brushed the tip of her nose with his finger.

~~ ** ~~

As the maid finished the last touches of styling Elizabeth's hair, a soft knock was heard. "Elizabeth, may I enter?" came the voice of Georgiana Darcy.

"Of course, Georgiana." Came the reply.

The door opened, allowing the young girl inside. "Elizabeth, you look so beautiful."

"I would argue with you, as Jane has always been the beautiful one in the family, as I cannot see my reflection, I will allow you to make such claims."

Elizabeth chuckled. "I am pleased you have come, for I had wished to speak with you."

"I was fretting whether or not to disturb you, after all that has happened today. But then, I thought it would be wise to do so. With all the happenings at Longbourn today, I am afraid I never had the chance to welcome you to the family. It pleases me so to have you for a sister."

"I am thrilled to have you as my sister as well. I am certain I will require your assistance when we make our way to Darcy House and Pemberley. William has told me of your learning the duties of the Mistress of the house, and I pray you will indulge me by teaching me what you know."

"I have no doubt you will be a perfect Mistress, as you are such a kind and caring person. William has told me so much of you, and he never lies."

Elizabeth laughed openly. "Such a perfect elder brother. Well, I am sure he exaggerated my abilities, for he is far too generous to me."

Georgiana stood beside her new sister, fidgeting a bit. It was clear to Elizabeth that the girl wished to say something more, though could not find the words. "Georgiana, would it be too bold of me to ask you to hold me? I feel a sadness creeping up and it would bring me comfort."

No more words were needed, as Elizabeth felt the

arms of the younger wrap around her. Returning the embrace, Elizabeth could feel the tears which were streaming down Georgiana's cheek.

"There, there, shush. All will be well." She continued to pat her hand on Georgiana's back as she held her.

"Seeing your father...oh, I am being a baby. Please...forgive me for behaving so." Georgiana sobbed.

"Something tells me this is more than what has happened today."

"Seeing your father in such a state, it reminded me of the day my father died. I was only ten when it happened. After my lessons, I went to his study. When I knocked on the door, there was no answer, though I knew he was inside. The door was unlocked, so I entered the room. Father was slumped in his chair, behind his desk. I shall never forget it, as I was so frightened. Mrs Reynolds, our housekeeper, came when she heard me shouting for help."

"Where was your brother when this happened?"

"William was at Matlock, assisting our uncle with something. By the time he arrived at the house, the servants had moved Father."

Knowing her own pain, Elizabeth could imagine what this poor girl had gone through at such a tender age. "I wish today had not sparked such a memory for you, Georgiana. It pleases me that you felt you could speak with me, for I wish for us to be close. You are always welcome to speak with me."

"I knew having a sister would be wonderful, and it is already. Not only have you made William happier than I have ever known him to be, you have comforted me already. I have always feared my brother marrying one of those ladies from society, you know the ones who are so...self-important."

"Like Miss Bingley?" Elizabeth asked with a hint of humor.

"Believe me, I have had nightmares of brother marrying the likes of her. Whenever she comes near me, she fawns over me as if I were a priceless china doll. She does not know I detest her behavior, and she is unaware I heard her speaking in a disreputable manner concerning William some months ago."

"Disreputable?"

Georgiana was pleased to have someone to confide in. "I heard Miss Bingley telling her sister how she would attempt to compromise herself at my brother's expense. She does not love William, she only cares for the power and status she would have as his wife."

"Goodness. I knew there were ladies in the world who behaved so, but I must say, I am shocked to know Miss Bingley is such a lady. Though, I cannot see she is much of a lady, if she behaves in such a manner."

Darcy entered the room just then. "Ah, what a wonderful sight. My two favorite ladies together."

Georgiana stood and flew into her brother's embrace. "William, I am so pleased you have married Elizabeth. She is the sister I have always wished for."

"And she is the wife I have always dreamed of." Darcy claimed as he placed a kiss on his sister's forehead. "Come, ladies, let us go down to dine."

~~ ** ~~

The Darcys joined the Bingleys and Richard in the drawing room prior to dinner being announced. Seeing his new brother, Bingley stepped over to speak with him. "Forgive me, Elizabeth, Georgiana, but I must have a word with Darcy."

Georgiana took Elizabeth's arm and led her to the sofa where Jane sat. Richard made his way to the men, for he was certain Bingley would have news to share with both men.

"I received a message from Colonel Forster. The detail of men will be transporting Wickham to Meryton tomorrow, and the hearing will be held the following day. Colonel Forster will send us word if we will be needed to testify, though he is certain the outcome will be the same."

Richard nodded his head. "Wickham is guilty of

desertion, and, being that we are at war with France, it is a crime that is punishable by death. The abduction and attempted robbery are secondary and will not make much of a difference. You cannot kill him twice, though it is my opinion that he deserves to be hung, drawn and quartered, castrated, and then burned on a stake."

Darcy was only half paying attention, as he kept his eyes focused on his wife. He knew she was in pain from her loss, though she was putting up a tremendous front for everyone. Seeing her with Georgiana only moments before, had torn Darcy's heart.

"Well, with all hope, we will be rid of George Wickham, once and for all, and soon." Darcy stated.

"I cannot agree more, cousin. And, once this mess is over, I may return to my beloved wife, who awaits me at our home."

Bingley smiled as he looked at his own wife. "You should have sent for Anne to join you here, Richard."

"I have thought of it, though Anne does not travel often. It is best if she remains at Rosings. My mother is planning to make the journey there, to assist Anne in the changes she faces, now that she is the Mistress of Rosings."

"Forgive me, Richard, but it has slipped my mind to ask, your brother's child..."

"Is a strapping, healthy young lad. From what I have learned from Father's letter, he is deeply admired, as is to be expected. Mother has longed for a grandchild for so long. And now that Anne and I are married, Mother is already hinting as to when her next grandchild will be on its way."

"When she learns of my wedding, I am certain Aunt Rebecca will be hounding me of my duty to provide an heir, though I believe she is thinking more on terms of being a grandmother figure than protecting the future of Pemberley." Darcy shook his head. Lady Matlock had been quite persistent in her desires to see her sons and nephew well settled and having families.

The room became quiet as Caroline Bingley entered the room, her flare for the dramatic obvious to all. Bedecked in a hideous orange gown, which was covered in far too much glitz, and the daring cut was far too revealing for any occasion. Feathers adorned her hair, making her look like a ridiculous bird.

"Charles, do forgive me for being late. I pray you have not been delayed in dining." Caroline said as she traipsed to the trio of men. Clutching Darcy's arm, she cooed to him. "Mr Darcy, it is such a pleasure to be in your presence once again. After being in the north, with so many men who are beneath our standing, it is a breath of fresh air to be with like-minded individuals, such as yourself."

Prying her fingers from his arm, Darcy made his displeasure apparent. "If you will excuse me, Miss Bingley, I wish to be with my wife. We have had quite a day, as it is, after all, our wedding day." Once dislodged from her grasp, Darcy crossed the room to take the seat next to Elizabeth. He raised his wife's hand to his lips, placing an enduring kiss on the back of it.

"Caroline, remember yourself." Bingley hissed under his breath.

"I am behaving, Charles. Is it not more palatable to be with people of our own society, rather than those who are inferior? I am certain that Colonel Fitzwilliam agrees."

"Ah, Miss Bingley, I must inform you, I am a colonel no longer. I am now a gentleman, with an estate to tend and a loving wife to adore. But during my time in the service of King and crown, I have known some very delightful and pleasant people who are, what you would refer to, beneath our rank. But, if you are fortunate, with your brother's marriage to the former Miss Bennet, being the daughter of a gentleman, even one from small country estate, elevates Bingley's status, as he was born of a tradesman."

Darcy nearly choked on the sip of water he had just taken. Caroline Bingley had always looked down her nose at those she deemed beneath her, though her father's fortune was derived from trade. Her cool demeanor was a sign of Richard's remark finding the bull's eye. But Richard was not finished. "If memory serves me correctly, the Bennet family has been landed gentry for many generations."

"Your memory is correct, Richard." Darcy replied. "In fact, I remember Mr Bennet enlightening me on that matter while we were at Hunsford. He was the sixth generation of Bennets to own Longbourn. My wife and her sisters were raised to be gentlewomen."

It was Caroline's turn to choke on her drink. Charles was required to assist his sister by smacking her back with force. "Enough...Charles, there is no need to beat me so viciously." She fumed once she could catch her breath.

"I was only attempting to assist you, Caroline. There is no need to become angered."

The meal proceeded quietly, as Caroline boiled with fury, witnessing the gentleness Darcy was bestowing upon the woman he loved. *I must do whatever I can to make him see his mistake. He must leave that chit, Eliza Bennet. I would even accept being Darcy's mistress, as I would still be well kept. With her blindness, it will be simple enough to make it appear a disgrace in the eyes of the Master of Pemberley and his family members.*

"Miss Eliza, if I remember correctly, your family was quite taken with the militia being in the neighborhood."

Darcy was quite disturbed. "Miss Bingley, her name is Mrs Elizabeth Darcy, and I do not remember her ever giving you permission to refer to her by Eliza. As to her family, they have endured a difficult day, with the loss of Mr Bennet. And the militia is of no concern to them."

Something in his tone enlightened Caroline to there being more to his anger than what was said. "Forgive me, Mr Darcy, I meant no disrespect. I was just wondering if the young men from the militia would be visiting Netherfield, so I am able to inform Mrs Blaine."

"As the duty of informing Mrs Blaine of whom is welcome in **my** home is mine, I suggest you not fret over such." Jane stated politely, though firmly.

Richard could feel the temperature in the room rising. "Miss Bingley, I cannot imaging the militia having much time to socialize at the moment, as they are training hard. I know from experience, with a war raging, all soldiers are needed to concentrate on their duties, as it may save their lives."

Bingley realized that his sister would soon learn of the impending hearing and Wickham's deceit. "One of the men from the militia recently deserted his post, taking a fellow officer and a young lady captive as he fled the area. The man was found, and he is to be tried this week for his desertion. The officer and young lady were returned to the neighborhood, with only the officer being injured. Colonel Forster is of a mood to keep close watch over his unit, as he is furious with the traitor."

This news came as a surprise to Caroline. *Who could have been the lady? Was it Miss Eliza? Was this the reason Darcy married her, to protect her from a damaged reputation? Was she involved with the officer?* Caroline knew she would have to do some investigating to learn more. If she were correct, it could be of assistance in breaking the newlyweds apart.

~~ ** ~~

The officers pulled Wickham from the prisoner carriage, marching him into Colonel Forster's office. Looking up at the prisoner, Colonel Forster held a look of disgust. "Wickham, such a pleasure to have you returned." He said sarcastically.

"It is not my choice to be here, any more than it is yours to have me, I am sure." Wickham looked about the room.

"Do not think of escaping, Wickham. It will only speed your demise."

"You have already pronounced sentence against me? Without hearing my statement?" Wickham was furious. "If I am to die, then Denny should be beside me when the time comes. He was with me, every step of the way."

"According to statements from Mr Fitzwilliam Darcy, Colonel Richard Fitzwilliam (retired), and Miss Lydia Bennet, Lieutenant Denny was your victim as well as captive. In their statements, they spoke of Denny's protection of Miss Lydia while they were your captives, as well as Denny being injured as he attempted to protect Mr Darcy, when you were discovered robbing the man's house. There are no charges against Denny, and he will soon be back to his duties."

"Darcy and Fitzwilliam would do anything to blacken my name. And you believe them, as they are wealthy. How much did they pay you to condemn me?" Wickham gave his tongue free range. "Did you know Darcy cheated me out of an inheritance from his father? The son was jealous of the father's love for me, so he ignored the provisions for me in his father's will. I was cheated, and am now will pay the ultimate price for old Mr Darcy's fondness for me."

"Mr Wickham, you deserted your post, pure and simple. Or are you claiming you were abducted and held against your wishes? For I do not believe such. Even without your escapades in Town, I have learned from many sources, in the neighborhood, which proves you a scoundrel. I have two fathers who wish your hide for mettling with their daughters, one of which is now with child. Every shop in Meryton has brought debts you owe them. Some of your fellow officers have come forward, claiming you have cheated them when playing cards, and have stolen from them. Your days in my unit were limited, even without the current charges of desertion. I would insist you be sent to the battlefields immediately, but I know you would find a way to run from your duty."

"Is it my fault the young ladies find me irresistible? When they throw themselves at me, what am I to do? The temptations of the flesh are difficult to ignore when there is so much to enjoy."

The officer holding Wickham's left arm slipped his elbow into the prisoner's ribcage. "Watch your words, Wickham. Captain Chambers is a friend of mine, and I know his sister."

Wickham's bravado took a sudden withdrawal. Knowing Elise Chambers had been uncooperative when he had his way with her, it was natural for her brother to be furious. Elise had never recovered from the attack on her person.

"How am I to receive a fair trial if everyone involved in trying me already have prejudices against me? Prejudices for which I have never been tried or convicted, only based on conjecture, I might add."

"George Wickham, I would have to travel to the other side of the world to find someone you have not brought harm. Between your gambling debts, your debts to merchants, the young ladies you have ruined, and many other faults, I doubt anyone in England would come out unscathed by you." Colonel Forster explained. "So you will be tried by your fellow officers, and that is that. If you wished for better, you should have behaved better. Now, have him locked in the gaol we had constructed. We will have guards posted inside and out, for I have no doubts as to this foul creature's plan to escape."

The officers nodded their heads and yanked Wickham from the room. Colonel Forster was pleased to see the officers who had been sent with Wickham were some of the largest, strongest men Colonel Forster had seen.

~~~~~~~ ** ~~~~~~~

Chapter 17

Pacing in his bedchambers, Darcy could not expel his nervousness. He had not had time to consider the fact that as it was his wedding day, that night would be his wedding night. He had not discussed the sleeping arrangements with Elizabeth or whether she would wish to consummate their marriage that night. Thoughts of how to approach her and speak of such matters made Darcy blush.

Elizabeth had entered her dressing chambers when he walked her to their rooms. "Will you come to my dressing chamber in half of an hour?" She had asked. "I would like some time with you before sleeping tonight."

The lump in his throat only allowed him to squeak out an agreement. Quickly changing his clothing, Darcy now wore only his shirtsleeves and breeches.

A knock was heard on the door connecting the two bedchambers the newlyweds occupied. Darcy opened the door, finding the maid standing before him. "Mrs Darcy asked me to inform you she is finished changing her clothes."

Realizing he had been lost in thought, and forgotten the time, Darcy hurried into the dressing chamber to collect his bride. The sight before him was more than he could have ever imagined. Standing before the dressing table, Elizabeth wore a very shear silk nightgown in a pale lavender color. The form fitting gown showed every curve of her womanly body, making Darcy's breeches suddenly tight. Her long, dark chocolate curls flowed free of restraints, nearly reaching her waist. How he had longed to run his fingers through those curls.

"William, I was worried. You had not come to me, so I sent the maid."

"There is no reason to fret, my beautiful, loving wife. I was woolgathering, and lost track of the time. Can you forgive me?" Darcy reached for her hand and pulled her to him.

"Well, I will be so kind if you will do one thing for me." Elizabeth teased.

"And that might be?"

Tipping her head towards his face, Elizabeth smiled. "If you kiss me immediately. I desire to feel your lips."

Not wishing to delay his wife's pleasure, Darcy claimed her lips, slowly building with the passion he had held for her.

As they gasped for air, after several moments, Darcy could not prevent the smile which grew upon his lips. "My dearest, I have dreamed of tasting your lips for some time now. And I must tell you, they are even more delicious than in my dreams."

"I must admit that I find your kisses to be quite enjoyable, William. But before we kiss again, I wish to speak with you."

Slightly nervous as to what she wished to discuss, Darcy led her into the sitting room which was attached to the bedchambers. Taking a seat beside her on the sofa, Darcy encouraged her to speak.

"I know we have not discussed the sleeping arrangements for the evening. I must admit, I am nervous. Not from any lack of desire to be with you, but I fear I will not meet with your approval, with my blindness." Elizabeth said, biting her lower lip as she finished.

Darcy took hold of her hand, placing a kiss on the palm of it. "My love, you could never disappoint me, no matter what. I love you, and am so elated to be able to call you my wife. Now, as to the matter of sleeping arrangements." The look on Darcy's face was that of a young boy, being coy as he asked for a special treat. "I know it is not the way of society, but I would prefer if you would share my bed. And when I say this, I mean each and every night. I have no desire to sleep in a separate room from you. Waking up with my arms wrapped around you, holding you to me, is what I wish. Please, grant me this desire."

"I was hoping you would feel this way. My mother has always discussed the marriage bed as a chore or duty which must be endured. But my Aunt Gardiner explained to me that those who marry for love, sharing a bed every night is not uncommon. Obviously, my parents had no love for one another. I wish for a marriage like my Aunt and Uncle Gardiner."

"My parents were similar to your aunt and uncle. They were a love match, and shared their bed every night."

Elizabeth was silent for a moment. "William, I am an innocent when it comes to the aspects of being a wife, in such a manner. It has been said that men of your society are not strangers to acts of love, and that young men are able to find ladies...in houses...who are willing to...you know."

"I am not sure I wish to know where you have learned of such houses, but yes, there are brothels which are frequented by men of my society. I have an admission to make to you."

Her eyes dropped as if she were looking at her hands. All the while, Elizabeth feared what she was about to hear. She nodded her head for her husband to continue.

"When I was a youngster, my father sat down with me one day. He told me that I was old enough to know about certain things, as I was preparing to enter school. He knew it was common for young men to speak of their conquests. My father was adamant that I knew the importance of having relations with a woman, the possible problems which could arise from having a moment of passion with someone you are not married to. My mother's sister, Lady Catherine, had a difficult marriage. Lady Catherine was cruel to her husband, and he spent many nights in the arms of other ladies. Most of the ladies were the sort you spoke of, from brothels. It is not common knowledge, but my cousin, Anne, has two half-sisters, both of whom are younger than Anne. Now that Anne and Richard are in control of the inheritance, Anne wishes to acknowledge her sisters, setting funds for them to have better lives. Father realized the difficulties in my uncle's marriage, but Father did not approve of behaving in a manner which would leave unwanted children, starving and being forced into menial labor to survive, just for a moment of pleasure. There are also diseases which are contracted with such behaviors. A man Father went to school with came down with the French disease. Father stated it was horrible to watch the deterioration of his friend as the disease devoured him."

"I promised my father I would behave as he would, and would wait until marriage. Father stated that it was unfair for society to condemn a lady if she were experienced outside marriage, but it was expected of young men to be well versed in love making. Such double standards were infuriating to Father. He had remained chaste until he married my mother, and, after her death, he remained faithful to her memory. When my father died, Richard and his brother teased me for not having been with a lady.

They dragged me to a brothel in Town, and tossed me into a room with a young lady. She looked to be no more than six and ten, and I was sickened at the thought of my first experience being with such a child. My cousins do not know this, but I paid the young lady double the rate to lie to them and say that I was the best lover she had ever had. While we were in the room, all we did was talk. She had been born to a harlot, her father was unknown. Her mother died when she was birthing the girl's sister. This left the girl alone in the world, no family to protect her. The very sort of child my father told me of, the abandoned and unwanted children from a moment of pleasure."

"So your cousins believe you are not pure, though your virtue is the same as mine?" Elizabeth lifted her chin, a tiny tear visible in the corner of her eye.

"Making love to you will be the first time I have ever had relations with anyone. I admit that I am well read on the subject, as I have been as curious as any other man. The libraries at Darcy House and Pemberley contain some books, which I have locked away. I do not wish to have Georgiana find them by accident. But the books are quite informative on the ways of pleasing each other."

"And will you teach me these ways, as I am unable to peruse the books?" Elizabeth inquired, the look of passion in her eyes.

"I will be dedicated to teaching you, so long as you

teach me what brings you pleasure. Some men only worry of achieving their own pleasure, but if you are finding joy in the activity, I will have a greater pleasure myself."

Darcy led his wife to his bedchamber, sitting her on the side of the bed. Quickly disrobing, Darcy laid his beloved back on the bed. Their first lesson of lovemaking continued throughout the night.

~~ ** ~~

Entering the parlor at Longbourn, Jane and Elizabeth walked, leaning against one another for support. Their father's casket was there, with their cherished parent laid in his favorite clothing. "Jane, did they put him in his deep sapphire blue waist coat? It was his favorite."

"Mary saw to it he was dressed in it. He looks so peaceful, Lizzy, and so handsome. The strain he had with his illness has left him. There is no more weakness or pain."

"I wish I could see him, one last time." Elizabeth stated with a sob. "Could you place my hand on his face, Jane?"

Jane took her sister's hand and laid it gently on Thomas Bennet's cheek. Her fingers could determine what her blindness could not, and Elizabeth could sense how relaxed his features felt. "I love you, Papa. I pray you know how much I love and treasure every moment I spent with you. And I thank you for insisting William and I marry before you died. I love him, truly. You gave me a tremendous final gift, seeing to my happiness."

Darcy stepped behind his wife, placing his hands on her shoulders. "He gave us both a most treasured gift, insisting in our marrying yesterday. Though I regret the circumstances which brought us all to Hunsford, I will never regret the time I was able to spend with your father while we were there."

Sir William and Lady Lucas arrived, with their four children, to pay their respects. Charlotte moved directly to her dear friend, embracing Elizabeth. "Lizzy, my dear Lizzy, this is a tragedy. I know how close you and your father were. He told me once that having you for a daughter was better than having a horde of sons. Your intelligence and impertinence always made him smile."

Wiping a tear from her cheek, Elizabeth placed a kiss on her friend's cheek. "Thank you, Charlotte. It is so very difficult to believe he is gone from us."

Pulling back, Charlotte looked upon her friend. "I have heard a rumor, and I wish to ask you if it is true. Did you marry Mr Darcy yesterday?"

"Papa insisted on our ignoring propriety, as I was officially in mourning for Mr Collins. Papa wished to be with us when I married William. He was strong enough to walk me down the aisle and place my hand in William's. At the end of the ceremony, Papa was gone."

Tears were free flowing between both of the ladies. "What a precious memory your father gave you, Lizzy. His final act was to give you to Mr Darcy for safe keeping. He knew you would be loved."

"How are you so certain of William's love?" Elizabeth was curious.

"Lizzy, when he stayed at Netherfield last year, it was obvious to me that he was in love with you. Whenever you were in the same room, he could not keep his eyes from you. The look he had, I was certain he was madly in love with you."

"I was, indeed, Miss Lucas." Darcy said as he interrupted their conversation. "I was a fool not to have realized how dear Elizabeth was to me at that time. So many things could have been changed. But now, we will look to the future, not dwelling on the past."

"Oh, yes, think of the past only as it brings you pleasure." Charlotte remarked.

"A philosophy I intend to keep close to my heart, Miss Lucas. And I pray that in years to come, we will look back on many happy memories which will bring us pleasure."

"As I have already said to Lizzy, I was quite certain that your marriage is a love match. I could tell last year how dear my friend is to you." Charlotte smiled.

"I would like to introduce you to my sister, Miss Lucas." Darcy led her to the chairs in the corner of the room, where Georgiana was attempting to blend in with the décor. "Georgiana, I would like you to meet Miss Charlotte Lucas. Miss Lucas, this is my sister, Miss Georgiana Darcy. Georgie, Miss Lucas has known Elizabeth all of her life, as Lucas Lodge is only a few miles from here. Miss Lucas and Elizabeth have been very close friends through the years."

"It is a pleasure to meet you, Miss Lucas." Georgiana said in barely a whisper, her shy nature amongst strangers making her nervous.

"And it is my pleasure to meet you Miss Darcy. When I met your brother last year, he spoke of your talent at the pianoforte. He says that you are quite proficient."

"My brother is far too kind when it comes to praising me." Georgiana said.

"I am sure your brother speaks the truth." Charlotte smiled to the shy girl. "Miss Darcy, my younger sister is near your age. Would you care to meet her?"

When Georgiana nodded her head, Charlotte led her across the room to meet Maria, who was in conversation with Lydia and Kitty Bennet.

Elizabeth turned her head from the conversation

she was having with Lady Lucas, hearing a familiar voice entering the parlor. Mrs Gardiner walked directly to her niece, pulling her into her embrace. "Lizzy, my dear girl, I have so longed to see you for myself. I feared you were lost to us forever after the accident. Are you well?" She pulled back enough to look upon Elizabeth's face.

"I am better each and every day. Recently I have begun to see bright light when the sun is out. The physician is pleased with the news, and holds hope in my recovery."

"Elizabeth, you are never to give me such a start again. Do you hear me? No further frights, for I doubt I could live through them." Mrs Gardiner kissed her niece's forehead. "Now, where is this young man of yours? I have developed quite a liking for him, as we met in Town."

Laughing, Elizabeth shook her head. "I do not know for sure, but I would hazard a guess that he is nearby."

As if summoned, Darcy was at Elizabeth's side. "Ah, Mrs Gardiner, a pleasure to see you again. I do wish it had been under more pleasant circumstances though."

"Unfortunate situation, is it not? Though I have it on good authority that you are now my nephew." Mrs Gardiner said with affection. "I could not be happier for the two of you."

"It is hard to be sad, when my heart is bursting with joy at the fact that Elizabeth is now my bride. I have caught myself wearing an ear to ear grin, and had to remind myself that we are here due to a tremendous loss. I would not have the neighbors believe I am overjoyed at the death of my father in law."

"Anyone who can see the two of you together will understand the smiles are due to the joy of your marriage. And you should be pleased, as you fulfilled Thomas' last wishes. Lizzy is happily married to a wonderful man, one who will cherish her as the treasure she is. It is my belief that Thomas is here with us, relieved that his dearest daughter is secured and loved."

"Thank you, Aunt." Elizabeth said as she leaned into her arms. Wrapping her arms around Elizabeth, Mrs Gardiner could not help but be relieved herself.

"Now, dearest, do not monopolize my niece. I wish to have my share of hugs." Came the voice of Mr Gardiner as he approached the trio. "Ah, my dear Mrs Darcy. What joy it is to see you. You are radiant."

"Uncle, you are always too kind in your praises." Elizabeth giggled. "I believe you are familiar with my husband."

"Indeed I am. And I must inform you, Lizzy, that he and I are interested in a business venture together. So it may come to be that he is not only my nephew, but also a business partner." Mr Gardiner gave his niece a bear hug, kissing her on the cheek. "My dear Lizzy, I have missed you terribly. I wish we had insisted on your coming to Town after Christmas, and forced the delay in you marrying Mr Collins. Perhaps we could have prevented all of the calamity from happening."

"But we do not have the gift of hindsight, Uncle. And rather than thinking of changing the past, we must look forward to the future. If I had gone with you, I may have been able to avoid the accident, but, then again, I might not have been reunited with William and we would not have been married at this moment. No, even though I nearly died, and so much has happened, I am where I am supposed to be."

"You knew your father's heart was failing, did you not?" Seeing his niece nod her head, Mr Gardiner continued. "It was difficult to keep the secret, as Thomas did not wish for many to know the truth. I felt it a tremendous burden to carry, and you were put upon far greater than I was."

"We have all suffered greatly, Uncle. You and Uncle Phillips have been given heavy loads with all Papa's affairs to be handled. Jane has been through so much, looking after all of us, as she usually does, only to a greater degree. Mary, Kitty, and Lydia have all given us support and love through all the trials we have been through. I am proud to see my family pulling together to make our way through this time."

"Lizzy, you are always too kind." Mary said as she joined her family. "Uncle, Aunt, welcome. Your support is a blessing."

The Gardiners embraced their middle niece. Mr Gardiner looked about the room, noticing his sister's absence. "Where is your mother?" He asked Mary.

"She is in her rooms, stating she is far too ill to come down. Kitty is sitting with her at the moment, though I will relieve Kitty in a few moments. My poor sister has endured Mamma's ranting far too much of late." Mary shook her head.

Elizabeth was nervous. "Does Mamma know of my wedding yesterday?"

"Jane told her, and Aunt Phillips spoke with Mamma this morning. Both of them explained how Papa knew he was dying, so he wished for you to marry before he was gone. You remember how she was when she learned of Papa's death. It seems to be worse today."

Mr Gardiner frowned. "How so? What is Fanny saying?"

Mary looked down at her shoes as Darcy wrapped a protective arm around Elizabeth. After several moments of chilling silence, Darcy spoke. "By the time we left for Netherfield last night, Mrs Bennet had determined that Mr Bennet died due to our wedding. She said the stress of the wedding and seeing his favorite taken away for a second time caused him to die. The screeching which came from her was unbearable. It was only when Mrs Hill gave Mrs Bennet a cup of tea laced with laudanum that we were able to calm her."

"Good God, has Fanny completely lost her mind? How could she come to such a conclusion?" Mrs Gardiner was beside herself with frustration towards her sister in law.

Darcy continued. "It will be far worse when Mrs Bennet learns that Elizabeth is the heir, as Mr Bennet signed papers yesterday before the wedding. Mrs Bennet is to be moved to a cottage at the furthest reaches of the estate. Mary, Kitty and Lydia will remain in the main house, and we are hiring a governess to stay with them. Jane and Charles will be close enough to watch over the girls. But it will be difficult to remove Mrs Bennet from the house."

"Leave my sister to me, Mr Darcy. I have had enough of her behavior to last a lifetime. She will listen to me or I will see that she is cut off from any income. See how she will act if she thinks she will have to find employment." Mr Gardiner stated, standing tall and erect.

Sounds of voices speaking angrily was heard from the hall. "Whatever could be happening?" Mrs Gardiner asked as everyone turned towards the door. Just then, Fanny Bennet entered the parlor.

"You, out of my home this moment." She declared as she walked directly to Elizabeth. "You are to blame for your father's death. The humiliation of your failure to fulfill your obligations to our family, allowing Mr Collins to die without an heir, leaving all of us in jeopardy of being tossed to the shrubs. Your poor father was devastated by your failures, and then you forced him into witnessing your ridiculous marriage to this man, before having a proper mourning period. It was the straw which finally killed him. You may have been his favorite, but he was greatly disappointed in your behavior."

Darcy stepped between his wife and her mother. "That is quite enough, Mrs Bennet. I suggest you return to your rooms."

"It is my husband who has died, and our friends and neighbors who have come to pay their respects. I should be here, receiving them in my home, not my worthless daughter who has ruined us all."

"Fanny, that is quite enough." Mr Gardiner took hold of his sister's arm and began to drag her from the room. Unfortunately, Mrs Bennet yanked her arm from her brother's grasp and turned back towards her daughter. "This is my home and I demand you leave and never come back." She reached out her arm before anyone could realize what she was doing, bringing her hand down hard against Elizabeth's cheek. Elizabeth stumbled backwards, before falling to the floor, striking her head on the side of the casket.

Chapter 18

Mr Lowe was preparing to depart from Netherfield when he heard a loud, masculine voice calling out his name. Stepping into the foyer, Mr Lowe could see Darcy carrying his wife into the house, heading for the stairs as rapidly as possible. "Good Lord, what has happened to Mrs Darcy?" Lowe inquired.

Bingley was aiding his wife from the carriage and they were making their way into the house in a hurry. "Mr Lowe, my sister has been injured. She received a blow to her cheek, knocking her backwards and she struck her head on the corner of the casket. She has been unconscious since."

Lowe took the stairs two at a time, hurrying after Darcy into the bedchamber of the newlyweds. A red mark could be seen on Elizabeth's cheek, and, upon inspection, a lump with a cut were found on the back of Elizabeth's head. The wound was quickly cleaned and ointment applied, wrapping bandaging around her head to protect the cut. Fortunately, the wound was not severe enough to need stitches.

While Lowe was busy tending to her injuries, Darcy was holding his wife's hand close to his lips. "Will she be well?" He begged of his friend.

"If she regains consciousness soon, I have a strong

feeling she will be fine. The longer she is unconscious, well, let us think positively. What has happened to put her in this condition?"

"The worthless beast of a mother she has. Mrs Bennet is holding Elizabeth responsible for Mr Bennet's death." Darcy spat the words. "I will see that woman tossed from Longbourn, homeless and starving, if anything happens to my wife."

Shaking his head, Lowe was astonished. "She is the sort who will never take responsibility for her own actions. The stress she caused her husband is more responsible than anything else, for his death. The discussion I had with Mr Bennet, not long after I began treating him, disclosed the fact that his wife has always been difficult to bear and she did not allow him time to recover from his illness which had originally weakened his heart. Had he been treated properly by a physician when he had the original illness, Mr Bennet may have lived many more years. He told me that Mrs Bennet refused to send for a physician from Town, as she felt it would be too expensive. She would only allow the apothecary to come, saying that her husband needed no further care than what he could provide."

"Dear God, what is wrong with that woman? Does she not have a rational thought in her head?" Darcy was disgusted. As he looked at his friend, a sudden movement on the bed brought both of their attentions back to the young lady lying there. "Elizabeth, my love, can you hear me?"

Waking, Elizabeth groaned as she brought her hand to her head. "Oh my, what happened? I feel as if I had horses trampling my head."

"No, dearest, only a blow which knocked you backwards. Your head struck the corner of the casket."

"Mamma struck me on my cheek, did she not?" Elizabeth turned her face towards her husband. "William, oh, my."

"What is wrong, dearest? Are you in pain?"

"William, oh, can it be real?"

Mr Lowe was concerned for his patient. "Mrs Darcy, what is wrong?"

"It is blurry, but I can make out my husband's being. I can see him."

Tears were flowing freely down Darcy's cheek as he scooped his wife into his arms, kissing her, forgetting Lowe's presence. As he began to remember her injury, Darcy placed her gently back on the bed. "Forgive me dearest, I was so excited."

"What could be the reason for my vision to be recovering?" Elizabeth asked Lowe. "Oh, my, I can finally tell you are tall with light colored hair."

Smiling at the development, Lowe shook his head. "I cannot explain what has happened, Mrs Darcy.

There may have been some blood pooled in the area of the brain which controls vision. Perhaps the blow to the head moved the blood enough to remove it from the area. This is truly quite amazing."

Darcy sat staring at his wife, joy filling his heart. Elizabeth looked him directly in the eyes, lifting her hand to caress his cheek. "I am so pleased to see your face again, William. You are blurry, but I can see a dimple in your cheek. My sister is correct, you have a most becoming smile."

Mr Lowe interrupted the couple. "I insist you rest for the remainder of the day, Mrs Darcy. You will, most likely, feel the lump on the back of your head giving you pain."

"Indeed, it does. It is not too painful though." Elizabeth smiled.

Lowe made his way to the door to leave the room, stopping as he prepared to exit, turning to look at the newlyweds. The sight of Darcy embracing his wife, with a fervor of pure love, was an overwhelming sight.

In the hallway, Jane, Bingley, and Georgiana nearly pounced upon Lowe for news of Elizabeth's health.

"It is with great pleasure, I am able to announce that Mrs Darcy is awake and doing remarkably well. As a matter of fact, the blow to her head seems to have made some improvements for her. She can actually see things, though not clearly as yet."

Bingley assisted his wife to a nearby chair, as the shocking news had made her legs weak. After a moment, Jane looked at Lowe with tears of joy welling up in her eyes. "How could this be? How could hitting her head have improved her eyesight?"

"I am not certain, but when Mrs Darcy informed me of being able to see bright light, I sent a letter to a friend of mine who specializes in head injuries. If I am correct, in the carriage accident, her head was most likely bounced about, causing bruising to her brain. The blood may have been pooled, which was putting pressure on the brain, in the section which controlled vision. If this is so, it would make sense that the blow she received today dispersed the pool, moving it from that location. Her sight should restore itself completely, though she must rest and use caution so she is not re-injured."

Georgiana was bursting with joy for her sister. "This is the most wonderful news possible. William and Elizabeth must be so very pleased."

"They are, Miss Darcy. I cannot help but wish for a marriage such as your brother's. To be loved as openly as they do, makes me quite envious." Lowe said with a smile.

~~ ** ~~

Wickham was escorted into the room by two very strong officers. He had been uncooperative with everyone, knowing his days were numbered and he was determined to end his life kicking and screaming all the way.

Roughly pushed into a wooden chair, Wickham complained loudly. "There is no reason to treat me so roughly. It is bad enough that you have me in shackles on my hands and feet, you did not need to slam me so hard onto the chair."

"Be quiet, Wickham. We have had enough of your foulness." One of the men stated with obvious distaste for the prisoner.

"If you feel we are mistreating you now, just wait until later." The other man smiled. "There are a good number of men who wish to get a few licks in before you dance on the rope. My, my, you have made a number of enemies. They all would like their pound of flesh before it is too late. And most are willing to pay to have a go at you."

The lump in Wickham's throat made it difficult to swallow. He was certain that his remaining days would be torture.

Richard Fitzwilliam and Fitzwilliam Darcy entered the room, with Colonel Forster and Denny close behind. Wickham glared at the men, furious with his fate, in comparison to others.

"Darcy, I will find a way to get even with you. You will be damned for your lies and cruelty. Do you hear me? I will make you pay for all the wrongs you have forced me to suffer." Wickham shouted at his childhood friend. "And you, Denny, you should be facing this trial beside me. You know you should. I should have killed you."

"That is quite enough, Wickham." Colonel Forster demanded. Turning to his aide, Colonel Forster had the young man read the charges against Wickham. When finished, the colonel faced his former lieutenant. "Do you understand the charges against you?"

"I understand I am being cheated, once again, by Fitzwilliam Darcy. If I hang, he is as good as a murderer for what he has done to me."

The trial began with Denny describing Wickham's behavior when he stopped to abduct Lydia Bennet. The description of the event were altered, as had been discussed previously, omitting Denny being with Wickham when they found Lydia. During Denny's testimony, Wickham seethed with fury. He muttered of his desire to avenge himself against Denny, if it was the last thing he did.

After Denny, Darcy testified as to his role in the search for Lydia, as well as finding Wickham in his townhouse, attempting to rob Darcy and the attack against Denny with a knife.

Finally, Richard Fitzwilliam was called upon to verify the information that had been given by Denny and Darcy. The trial took all of two hours, before

Colonel Forster was given the verdict from the officers who served in judgment.

"George Wickham, you have been charged with willingly deserting your post with the ___shire Militia unit. The other charges against you are secondary to desertion in wartime. For that crime alone, you are sentenced to hang by the neck until you are dead. The sentence will be carried out tomorrow morning."

"I will haunt each and every one of you for the rest of your lives. I will curse you all with misfortune and despair for what you have done to me. Darcy, if you had not swindled me from my inheritance, I would never have had to join the militia. It is all on your head, you are murdering me for your selfishness and your petty jealousy. Your father loved me more as a son than he did you. If he knew how you are treating me now, he would roll over in his grave."

One of the guards roughly took hold of Wickham's arm and yanked him from his chair. "Come, Wickham, we have a celebration planned for you tonight. Some of your old friends wish to send you off to hell in style."

Realizing the night which would be in store for him, Wickham turned back towards Darcy. "Please, Darcy, you must protect me. You have no idea what I will be facing tonight. You must protect me, in honor of your father's memory."

Darcy shook his head for several moments. "You

have never learned to take responsibility for your actions. My father thought you were amusing. The only reason he treated you as well as he did was his respect for your father. You deserted the militia, I had nothing to do with it. I did not tell you to run away from the duty you swore to serve. I did not tell you to abduct anyone, and I certainly did not make you enter my home to steal from me. It is time you paid for your crimes. This is the last I will speak to you, so I wish to tell you to burn in hell for all the harm you have done to everyone. As of this day, I will no longer think of you, as you no longer exist."

Darcy and Richard made their way from the room, with Denny following close behind them. Wickham was begging for Darcy to protect him, pleading for his life. Gone was the bravado and disdain he held, and in its place was fear.

~~ ** ~~

After the trial, the cousins made their way back to Netherfield. Elizabeth had decided to remain at the house rather than accompany her sister to Longbourn, preferring to wait for her husband's return.

Though Darcy was grateful for the verdict, there was a part of him which still remembered the boy he had grown up with. When they were young, Wickham had been a good friend and playmate. It was only later, after his mother's death, when Wickham began to change for the worst. By the time they had left Pemberley to attend school, Wickham's predilections for gambling and fornication were set in his nature.

Darcy's mask of indifference was visible to all, though his wife was coming to know him well enough to know there was something bothering him. "William, would you take me for a walk? It seems like a lifetime ago since I have been to Oakham Mount and it would do us both good to enjoy the fresh air and sunshine."

A small smile grew on Darcy's lips. It was clear that his wife had already come to know his moods. "I would be delighted, my love. Do you feel well enough for such a long walk?"

"I do, William. There is still a bit of a lump on my head, but there is no pain anymore. Mr Lowe was just in to check on me, and he said I may go for a walk when you returned."

"Very well, allow me to change into my boots and we will be off."

~~ ** ~~

Holding tightly to her husband's arm, Elizabeth enjoyed the pleasure she had always found in walking in the neighborhood where she had spent the majority of her life. The familiarity was soothing to her, with all the upheaval which had plagued her of late.

Upon reaching Oakham Mount, Darcy led his wife to a nearby tree which had fallen over many years before, leaving itself as a makeshift bench. Elizabeth sat down, pulling Darcy down beside her. "Now, would you care to speak of today? I am sensing something is causing you pain."

"Elizabeth, it is shocking to me how quickly you have come to know me. To think, it was only mere weeks ago that you were unaware of my love for you, and now it is as if we have been together for many years."

"Perhaps, due to my inability to see, my other senses have made me more aware of what was happening around me. I am pleased to know you better, you are completely different from what I thought I knew last year."

"Oh, do not remind me of my gruff and careless behavior at that time. I am surprised you allowed me a second chance, as I can now see why you would think ill of me."

"Shush, that is over and done. Now, we are moving forward. What is giving you such despair today?"

Darcy pulled Elizabeth into his arms, placing a kiss on her hair. "I am saddened by the waste of life that Wickham has become. He was a different person when we were children. He played fair and was a loyal friend. My heart sank the first time I discovered him lying and stealing from me. When we were at the university, his gambling debts were outrageous, so he would steal from me to pay his debts. And he would bring young ladies to our rooms. It was quite embarrassing to find nearly naked women in such inappropriate acts with him."

"Why did he attend the university with you? He was not the son of a gentleman." Elizabeth inquired.

"His father was a devoted steward to mine. When I was near six years of age, I remember coming down from my room to servants rushing about my father's rooms. My father was severely injured when a bridge on our property collapsed, pinning him under rubble and half in the water. Mr Wickham, senior, was nearby and rescued my father. Between his dedicated services as a steward, saving my father's life sealed Father's devotion. He promised Old Mr Wickham that George would receive a gentleman's education and a start in life. Father hoped George would take orders and left the request in his will that a valuable living be given to George if he did so. George did not wish to take orders, stating he preferred to study law. Instead of the living at Kympton, I gave George three thousand pounds in addition to the one thousand my father bequeathed him."

"With such a generous gift, why would Wickham join the militia? He could have done so much with his life." Elizabeth was shocked.

"You would think so, but Wickham's penchant for

gambling and women must have depleted his funds quickly." Darcy replied. "He attempted to obtain further funds from me, even going so far as attempting to convince Georgiana that she was in love with him, hoping he could convince her to elope. That was only last summer."

"Georgiana is so young, she is just a child." Fury had grown in Elizabeth at such a crime perpetrated against her newest sister.

"Indeed. Fortunately, Georgiana wrote to me and mentioned Wickham's attention to her. I quickly made my way to remove her from his presence. I later discovered that Wickham had planned to force Georgiana into marrying him, if she would not elope with him. Either way, he would have had access to her dowry, which was what he was after all along. Thirty thousand pounds would have kept him afloat for a few years, until he squandered it away as well."

"William, it is time for you to release the pain you have suffered by your acquaintance with this man. The past is over, you cannot change it. What George Wickham became was from his own doing. He had a proper upbringing, was given a generous gift to better himself, and he threw it all away for a decadent lifestyle. I agree with your words, that it was a waste. So many young men would be jealous of the education alone, not to mention the four thousand pounds on top of it. Now it is time for you to wash your hands of the man, once and for all. You cannot punish yourself any longer. Do you understand me?" She reached up and placed a hand gently on his cheek. "I love you William, and I know what a decent and caring man you are. You have taken such care of me and my family, not to mention all of those you employ. My aunt has told me how revered you are at Pemberley and Lambton. You take such tremendous care of those around you. Think of all the good in your life and move away from this horrible man."

Darcy could not erase the smile from his face as he thought of his future with the woman he loved. "I am quite fortunate to have you, my dearest love."

"Of course you are, and it is good that you recognize my worth." Elizabeth teased.

"Oh, I recognize how valuable a treasure I married. It may be horrible to say, but your accident was one of the best things that ever happened to me. Finding you there, at Hunsford, woke me to what life could be with you at my side, and how close I came to losing you. That is one lesson I will never forget."

"Good, for I have no plans to be in another carriage accident to remind you." Elizabeth turned to place a kiss on her husband's lips, igniting his passion for her. The two remained entwined in their amorous embrace for several moments before the lack of air commanded their lips to part.

"Well, we have tackled one catastrophe, shall we speak of another?" Darcy said as he gathered his wife back to his chest.

"As there is only one catastrophe remaining, I assume you wish to discuss my mother."

Darcy nodded his head. "We must discuss how we will treat her after her behavior yesterday. I will not allow her to strike you again, even if it means I must cause her harm. I simply refuse to allow her to harm you."

"I wish I knew what my uncle has said to her. Uncle Gardiner is a gentle man, for the most part, but never make him angry. He has a temper when provoked. And yesterday, Mamma provoked him terribly." Elizabeth sighed. "Though I have a deep sadness at her behavior, I know it is fear which is speaking, I realize that she has brought most of her problems upon herself."

"Indeed." Darcy nodded his head. "It is quite foolish of her to take her fury out on you, with your inheriting everything. Your mother would be wise to be kind to you, so you would be willing to take greater care of her."

Elizabeth chuckled lightly. "That would be the intelligent manner in which to approach the situation, but my mother is far from being intelligent. She reacts with fear and frustration rather than rationality."

"Perhaps it is time she has her eyes opened to some rational thoughts." Darcy said, tipping

Elizabeth's head to allow her lips to be positioned for
his to take more delight."

When they finally broke apart, the newlyweds
made their way down the hill and walked onto
Longbourn. As they neared the house, Elizabeth
stopped for a moment, steeling herself for what was
to come. Taking a deep breath, Elizabeth shook off her
fear and held her head high as they continued on to
the main house."

~~~~~~~ ** ~~~~~~~

Chapter 19

The stable hand brought forth Caroline Bingley's horse, ready for her to ride. Frustrated by the turn of events which had happened, she decided a long and strenuous ride would be beneficial to calm her.

I should have insisted on traveling to Hunsford as soon as I knew Charles was on his way there. I should not have allowed Louisa to talk me from making the trip. If only I had gone there, my brother and Mr Darcy would not have married those wretched Bennet sisters. Now what am I to do? Just this morning, I overheard two maids discussing Eliza Bennet's improved health. How am I to ever convince Mr Darcy to rid himself of her and marry me?

Caroline mounted her horse and took off rapidly, making the men of the stables concerned for her safety.

Eliza Bennet is all wrong for Mr Darcy. She is too plain, too impertinent, too...oh, she is simply not nearly as perfect as I am. I was trained at one of the best finishing schools in all of England, am talented at the pianoforte and the harp, speak three languages, and am quite beautiful. I should be the next Mistress of Pemberley. It is not fair. Louisa caused all of this to happen, as she delayed me from arriving in time to protect Charles and Mr Darcy. That drunk she married is a fool. She must have been jealous, refusing to aid me in marrying better than she had. It will do her good to have a piece of my mind when I see her again.

Suddenly, the horse reared up, front legs pawing at the air. Miss Bingley was thrown from her saddle, landing on the ground hard, feeling something snap in her leg. Pain overrode all other senses. Caroline quickly succumbed to the waves of pain which caused her to black out.

~~ ** ~~

Entering Longbourn, Elizabeth made her way to the parlor. With her sight improved, she would be able to view her father, albeit still fuzzy, but she would have a final chance to see the man who had loved her all her life. Mary was sitting quietly, by herself, in the parlor, reading scriptures. Seeing her sister's arrival, Mary quickly stood. "Lizzy, I have been worried for you. Jane has told us of your improvement, but I was still worried."

Gathering her sister in her arms, Elizabeth embraced her and placed a kiss on Mary's cheek. "Have no fear, Mary. I am much improved. Nothing is quite in focus yet, but I am able to make out objects and people. Everyone is fuzzy, but I can distinguish much."

"When William left, carrying you in his arms, blood from the wound on his coat, I thought we would certainly lose you. Mamma was so lost to rational thought, but to strike you, I do not know what we would have done if Uncle Gardiner had not been here to take charge of her."

"Where is she now?" Elizabeth asked.

"Sleeping. It was determined that keeping her sedated with laudanum would be in everyone's best interest for the moment. Jane, Kitty and Aunt Gardiner are at the cottage, preparing it for Mamma. They decided to carry her there while she is sedated, and have us wait there for when she wakes. Then it would be easier to move her."

"It pains me that she has to be moved. I would much rather have been able to allow her to remain here, but Mamma's behavior has sealed her own fate."

"Do not fret, Lizzy. We have all spoken of the situation. It is best for Mamma to be on her own. Perhaps she will finally realize the truth of the situation. And we are looking forward to having a governess. Kitty and Lydia are actually excited to learn. Is that not wonderful news?"

Elizabeth smiled. "Indeed, and what has caused such a change in their behavior?"

"They both wish to be fashionable young ladies, much like Miss Darcy." Mary stated clearly.

Georgiana was just entering the room. "Like me? Goodness, I am far from fashionable."

The trio laughed softly. "Georgiana, in comparison

to all of my sisters and the other young ladies in the neighborhood, you are very fashionable and a proper young lady." Elizabeth said with a smile. "And I am proud that Kitty and Lydia wish to emulate you."

"As am I." Darcy exclaimed. "Having such fine younger sisters would be very pleasing."

Elizabeth finally turned from her sisters, towards the casket. Darcy placed a hand gently on her shoulder, squeezing lightly.

"Would you prefer a moment alone?" He asked.

Nodding her head, Elizabeth kept her eyes towards her father. Darcy and the younger sisters quietly left the parlor, leaving Elizabeth to say her farewell.

Moving to the side of the casket, Elizabeth caressed her father's cheek lightly. The coldness of his body made the realization clear in her mind. *This is just the shell that remains of what was my father. Nothing more than the shell which had contained him.*

"Papa, I miss you. It is so difficult for me to realize you are gone and I will never be able to debate a new book or play a game of chess with you again. I do not hold any animosity towards you for demanding my marriage to Mr Collins. You were attempting to protect us. It was difficult to go through, but it is in the past. I wish to remember the past that brings me pleasure. I wish to remember your voice, your strength in educating me against Mamma's demands, and remember how dearly you loved me. And I will always remember the moment you placed my hand in William's, giving me to a man who loves me dearly. You protected me in your final moments with us. How can I ever thank you for the treasured gift you gave me?"

"Do not fret for Mamma and my younger sisters. They will be watched over, given the same opportunity for education as you gave me, and protected by William and me, as well as Jane and Charles. Mamma is beside herself with fear at the moment. But I will make certain she is protected and looked after as well as my sisters. She has always been...unique, but, if it were not for her, I would not be here. Mamma had a part in making me who I am, both physically and emotionally. I had to become strong, to endure her insults and aggravation. But there were also tender moments, when I could feel she cared for me. They were few, but they are cherished memories. It is for those memories, I make you a promise to watch over Mamma. Though, I must tell you, I will be watching over her from afar. I would not wish to be close enough to feel the sting of her hand striking me again."

Elizabeth leaned over the casket and placed a kiss on her father's forehead. "Papa, you will be missed, terribly. But I will do my best to make you proud. Keep watch over us from heaven."

Standing straight, Elizabeth took a handkerchief from her pocket and dabbed at her eyes. Blowing her nose, Elizabeth stepped away from the casket and turned, leaving the room. It would be the last time she would view her father, as Elizabeth did not return to the parlor again until after the casket was closed.

~~ ** ~~

The Bingleys and Darcys returned to Netherfield that evening, finding the head groom awaiting their arrival. "Mr Bingley, I was about to ride over to Longbourn to fetch you. It is your sister, Sir. She went out on her horse earlier, and when her horse returned without her, I sent some of the lads out to search for her. They found her quickly enough and we brought her back to the house. Mr Lowe is tending to her as we speak."

"Was she injured terribly?" Bingley asked, concern was apparent on his brow.

"A broken leg, and some bumps and bruises. Nothing too severe, from what the physician said, though she will be in some pain when she wakes."

"I will go to her rooms, straight away." Jane offered.

Elizabeth looked at her husband, and made her own offer. "Jane, you were not feeling well this morning, perhaps you should rest. I will see to Miss Bingley."

Everyone turned towards Elizabeth, astonished at her offer. "Lizzy, I know you are improving, but do you wish to endure Miss Bingley's barbs? She makes no attempt to hide her disapproval of you." Bingley said.

"Charles, none of us are at our best when we are injured or ill. I have had my moments that you have all endured. I am more than well enough to take Miss Bingley's venomous words."

Darcy was reluctant, but finally gave in to his wife's choice.

~~ ** ~~

Elizabeth joined her husband and family for dinner. She reported Miss Bingley was resting, with the assistance of the laudanum Mr Lowe had given her. It was doubtful she would wake for several hours, and Elizabeth planned to visit her the following morning. She had left word with the maid who was to remain in Miss Bingley's room, if Caroline needed anything in the night, the maid was to send word to Elizabeth.

Darcy was proud of his wife's behavior, pleased that she could see past the slights and outright rudeness of Caroline Bingley, doing what she could for the lady. He knew it would be difficult to do so if he were Elizabeth.

After dinner, Darcy and Elizabeth excused

themselves, as they wished to retire early. The next day would be filled with many challenges, and Darcy wished to ensure his wife was rested enough to meet the day.

Bingley and Richard decided to play a game of billiards to unwind, while Jane and Georgiana spent time in the drawing room, Jane stitching some clothing she was making for one of the tenants who was expecting a babe, and Georgiana reading a book her brother had purchased for her.

~~ ** ~~

At the crack of dawn, the soldiers gathered. The men lined up in formation, most unprepared for what they would witness. Most of the men in the militia had never seen death or fighting. And witnessing a hanging could be quite distasteful. Watching a man drop on a rope, the sound of the neck snapping, or, if the neck did not break, the man thrashing about as he was strangled; this was not pleasant. But Colonel Forster had decided to make an example of Wickham. He insisted all of his men be present and witness what happened to deserters.

Wickham was led towards the location of the makeshift gallows. The officers who escorted him yanked him forward, as he attempted to break free from them at every step. He did not want to die, and he would not go to the gallows willingly.

It was clear that more than one of his fellow militia

had extracted their pound of flesh. Wickham's face was battered, a few teeth missing, and even a few ribs were broken. The beating he had received lasted throughout the day and night, after the verdict had been pronounced.

The noose was finally placed around Wickham's neck, tightened into place, and a cloth sack was placed over his head. All the while, Wickham pleaded for his life. His sobs could be heard, though no one felt sad for him.

Colonel Forster stood before his troops, and read the charges and verdict aloud. With a wave of his hand, the lever was thrown and the floor gave way under Wickham's feet. Wickham's body was left hanging there for several moments after he was dead, as Colonel Forster insisted his troops remain, watching the fate of a man who had shown himself a coward and been a disgrace.

Denny was standing beside Richard Fitzwilliam. Though Darcy did not care to witness Wickham's death, Richard felt duty bound to do so. He wished to make absolutely certain that Wickham would never be able to cause harm to anyone again. Denny swallowed hard as he watched Wickham's body drop, hearing the sounds of gagging coming from Wickham as he gasped for air until he died. When Wickham's body was taken from the rope, Denny realized how dear a gift Darcy, Richard and Miss Lydia had given him. He made a solemn vow that very moment, a vow that he would strive to make his life worthy of the gift he was given.

Richard stepped over to the wagon where Wickham's body had been deposited, to be hauled to the Meryton cemetery. Reaching out his hand, he felt Wickham's neck for any signs of life. Finding none, Richard was finally able to accept that Wickham was dead.

~~ ** ~~

At ten o'clock that morning, the men from Netherfield made their way to Longbourn's chapel. The service for Mr Thomas Bennet was held quietly, as was in accordance with Mr Bennet's wishes. Mr Phillips, Mr Gardiner, Sir William Lucas, and many other neighbors were present to bid the Master of Longbourn farewell.

Jane and Elizabeth had also gone to Longbourn, as they would spend the morning with their sisters and aunts. "It is unfair for ladies to be denied attendance to funerals." Elizabeth declared. "What makes it inappropriate for a lady to bid farewell to her father or husband? We feel the loss and must be strong in our dealing with the loss. It is not as if we are too delicate to witness a casket being placed in the ground."

"Lizzy, you cannot mean you would have gone with your husband to the service and to the cemetery." Mary was astonished.

"Why not, Mary? We were here when Papa died. We have sat beside the casket as neighbors came to pay their respects. We know that he is dead, the casket is closed, and they are saying some prayers over his grave. What of that can be determined as too difficult for the delicate females?"

"I agree with you, Elizabeth." Mrs Gardiner stated. "I have found it quite disturbing to be denied something as simple as bidding farewell to our loved ones."

"Aunt Gardiner, you shock me." Jane replied. "I never would have thought you to be a rebel."

Mrs Phillips nodded her head. "I agree with my sister in law. It is ridiculous for us to remain at home with our grief while the men are allowed to express theirs openly. But they feel we are all too delicate to attend."

"Men have always had more rights and privileges then women, and I do not see that this will change any time soon." Mrs Gardiner agreed. "When we are young, our fathers make decisions for us. When we marry, our husbands take control. Only if we marry for love, and our husbands grant us the freedom of choice, do we have any hope. I am grateful my husband is kind and caring. I do not envy those in society who are bargained away to men who only want their money or property, and then are treated worse than the servants."

"There are many such ladies in Town who live as you describe, Aunt." Jane agreed. "Lizzy and I are fortunate in our husbands, and I would hope our sisters find equally kind husbands when they are ready to wed."

~~ ** ~~

The men returned to Longbourn to partake in the refreshments which had been laid out for them. Mr Goulding and Sir William Lucas approached Elizabeth. "Eliza, I wish to convey my deepest regrets at the loss of your father." Sir William declared. "I counted Thomas as my dearest friend. I have known him since we were children and he was always good to me."

Mr Goulding agreed. "You have so many of your father's traits. Your wit and humor are so like Thomas was. I agree with Sir William, your father was a good friend and will be deeply missed."

"I thank you both for your kind words. It has been a difficult time, so much has happened in such a short time. I must admit, I half expect him to step out from his study and ask me if I wished to play a game of chess." Elizabeth smiled.

"I am pleased to see you are well married, Eliza." Sir William informed her. "Thomas told me, just the day before he died, that he prayed he would live long enough to give your hand to Mr Darcy. Thomas was certain you would be happy and well taken care of when you were married to Mr Darcy."

"William is a good and caring man." Elizabeth replied. "Papa was determined to see me wed, I only wish he had survived a little longer with us. But he is no longer in pain, and that is important. This past year has been difficult for him, and I am pleased he was with us when I married Mr Darcy."

"You and your husband will be leaving soon, I suppose." Sir William said.

"We plan to remain here for another week, and then we will stay in Town for a few weeks. My husband wishes to take me shopping and to the theater, as well as to the museums and the parks." Elizabeth chuckled. "I do believe he plans to spoil me."

"I do, indeed." Darcy said as he walked up behind his wife, placing a hand gently on her shoulder.

"Mr Darcy, you could not bestow your love on a more deserving young lady. Eliza has been a dear friend of my Charlotte, and has always been a delight to be around."

"I look forward to many years spent at her side. And I appreciate your kind words with regards to my beloved. It warms my heart to know she is well thought of by those who have known her all her life."

Mr Goulding agreed with Sir William of how highly thought of Elizabeth was. After a few more moments, Sir William leaned closer to the couple. "Goulding and I have decided to keep a close watch over Longbourn, in your absence. I promise you, if there is any problem, I will write to you immediately. Mrs Bennet has been cruel, and I am certain she will need to be reminded by all of us as to her standing. She is no longer the Mistress of Longbourn. And we will look after your sisters. I know Jane and her husband will be at Netherfield, but they are newlyweds, and deserve someone giving them some time to enjoy their lives."

"Sir William, Mr Goulding, I cannot find the words to thank you. I have been worried for Mary, Kitty and Lydia. They have never been able to stand up to Mamma, especially when she has built up her steam." Elizabeth stated. "Jane and Charles have been so good to William and I, being at Hunsford while I was so ill, separated during the ordeal with Lydia, and now in mourning for Papa. I can only pray they have some time to be alone. Jane has already told Mamma that she will only be welcomed at Netherfield if she were invited or in the case of a severe emergency."

"I plan to call on your sisters often, to make sure all is well." Mr Goulding remarked. "And Sir William has already informed your sisters that they are welcome to send for him if they have need of assistance."

"Now, I had best be on my way home. My dear wife will be expecting me. Charlotte wished for me to pass along her hopes of seeing you before you leave the neighborhood, though if she does not, she expects to receive letters on a regular basis." Sir William smiled as he held Elizabeth's hand. "Be well, Eliza. And be happy in your life. You deserve it."

~~ ** ~~

Returning to Netherfield, Mr Lowe informed everyone that Miss Bingley had taken a fever. "It is slight, but, if we do not act to control it, she could become quite ill."

"I will sit with her." Elizabeth volunteered.

"Elizabeth, you sat with her last night. I would prefer you rest, as you have had much to endure of late. Please, my love, rest until dinnertime." Darcy attempted to persuade her.

"William, it will not harm me to aid Miss Bingley. I am well, and my vision is even improving a bit. Please, understand. I feel the need to do my share of caring for Miss Bingley."

"But why, Elizabeth? Why do you need to care for her, of all people? If it were you who was in need of care, I can guarantee that she would not come to your aid."

"That, my dear husband, is the point. My kindness may never be appreciated, but how can I ask for aid when I am in need, if I am not willing to do so for someone else, no matter if they like me or not? We reap what we sow, William, and I plan to sow as much kindness and love as I can."

"Very well, but if you become fatigued in any way, you are to rest. Do you understand me?"

Smiling, Elizabeth reached up on her toes and placed a kiss on his cheek. "Thank you, William. I will come down for dinner."

Elizabeth made her way to Miss Bingley's room and found the lady to be thrashing about, her fever had taken a drastic rise. "Mr Lowe, you had best come quickly." She called out to the physician who was still speaking with Darcy in the hallway.

Mr Lowe was displeased with the development. "This is not good. We need to cool her down with cold compresses. Can you do so, Mrs Darcy?"

"Of course." She replied, moving to the table where a pitcher and basin were sitting, and cloth was nearby. For the next four hours, Elizabeth worked side by side with Mr Lowe and the maids to cool Caroline's fever.

Fortunately, the fever broke nearly as quickly as it had begun. At last, Miss Bingley slept peacefully. Elizabeth then left the room and made her way down the hall to her own room.

"Lizzy, I have been so worried for you." Darcy stated as she entered the bedchamber. He had been sitting by the fire, book in hand, unable to read.

"I am well. Miss Bingley's fever was high, and we needed to lower it. It took some time, but she is resting peacefully now. When I first went into the room, she was thrashing about from the fever. She looked so vulnerable, it nearly broke my heart to see her in such a manner."

Darcy pulled his wife into his lap, wrapping his arms around her. "Dearest, you should have allowed Jane to take care of Miss Bingley, after all, she is her sister."

"William, Jane has not told Charles, but she believes she is with child. You cannot tell him, she wishes to wait a bit longer. She has been ill in the mornings, and certain smells makes her stomach quite upset. One of the scents is the fragrance Miss Bingley wears. I do not believe she would be of much help to Miss Bingley if she were constantly losing her stomach contents."

Darcy chuckled. "There are times I feel nauseous from Miss Bingley's fragrance, and I am not with child."

"So you can understand why I volunteered to aid Miss Bingley, in Jane's place? It is more for protecting my sister from becoming ill, though I do not believe it will harm me to show Miss Bingley some kindness."

"Very well, but I insist on having a tray prepared for you. You have not eaten since we returned from Longbourn."

Smiling, Elizabeth agreed with her husband. "You

are too good to me, my love. Far too good."

"As you stated earlier, we reap what we sow. I am sowing my love for you, and expect to reap the benefits later." Darcy hungrily devoured her lips in a manner leaving no doubt as to his plans for the night.

~~~~~~~ ** ~~~~~~~

Chapter 20

The following three days saw Caroline Bingley at her absolute worse. Between the pains she suffered, the humiliation she felt, and the fever which attempted to take hold, she had never felt angrier. And having her least favorite person in the world lending aid to her was beyond frustrating.

Late in the afternoon on the third day, Caroline was ready to scream. Finally, as Elizabeth was fetching a glass of water for her, Caroline lost control of her tongue. "Why, **Mrs Darcy**, are you being so kind to me? You know I despise you. You took from me the one man I wished to marry. You are not fit to be Mistress of Pemberley. So, why in the world would you do so much to assist me?"

"Miss Bingley, I was taught by my father to be kind, even to those who would do me wrong. After all the kindness which has been bestowed on me since my carriage accident in January, it would be a pitiful way of being grateful, if I ignored you." Elizabeth brought the glass of cool water and assisted Caroline to sit up enough to drink from it. Once Caroline was settled back on the pillows, Elizabeth smiled. "And another reason for my aiding you is a battle strategy. Keep your friends close, but your enemies closer. Now, I am going down to take a walk with my husband."

Walking to the door, Elizabeth prepared to open the door, though stopped and looked back at the lady on the bed. "You are looking much better today. I am truly pleased to see you improving."

As she opened the door and began to walk through, Caroline spoke. "Mrs Darcy, I...I...am grateful. You have been kind."

~~ ** ~~

Mrs Bennet settled into the cottage, though she never found comfort in her home. She constantly fumed at the fact that all of her daughters had turned against her, not allowing her to remain as Mistress of Longbourn and live in the main house. She was not allowed to visit the main house or Netherfield without invitation. And the distance to walk to Meryton was twice as long as it had been from the main house, so she rarely made the trip to visit with her sister. Invitations came once in a while, though not as often as she felt they should. Bitterness began to permeate every fiber of her being. The one servant she was allowed was paid handsomely by the Darcys and Bingleys, as they knew the abuse she had to endure.

~~ ** ~~

Darcy and Elizabeth made their way to Town briefly, then on to Pemberley for the next three months to be alone. As Elizabeth was in mourning for her father, they deemed it to be their private time. By fall, Darcy and his bride made their way to London for an extended trip.

Proud of the young lady he had married, he wished to show her off to all his friends and family. Lady Matlock had journeyed to Town to be with her husband. Richard and Anne had also traveled to Town, as Lady Matlock had deemed it necessary to throw a ball in honor of the two couples. Charles and Jane decided to remain at Netherfield, as Jane was quite heavy with child by then.

One of the first places Darcy took his wife was to the modiste Lady Matlock had recommended. Usually Darcy would have found a way to abstain from such activities, as he would rely on his aunt to take Georgiana shopping. He wished to be involved in choosing the clothes his wife wore, and give his input on what he liked. He adamantly opposed any gown which had tiny buttons, as he had already discovered their hindrance when he wished to quickly disrobe his wife. Darcy also made certain that his wife ordered what he thought to be the necessary amount of gowns, rather than the few she would have ordered if left to her own choices.

First the modiste, then the milliner, the cobbler, and finally, a stationary store. Darcy ordered supplies for his wife's study at both Darcy House and Pemberley, including the finest paper and her very own seal. By the time the couple had returned to Darcy House, Elizabeth was exhausted.

The following day, Darcy escorted his wife and sister to a museum for a particular display Georgiana had wished to see. She was staying at Matlock House, as she wished her brother and new sister to have time to themselves, but the newlyweds wished to include her as much as they could. Finishing with the museum, the Darcys visited a shop which was a favorite to all three. Pratchard's Book Emporium kept the trio busy searching the many shelves of books. When they were finally able to drag themselves from the shop, they went across the street to the confectionary shop. Choosing from all the sweets was a difficult task for Elizabeth, as many of them were new to her. Darcy had a sampling of many treats packed up and sent to their townhouse. Once his wife had tried the sampling and discovered which treats she liked, Darcy would order more.

Elizabeth was thrilled when they went to the theater. It was the first time she had ever sat in one of the boxes, having always attended with her aunt and uncle, sitting in seats on the floor level. Her beloved husband invited her Aunt and Uncle Gardiner to attend, making Elizabeth's pleasure greater.

The night of the ball came quickly, two days before the Darcys were set to travel to Pemberley. Darcy paced in the foyer of his townhouse, waiting impatiently for his wife to join him. She had refused to allow him to see her until she came down the stairs, as she wished to see his expression when he first saw her. Her demand was well repaid, as the look of adoration in his eyes was pure pleasure. Hearing his wife on the steps, Darcy raised his eyes to watch Elizabeth descend the stairs.

The gown she wore was the palest shade of yellow, with golden threads stitching the intricate patterns in the fine silk fabric. The décolletage was far more daring than Darcy had ever seen his wife wear, and for a moment, he questioned whether he should allow her to leave their house looking so fetching. Being of a jealous nature, Darcy was not certain he wished any other man to see his wife in such a gown.

She wore a choker of pearls with matching earbobs, and tiny seed pearls were pinned in her dark chocolate curls. Her new maid, Sara, had styled Elizabeth's hair high on her head, with some of the curls hanging down, especially on the back of her neck. The way those curls danced about on her delicate skin was nearly Darcy's undoing.

"Well, Husband, do I look elegant enough to be seen in public with you?"

"No, as a matter of fact, I was just considering asking you to go up and put on one of your mourning gowns. This gown is far too daring, I do not wish any other man to see you looking this perfect. I do not like the thought of others leering at your perfect figure and having thoughts of you which only I should have."

"As much as I wish we could remain here, I am afraid of what your aunt would do to us. She has made it clear that we are to be at Matlock House early, as we are to be in the receiving line, next to Richard and Anne."

"Can we not say you were feeling faint or had a headache and we were required to remain home? I despise such gatherings." Darcy sounded much like a petulant child.

"I am sorry, my love. We must attend. But you have three dances reserved with me, and, if you are a good boy, when we return home, I will have a surprise for you."

Darcy's face lit up at the thought of the potential surprise his wife might have for him. "I promise to be on my best behavior."

~~ ** ~~

The night was long, with Elizabeth dancing nearly every dance. Along with the three dances he shared with his wife, Darcy danced with his aunt and Anne, as well as the wives of two of his friends. When he was not dancing, he was watching his wife, witnessing her smiles and her radiance. How pleased he was to see how well accepted Elizabeth was amongst those of the *ton*.

As promised, Elizabeth saved three dances for her

husband. They danced the first, the supper and the last sets of the night. Everyone who watched them commented to Lord and Lady Matlock on how happy the couple seemed. There were, of course, several disappointed young ladies who would have preferred it was them in Elizabeth's place, but no one had the audacity to berate Lady Matlock's new niece. If they had, they would find themselves facing the wrath of one of the most powerful ladies of the first circle of society. Lady Matlock had made it clear she would not tolerate anyone being disrespectful to her niece, as she adored Elizabeth.

When the last song finished, Darcy was quick to take their leave of their loved ones, as he wished for his prize for behaving as he had.

Elizabeth found Sara in her dressing room, waiting for the Mistress to assist her in changing into her night clothes. Elizabeth decided to wear her favorite nightgown, wine colored silk with a matching dressing gown. It was not long before her husband was knocking on the door of her dressing chamber.

Darcy needed only a couple steps to cross the room and wrap his wife in his arms. Her long locks were hanging down, as Darcy preferred. Tangling fingers in her curls, he brought her face up to his, claiming her lips.

After several moments, he scooped her into his arms and carried her to their bed. "I believe you promised me a reward for being a good boy tonight. It is now time to collect my reward, as I was on my best behavior at Matlock House."

"You were, indeed, my love." Elizabeth said as he slipped the dressing gown off her shoulders. Lying back on the bed, she motioned for her husband to join her. "I have been keeping this surprise for more than two months, but I believe it is well worth the wait." Taking his hand, she placed it gently on her abdomen.

Curious, Darcy looked in his wife's eyes, attempting to determine what she was telling him. Suddenly, he felt a movement inside her belly. "My love, what was that? Are you well?"

Elizabeth laughed. "I am well, dearest. That is your reward. Your child decided to greet you."

Darcy's eyes grew round, like saucers. "My...my...my..."

Placing her hands gently on her husband's cheeks, Elizabeth smiled at him. "Yes, my dearest love, your child. You are to be a father."

"Oh, Elizabeth Darcy, you have given me the greatest gift I could ever imagine. A father." Darcy feathered kisses on her lips and along her jaw. He then moved to place kisses on her abdomen. He realized there was a slight swell there, and he had not noticed before. Her breast appeared larger as well. "How is it I can make love to you nearly every night, and never noticed the changes in your body?"

"Love is blind?"

Darcy began laughing. "You have given me the most wonderful gift I could ever receive. Our love has taken life."

~~ ** ~~

Darcy wandered into his wife's study, finding her sitting on the window seat, gazing off at nothing. "Are you well, my love?"

Elizabeth smiled as she turned her face towards her husband. "Forgive me, William, I was woolgathering."

Taking a seat beside her, Darcy lifted her hand to his lips. "Tell me of what you are thinking."

"So much has happened in the past year. It is difficult to realize how much we have endured, only to be so happy in life now."

"You do not think a lady should be married twice in one year?" Darcy teased.

"I do not plan to ever marry again. You had best live to a ripe old age, for I plan to spend many years with you." Elizabeth declared, as she squeezed his hand.

"I plan to live many years to come, for I do not wish to miss a moment of loving you." Darcy pulled his wife into his arms, holding her to his chest. "You remind me of a tree at Pemberley. I noticed one day, several years ago, there was a sapling growing in the shallow section of the pond. I thought it was odd, given its location. Trees rarely grow in pools of water. But each month, I noticed the tree grew. Against all odds, the tree thrived and grew. It has grown quite strong and sturdy. You, my dearest love, are just like that tree. Rare, yet strong and beating the odds of survival. You are strong and flourishing, now increasing with new life."

~~ ** ~~

It was a cold February morning, when the calm was disrupted by the cries of Pemberley's Mistress crying out in pain. The Master was quickly calling out for the midwife and the physician, his voice strained as he endured the agony his wife's labor pains were bringing him.

Darcy was forced from his wife's room, though he would not follow the suggestion from the midwife to retire to his study. He remained steadfastly pacing outside his wife's bedchamber door. Every cry from his beloved sent chills down his spine, as he desired to be in the room, holding her and bringing her comfort.

For six hours, Darcy refused to leave the hallway outside his wife's door. Refusing food and drink, Darcy continued to pace, desperate for his wife's pain to be over and their child to be born. Six hours, and Darcy was ready to force his way into the room, no matter what anyone said. He was the Master of the house, if those he employed did not approve of his being at his wife's side as she brought their child into the world, he did not care.

As he reached for the doorknob, the door opened wide. The housekeeper, Mrs Reynolds, came out of the room wearing the biggest smile Darcy had ever seen. "Master William, please, come in. Your wife wishes you to come in."

Taking the steps in his long strides, he had crossed the room quickly. "Lizzy, are you well, my love?"

Squeezing the hand which had taken hold of her own, Elizabeth gave him a fatigued smile. "I am more than well, William. I am perfect. So is our daughter."

"A daughter? We have a daughter?" Darcy's heart nearly soared.

"Indeed, Master William, your wife has given you a beautiful baby girl." Mrs Reynolds said as she brought the babe, wrapped snuggly in a blanket.

The babe was a perfect copy of her mother, with dark chocolate curls, her mother's eyes, and even the small birthmark behind her left ear. Darcy lifted his daughter and placed a kiss on her forehead.

Turning his eyes to meet his wife's, tears were streaking down his cheeks. Elizabeth was worried. "Are you disappointed that it is a girl?"

Shaking his head, Darcy's dimples could be seen as he smiled. "No, I am far from disappointed, my love. I wished to have a daughter who looked just like her mother. A small version of my beautiful wife, whom I can spoil and cherish, as you should have been. Your mother did not appreciate the wonderful gift she was given. She did not treasure you as she should have. Our daughter will be loved for the precious jewel she is. I could not be happier."

Elizabeth was exhausted, but overwhelmed with love. Her husband shooed everyone from the room, as he laid down on the bed beside his wife and holding their daughter in his arms. Once they were nestled in together, the newly formed trio fell into a restful sleep.

Waking several hours later, Elizabeth kept her eyes closed as she listened to her husband speaking to their daughter. "And when we take you out for walks this spring, I will show you the Lizzy tree. You will love the outdoors, just as your mother does. She is a treasure, and so, my tiny love, are you. Though your Mamma does not like to ride horses, I will teach you when you are old enough. And one day, you will have brothers and sisters with which to play. I wish for a large family. As your Mamma has four sisters by birth, it is a fair chance we could have a large family. Pemberley should be filled with the sound of children."

~~~~~~~ ** ~~~~~~~

Chapter 21

The Darcys were indeed blessed with a large family. Cate Anne was the first of seven children born to Elizabeth and Fitzwilliam Darcy. After their beloved Cate, their first son was born a year later. William Charles Darcy was a copy of his father, except he had his mother's eyes. He was shy, much like his father, and very protective of his loved ones. Whenever Cate found herself in trouble, William was nearby to save her.

Two years later, a set of twins arrived. Thomas Gerald and Madeline Jane were adored by their parents and elder siblings. Cate, now four, was the motherly sort, and, as the children grew, it would be common for them to run to Cate for comfort when they skinned a knee or had some sort of sorrows.

A year later brought a third daughter, Mary Catherine. She was quickly followed by Lydia Rebecca.

Finally, the baby of the group was born three years after Lyddie. Edward Henry was loved by all of his siblings, for he had the sweet nature of his Aunt Jane and Uncle Charles. Elizabeth and Darcy loved each and every one of their children. Unlike other members of society, the Darcys never left their children to be reared by their servants, but were a part of their children's daily life. If there were no guests to dine, the children usually found their parents taking their evening meal in the nursery, as their children would regale them with what they had learned in their lessons that day.

The Darcys were not the only family to flourish. The Bingleys had five children, three sons and two daughters. They were all sweet natured children, though their youngest daughter had a bit of impertinence to her when she needed it. She was well named, Elizabeth Catherine, as she was also the one who was constantly reading and expanding her mind.

Richard and Anne were only blessed with two sons, but they were healthy and strong young men, the eldest of which, Henry James Fitzwilliam, fell in love with Cate, and they married when they were both twenty. Born only a week apart, Cate would tease her husband that he would never forget her birthday.

Mary Bennet married four years after her elder sisters. Her husband purchased the book shop in Meryton, and they were blessed with three daughters.

The next to marry was Lydia. After a successful career in the regulars, fighting in France, Colonel Jonathon Denny returned to Longbourn and asked for Lydia's hand. He had never forgotten her, nor she him. Whenever he was on leave, Denny would visit Longbourn and Netherfield, and had fallen in love with the young lady whose life had been saved by him those many years before. They had a son and a daughter, and lived out their days taking care of

Longbourn for Elizabeth.

Kitty (Katherine) Bennet was the last of the sisters to marry. When visiting London with her sister, Elizabeth, Kitty met a young man studying law. He had plans to one day become a barrister. Kitty waited for him, and was rewarded for her devotion the year after Lydia married. Eventually, she would give her husband four sons and one daughter.

Mrs Bennet died a year after her husband. She had been miserable the entire time, blaming her least favorite daughter for all the wrongs in her life. Though sad to lose their mother, the daughters all felt a sense of relief that her discontent with life was at an end.

Lord Matlock kept his word to Thomas Bennet, and assisted in making Elizabeth the rightful heir of Longbourn. Though Elizabeth was honored, she had no desire to be her childhood home's Mistress. Unofficially, she left that honor to Lydia to claim. The estate thrived under the care Mr and Mrs Denny, as they tended to its needs diligently.

Three years after being placed in an asylum, Lady Catherine de Bourgh died from a trifling cold. She had grown more difficult to manage in those years, and refused any assistance to treat her illness, leading to her own demise.

Shocking to everyone, especially her family, Caroline Bingley found her heart. She married a gentleman who owned a small estate near Scarborough, and was pleased in her love match. Caroline gave her husband a son and two daughters. Her son fell in love with young Lydia Darcy, and finally there was a marriage between the Bingley and Darcy families, as Caroline had always wished. Her heart had grown to be caring, as she had learned an important lesson from the generosity shown her by Elizabeth Darcy.

~~ ** ~~

Cate Anne Darcy Fitzwilliam was forty three years old when her parents had died. Her father had been in an accident, as he was attempting to rescue one of the tenant children from a burning cottage. A beam fell from the ceiling, pinning the Master of Pemberley to the floor. He succumbed to his injuries two days after the fire, his loving family at his side.

Elizabeth Darcy had sat beside her husband's bed, doing all that she could to save him. He was in such pain, and his breathing was difficult, as the beam had broken five ribs, pushing them into his body. When he was first brought to the main house, after the accident, Elizabeth begged her beloved husband not to leave her. By the second day, she realized the struggle he was having to remain alive for her, and, after speaking with the physician and her children, Elizabeth knew there was no real hope for him to survive.

Leaning close to her husband's ear, Elizabeth whispered to him. "It is alright to leave, William. Do not struggle on my account. I wish you to be at peace and without pain. Do not worry for me, my love. I will be well, until I am reunited with you. I love you, Fitzwilliam Darcy. And our love will never end, even in death."

Within an hour, Fitzwilliam Darcy died. Even after his death, Elizabeth sat beside him, holding his lifeless hand in hers, tears streaking her cheeks.

It was only a fortnight later, Cate kissed her mother goodnight and left for her own home twenty miles away from Pemberley. Elizabeth entered her bedchamber, walking to her dressing table, taking the pins from her hair. The maid came into the room to assist her in preparing for bed, brushing her long, dark curls. A smile graced Elizabeth's cheeks at the memory of her husband's enjoyment of playing with her curls, wrapping one about his fingers when they would rest together on their bed.

The maid noticed the smile and asked her mistress what had brought such a joy to her. When Elizabeth informed her of the memory, the maid smiled. She, too, knew of Mr Darcy's delight with his wife's locks.

Elizabeth wished to wear a particular silk nightgown, one which her husband had given her for her birthday the previous year. It was a pale, ice blue, with lavender flowers stitched along the neckline and hem. There was a matching dressing gown, though Elizabeth left it in the dressing chamber.

It was believed that Elizabeth suffered heart failure in her sleep. Though suffered was not the word Cate would use after seeing her mother's body, still lying on her bed. The smile which graced Elizabeth's lips was the same one she usually bestowed to her beloved husband, a smile which spoke of her love for him. Cate firmly believed that her father had come to escort his beloved into the next life.

A year had passed when Cate returned to Pemberley to honor her parent's memory. Bringing her own daughter and granddaughter, the three generations of Darcy ladies placed flowers upon the graves of Fitzwilliam and Elizabeth Darcy.

Cate's granddaughter, Elizabeth Jane, was eight years old. She had been fond of her great grandparents, who were often found spoiling their grandchildren and great grandchildren. Being named for her beloved Grams Lizzy, Elizabeth felt she was destined to be special.

After placing her bundle of roses and lavender on her Grams Lizzy's grave, Elizabeth looked up at her grandmother. "Grandma Cate, when did Gramps Will fall in love with Grams Lizzy?"

The Darcy's love story was well known by their children and grandchildren, as they wished for the future generations to realize love should be cherished and welcomed, no matter what possible obstacles were perceived.

Kneeling down beside her granddaughter, Cate took hold of her hand. "Elizabeth, I will tell you the story of your Grams and Gramps. It really began the moment Gramps found Grams had been in an accident and was injured terribly. At that time, Grams was Mrs Collins, against her wishes..."

THE END